Highland Blessings

"Jennifer Hudson Taylor has a winner with her debut novel, *Highland Blessings*. What's not to love about battling Scottish clans, a lady kidnapped, romance, intrigue, and a mystery that will keep you turning pages to the very end? This is the kind of book you can curl up with on a rainy day and forget all your troubles as you plunge into the adventure and romance of fifteenth-century Scotland. Highly recommended."
—*Bestselling author MaryLu Tyndall*

Highland Blessings

Jennifer Hudson Taylor

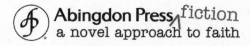

Abingdon Press fiction
a novel approach to faith

Nashville, Tennessee

Highland Blessings

Copyright © 2010 by Jennifer Hudson Taylor

ISBN-13: 978-1-4267-0226-6

Published by Abingdon Press, P.O. Box 801, Nashville, TN 37202
www.abingdonpress.com

Published in association with the Hartline Literary Agency.

Cover design by Anderson Design Group, Nashville, TN.

Library of Congress Cataloging-in-Publication Data

Taylor, Jennifer Hudson.
  Highland blessings / Jennifer Hudson Taylor.
    p. cm.
  ISBN 978-1-4267-0226-6 (pbk. : alk. paper)
  1. Forced marriage—Fiction. 2. Betrayal—Fiction. 3. Scotland—History—15th
century—Fiction. I. Title.
  PS3620.A9465H54 2010
  813'.6—dc22

                    2009047205

Printed in the United States of America

1 2 3 4 5 6 7 8 9 10 / 15 14 13 12 11 10

To my loving Father, who lifted me from my
knees more times than I can count,
who kept shining a guiding light in my heart
that wouldn't let me quit,
and who gave me the desire to write, I pray that
my work will glorify You.
Thank you for loving me, for not ever forsaking
me, and for this special birthday gift.
You are the Great I Am—my everything.

Blessed be the God and Father of our Lord Jesus Christ,
who hath blessed us with all spiritual blessings
in heavenly places in Christ.

(Ephesians 1:3)

Acknowledgments

This book couldn't have been completed and published without the loving support of Dwayne, my husband, best friend, and soulmate. Thank you for all the meals, laundry, and dishes while I wrote. Your thoughtful input on every manuscript, your listening ears through the rejections, and your encouragement . . . you believed in me and loved me through it all.

To Celina, my daughter, who gave up more mommy time than she should have, thank you for being patient with me to finish "one more sentence" and for making our special times so full of quality. You have taught me so much about patience and understanding.

ACKNOWLEDGMENTS

To my dad, thank you for giving me a love of history. To my mom, only a special mom would reread a twelve-year-old girl's handwritten manuscript in a spiral notebook. Your wisdom and encouragement inspired me. Aunt Judy, thank you for giving a child a box of thirty novels.

To the rest of my extended family, I appreciate all your love and support. To my in-laws, Helen and Winston, thank you for being so understanding when I hauled my laptop with me everywhere.

To my agent, Terry Burns, at Hartline Literary Agency, you never gave up and you were persistent in sending out my work. You are a legend—a cowboy who has touched so many lives.

To my editor, Barbara Scott, you believed in me and took a chance on *Highland Blessings*. How can I ever thank you enough? When I met you in person, I knew I had an author's dream editor. To the Abingdon staff, your help has been wonderful. To Anderson Design Group, your book covers are awesome!

To the ladies on the F.A.I.T.H. Blog, HisWriters, my critique partners, RWA, and ACFW, I needed your fellowship, prayers, and expertise. I'm a better writer because of you.

To my readers, I pray this novel and my future novels will bless you abundantly and inspire you with God's love and joy.

Prologue
Scotland
1463

Cedric MacPhearson knew he was going to die, but he glanced up at the low clouds brewing into a storm and raised a fist, determined he would last until one of his sons found him. The survival of his clan depended upon it. And as ornery and stubborn as he had been all his life, no one would believe he had agreed to a peaceful settlement with the MacKenzies if he died, least of all his sons.

Beads of sweat broke along his brow as he struggled to remain conscious, mentally listing every black deed he had ever committed and then muttering a whispered prayer for each one. As the MacPhearson chieftain, Cedric knew his word had been the unquestioned law. He had always thought himself a fair man with a firm ruling hand. Now as he prepared to meet his Maker, he wasn't so sure. It was imperative that he complete one last goodwill before he closed his eyes forever.

The restless wind twirled faster, rustling scattered leaves around him. The cool air was a comfort, giving him a feeling of being lifted high and floating away as the pain in his chest faded to numbness. Lightning flashed silently, highlighting a lone rider approaching at top speed.

Rumbling thunder echoed in Cedric's ears, drowning out the sound of a winded destrier pulled short and his son's voice calling to him. Cedric's head was gently lifted into the lad's lap and tenderly cradled in youthful hands, strong with promise. Bryce, his middle son, peered down at him with intelligent, gray eyes full of concern.

"Da! What happened to ye?" He reached over and carefully lifted Cedric's bloody tunic. Moisture gathered in his eyes at the sight of the large sword wound slightly below Cedric's heart. "Likely, the villain got yer lungs." His voice sounded like a man's, but it shook with desperation. He looked deeply into Cedric's eyes with painful certainty. "Who did this to ye?"

"A MacKenzie warrior struck me down. I came from signing the peace settlement with Birk MacKenzie, so I wasn't expecting an attack."

"I'll kill the MacKenzie responsible!"

Cedric could hear the anger in his son's voice and knew a century-old vengeance coursed through his veins. Pride swelled in Cedric's battered chest, and he was pleased that he hadn't missed this opportunity to give his final command and say good-bye. He clutched his son's shirt in his fist.

"Listen, lad. Birk MacKenzie didn't order this. Even now he doesn't know."

The effort to speak drained his energy and made his chest feel heavy. What blood had not drained from his body began to fill his lungs, and breathing became increasingly difficult. With a concentrated effort he motioned to his pocket and took a labored breath.

"Get paper." His hoarse whisper brought blood to his mouth.

Bryce shuddered. Knowing time was of the essence, he frantically searched his father's clothes and found a piece of paper. He unfolded it and scanned the signed documents.

Denial was on the tip of his tongue, when he looked at his father with defeat.

"Prom-ise . . . ye'll . . . make E-van . . . hon-or . . . my word."

A flicker of apprehension pierced him. He was uncomfortable making a promise of a lifelong commitment for his elder brother, and even more afraid to spend these precious moments arguing with his dying father.

With the last of his strength, Cedric grabbed his wrist. "Promise!" More blood spewed from his lips as the clouds opened with rain. Lightning struck and thunder roared.

Bryce bent forward, hating the entrapment of death he saw in his father's eyes, and cradled his father to him. "Da, don't die!" Tears blended with the downpour of rain. Cedric's cold fingers squeezed. Out of desperation Bryce yelled over the storm. "I promise! I promise!"

He couldn't bear the thought of his father dying without granting his last request.

Cedric released his wrist, and Bryce knew he was gone. Tears were difficult to shed. He couldn't ever remember a time in his childhood when he allowed one tear to slip from his eye.

Now, alone in the storm, a lad of ten and four, Bryce grieved for his loss and a promise he prayed he could keep.

1

Scotland

April 1473

Akira MacKenzie willed her knees not to fail her. She watched Gregor Matheson's blond head disappear through the astonished crowd that slowly parted for him. He would have made her a perfect husband, but now he deserted her, placing her safety in jeopardy once again.

She swallowed the rising lump in her throat and straightened her shoulders. Akira clasped her hands in front of her and turned to face the expectant gazes of her Scottish clan. Hushed murmurs flowed through the crowd until one by one their voices faded into the restless wind.

"'Twill be no wedding this day." She allowed her strong voice to echo over her kinsmen. The earth vibrated, and thunder rumbled in the distance. Akira paused, but naught seemed amiss. Green hills and hidden valleys lay undisturbed, draped with wildflowers and tall grass that rippled in the gentle breeze. Strands of golden-red hair lifted from her shoulder and brushed against her face. She whisked a wayward lock from her eyes.

She turned to Father Mike for encouragement. He stood in a brown robe gathered with a rope cord tied at the waist around his thin frame. Holding a small book in the crook of his arm, he shook his graying head. His aging face held laugh lines around the corners of his eyes and mouth, but today his wrinkles were pulled into a sad frown. His soft brown eyes settled upon her with understanding. Akira wanted to run weeping into his arms, but she held herself still.

More thunder rumbled and grew closer.

"'Tis the MacPhearsons!" A lone woman cried in alarm, pointing past where Akira stood on the grassy knoll.

Panic slashed through her clansmen, and they scattered to find shelter behind her father's castle gates. Unarmed MacKenzies sought their weapons before the riders reached them. Expecting a wedding celebration, few were prepared for battle.

Akira turned. The thunder she had heard was an army of warriors descending upon them. A savage barbarian riding a fierce gray stallion charged toward her, his army in quick pursuit. Together, the lead warrior and stallion embodied power. He led them as befit a king, but when his gaze fixed on Akira, her blood ran cold.

The MacPhearson chief wanted his bride. Akira hated her fear of him as it took root and gripped her insides.

"Lord, give me strength," she prayed.

She would not run. No, she would stand and wait for him. If it was peace he wanted, then peace she would give him. She'd be calm, meet his gaze, and remind him of the letter her father received six months ago from the MacPhearson chief saying he would not honor the betrothal their parents had pledged years ago when she and Evan MacPhearson were children. Accepting it as the insult it was, Akira's father granted his permission for her to wed a man of her choice. She had chosen Gregor Matheson, but now she realized even that had been a mistake.

Her brother Gavin broke through the madness and grabbed Akira's arm, propelling her toward the castle gates. The sound of horses' hooves pounding into the earth grew louder. One gray stallion erupted forth, his rider targeting her. Knowing Gavin held no weapon to defend them, she fretted for his life and tried to wrench herself free.

"Run, Gavin! Run!" she yelled above the chaos.

Gavin wouldn't leave her. He struggled to pull her along, but her heavy satin gown caught under her feet, nearly tripping her. While most wedding gowns of her clanswomen were of varying colors, Akira had wanted to look like a white dove. The front was simple, but elegant, with no beads or trim. The long sleeves widened at the wrists and the skirt portion draped over her figure like a long tapestry.

"Hurry, lass!" he urged as the material ripped.

The stallion's labored breathing almost pulsed down her back. Her skin crawled with tiny prickles. The dark rider would soon overtake them. Jerking free of Gavin's hold, she again urged her brother to safety.

"Leave me, Gavin." Tears of despair threatened to snap her control. "I'll not have ye die at the hand of a MacPhearson because of me."

"Nay. Never!" Gavin protested.

The MacPhearson warrior bent, and his heavy fist slammed against Gavin's jaw. Her brother landed several feet back. Iron fingers gripped her waist. The MacPhearson tightened his hold across her middle as he pulled her backward and up onto the horse. Akira screamed and kicked, lashing out blindly against him. He fought her with one hand while he guided his charger forward. The reins almost tumbled from his hand, and he lunged to grab them. His hard elbow rammed her cheek in the process.

"Don't fight me, lass," he roared. "Or else the blood of innocent men will be upon yer head!"

His words cut into her like a blade, and she ceased her struggles as he threw her over his lap and across the racing animal's back. Akira believed him. A MacPhearson could have no compassion in a heart as black as death.

"How dare ye, MacPhearson!" Akira's father bellowed behind them. She stole a glance through her tumbling hair. He ran after them with a fist raised in mid-air. He roared another promise of revenge before bending over his knees to catch his breath. Her father shook his graying head in disbelief.

"I love ye, Da," she whispered, committing his image to memory.

The forest swallowed them, and for hours the MacPhearsons kept their fast pace. Akira tried to calm her heaving stomach, but it continued to twirl as she lay over his lap. The ride would have been much more tolerable had she been able to sit on her backside. Instead, her stomach suffered from the jarring of the stallion's movements. The nausea finally overtook her, and she vomited.

They stopped. Left with no other recourse, she tried to wipe her mouth with her hand.

The warrior ripped off part of his plaid hanging over his tunic that reached down to his knees like a long shirt and belted at the waist. He wet it with water from his flask and offered it to her. His plaid of red and gray colors fell forward, and he shoved it back over his shoulder. Since the MacPhearsons lived in a different region, their plaids were made by a different weaver from the MacKenzies'. Akira's clan often wore plaids of blue and green.

She lifted her gaze to his menacing glare. Akira trembled in spite of her silent resolve not to fear him, for he looked as if he wanted to beat her, and she felt certain it wasn't beneath him.

He leaned forward, thrusting the material in her face. "Take it and clean yerself," he demanded, as if the sight of her disgusted him.

Grimacing, she looked down at his leg covered with her sickness. Her cheeks grew warm. He deserved what he had gotten for throwing her on his stallion and hauling her off like a prize he had won.

"Lass, don't make me repeat myself." His lack of patience was quite evident in his tone, but even more so as he shoved the damp material in her face.

Akira snatched it out of his hand and glared back, momentarily forgetting her danger. "Ye blunderin' fool, 'tis yer own fault it happened. Ye got no more than ye deserved."

He leaned forward, his nose barely an inch from hers, and she leaned back as far as she dared without toppling off his stallion. His dark gray eyes turned black, and a vein pulsed rapidly in his neck as he stared down at her.

Once again her temper and boldness had gotten the better of her. *Lord, help bridle my tongue*, she silently prayed. Deciding she had pushed him far enough, Akira gripped his leg while she stroked the damp cloth over his skin in hopes of diverting his attention from her angry outburst. He flinched at her touch. She dropped his leg with a questioning gaze.

"I told ye to clean yerself, not me."

"I'm not quite as messy." She turned back to her task.

He lifted her from the stallion and dropped her on her unsteady feet. It took her a moment to recover. When she did, she found herself staring at her captor's chest. Tall for a woman, Akira wasn't used to a man's height equaling her own, but this MacPhearson was a giant. His massive shoulders blocked the sun's rays, filtering through the trees.

He bound her hands with a leather strap, pulling the knot secure against the flesh around the fine bones of her wrists. She noticed his skin was a shade darker than hers.

Akira stole the moment to study his profile. Shoulder-length hair the color of potted soil framed an authoritative, square face. His gray eyes were sharp and purposeful as he tended to his task. Up close he appeared more handsome than barbaric. His bronze face bore a recent shave. The bridge of his nose smoothed over his face to striking, high cheekbones. He radiated confidence, but she sensed a stubborn streak hid behind his determined expression.

As he towered over her, she felt a rare fear and trembled. His hands gentled, and his voice softened.

"I'm sorry I was so rough with ye. I didn't mean for my elbow to hit yer cheek." He pulled the leather tighter, making her wince. "I apologize for this inconvenience, but I must see to it that ye canna escape."

He stepped back, rubbing his chin in thoughtful concentration as if contemplating what to do with her. "Ye're no ordinary woman." He crossed his arms and circled Akira, observing her. She could feel the heat of his blazing gaze travel the length of her. "Any other woman would have fled." He paused in front of her and looked into her eyes. "'Twas as if ye were determined to stand yer ground and wait for me until that man encouraged ye to run." He raised a black eyebrow. "Why?"

"They're my family and clansmen. If ye were coming to claim yer bride, then I was the one ye wanted, not them."

"So ye're a courageous lass. Willing to sacrifice yerself for their lives. Is that the way of it then?" He spoke in a firm, yet gentle tone. He touched her swelling cheek with the back of his knuckles. Akira flinched from the uncharacteristic gesture. He dropped his hand.

"Regardless of what ye think, I'm not in the habit of mistreating women." He looked at her intently, his eyes almost willing her to believe him.

She stared over his shoulder at the dark forest, refusing to relieve him of his guilt—if he was human enough to feel any. "My brother did naught to ye. Why did ye hit him?"

"Yer brother would have interfered and caused a massacre of yer people. I had no wish for that to happen, so I took the only option I had. I took care of him before he could strike me and my men retaliate on my behalf."

Akira stepped back in disbelief. She craned her neck to see into his dark gray eyes. "'Twas not the only option. He could still be unconscious this verra moment."

He sighed, crossing his arms over his chest as if she were trying his patience. "I assure ye, lass, yer brother will be fine. I didn't hit him hard."

She leaned up on her tiptoes. "Then my eyes must have been deceiving me, for ye knocked him plumb out."

"Aye, that I did." He grinned with pride, as white, even teeth flashed in contrast to his dark profile. "But the blow will not cause any lasting effects, I assure ye."

"There's not a guilty bone in yer body." A lock of golden-red curls fell forward covering her right eye. She reached up with her bound hands and tossed her long tresses over her shoulder. "Ye had no right to take me from my family."

"Believe as ye wish." He shrugged. "I may have taken ye against yer will, but I never commit harm unless I'm forced." He placed a finger under her chin and tilted her face.

Her mind whirled in a daze. Akira purposely closed her heart to any generosity he might bestow upon her. "Gavin gave ye no reason to hit him. I hope I do naught to force yer mistreatment of me before ye return me to my family." The sarcasm in her voice overshadowed her fear.

A sudden frown perplexed his otherwise perfect face, and she sensed a change in his demeanor. In one fluid motion, he lifted her upon his stallion. This time she was properly seated as he mounted up behind her. He urged the beast beneath them forward, signaled to his men, and they were again on their way. Akira had nearly forgotten that others were present to witness their exchange.

Under the circumstances, he set a much slower pace than she would have anticipated, knowing the MacKenzies could be following close behind. They traveled a good distance in silence.

After a long while had passed, he bent toward her ear. "I'm sorry."

His warm breath floated over the skin at her nape, and she fought the urge to shudder. His apology stunned her speechless. Warriors did not apologize, least of all to bound prisoners or to women.

"Whether ye believe me or not, I do not mistreat women. And the blow to yer cheek wouldn't have happened if ye hadn't put up such a struggle."

Akira remained silent. How was she supposed to have responded while being kidnapped away from her family and all that she held dear? She had no idea what to expect. All she knew was that she depended upon the Lord to give her sufficient grace to get through whatever she would be forced to endure at their hands.

"I see ye've naught else to say." Disappointment carried in his voice.

She arched an eyebrow. He expected friendly conversation while he carted her halfway across the country against her will and kept her in bonds? "What would ye have me say?" She turned sideways in the saddle. "I can only wonder at what ye plan to do with me. Should I beg for mercy in hopes ye'll spare my life? Or should I wait 'til ye've no more use for me?" She straightened away from him.

He chuckled. "I appreciate the ideas."

"Why not take me home now before my da comes after me and more blood is shed?"

He tensed as if her words had struck some deep chord within him. "Believe me, lass, more bloodshed is not my intention. I took ye because I had to and that's the end of it."

Akira wisely remained silent. The man seemed to contradict even his own character. He didn't want her to believe him a barbarian, yet he had ridden onto MacKenzie land with warriors and carted her off against her will, thrown across his lap like a sack of potatoes. Then he bound her wrists with a leather strap and tried to convince her that he was a caring gentleman with good manners. There could only be one explanation. The man was daft.

They rode well into the night. Bryce's heavily muscled arms shielded her from branches and other brush in their path. They came to a clearing and Bryce halted. "We'll camp here for the night. There's a small brook beyond those trees." He gestured to the right. He called two men over. "Backtrack and station yerselves to keep watch. I want to know of the first sign of a MacKenzie."

Before she could object, large hands circled her waist and lifted her down. "Follow me." He turned on his heel, leaving her with no choice but to do as directed. He led her into the dark woods, and she wanted nothing more than to turn and run the other way. Twigs cracked beneath the weight of their footsteps. An owl hooted in the distance. A small animal shifted and darted through the leaves. She wondered if it was a rabbit. Crickets sang around them. Akira rubbed her arms in discomfort and crouched close to his back to avoid the leaves and limbs he shoved aside. They reached the brook, and he motioned for her to kneel beside him. She bent and watched him remove more of his plaid. He dipped it into the water and brought it against her face.

She jerked at the cold contact. What was this about?

"I merely want to bathe yer face."

She leaned back. "Nay!"

His hands fell to his sides, still holding his wet plaid in one hand. "I can see the swelling and darkness just below yer eye, even in the moonlight."

As if brought on by his words, the skin under her left eye tightened and grew numb. Her fingers inched to her cheek as she stared at him. He was stern with his men and they rushed to do his bidding. A man did not earn that kind of respect and power with a gentle nature. They feared him, and they wanted his approval. She could see it in their faces when they looked at him. Admiration shone in their expression.

"Ye've no reason to fear me, unless ye plan to make it so," he interrupted her thoughts. "I'll treat ye with all the respect owed and due a lady, but heed my warning: Don't anger me by trying to escape. There is naught I despise worse than distrust and betrayal."

Akira stood to her full height, prepared to challenge him. "As yer prisoner I owe ye no trust or loyalty."

He rose beside her. "Consider yerself warned. 'Twould ease yer fear of me." He lowered his voice, and she sensed his tone carried great meaning.

"I'm not afraid. I simply wish ye not to touch me." She hoped her tone carried the contempt she felt.

"As ye wish." He stepped closer, pointing a finger in her face. "But I warn ye. Ye'll remain bound, for I'll not give ye the opportunity to flee. If ye eat, I shall feed ye. If ye wash, I shall help ye. Ye belong to my brother, and I trust no one else save Balloch."

Akira stood still, stunned. He was not the MacPhearson clan chief? She belonged to his brother? "Yer not Evan MacPhearson?"

"I am Bryce MacPhearson, the middle son." He grinned. "I see ye've managed to remember the name of the man ye should have been saying yer vows to when I found ye, instead of that oaf ye were about to commit yerself to."

He started to turn from her, but she gripped his arm. "Gregor is not an oaf. Though that is the best I can describe of ye." She felt almost breathless. "What lies do ye speak? Evan MacPhearson sent my father a letter saying he had no intention of wedding me."

"I speak no lies. The letter was a mistake." He turned his full attention toward Akira and placed his hands on his hips, towering over her. "And as to a better description of me, do ye really lack that much imagination, lass? If this Gregor deserves such defense, then where was the brave groom when I found ye?"

Akira hated the truth of his words. Shivers ran up her spine, and she consciously tried to shake them off, but his last question brought her blood to a boil. Her thoughts turned to the humiliating scene. Warmth crept up her neck and into her face.

"Perhaps he was a wee bit late?" he taunted.

She refused to give him the satisfaction of seeing how much his words hurt. "Maybe he knew how miserable I could make his life, which would be my full intention if yer brother were to succeed in wedding me."

His lips twisted into a sardonic grin. "As laird, Evan is only performing his duties by wedding ye. Marriages of convenience occur every day. I doubt he plans to spend enough time with ye to allow ye to wreak havoc in his life."

"I haven't agreed to wed Evan. And ye know naught of Gregor to throw insults in his absence." She hated the fact that she felt forced to take up for Gregor. He did not deserve her loyalty any more than the MacPhearsons.

"I know enough." His gray eyes grew darker and his voice a bit louder.

"What do ye know of him?"

"Enough."

"If I must hear these accusations against him, then tell me."

He reached for her, and not knowing his intention, she flinched. His palm rested on the side of her face, surprisingly as gentle as a breeze. "I know he is a complete fool to give ye up." His voice broke to a husky whisper.

Akira blinked, wondering if she had heard him correctly. "Then I suppose yer brother would be an even greater fool, because my da received Evan's letter releasing me from the betrothal agreement just six months past."

Bryce's expression didn't change. "He is the fool of all fools." He turned and walked away. Akira followed him.

"Did he send ye for me?" She wanted to know if she was an unwelcome necessity in Evan's life.

"Ye'll know soon enough."

Akira caught up with him and tugged on his arm. She needed answers. "Why didn't he take me?"

He shook off her arm. "Ye'll sleep close by me."

"I think not." She turned from him and stomped off in the other direction, only to realize she still desired to know more about Evan MacPhearson. "Why did he not come for me himself?"

Bryce turned from her, rubbing his palm against his forehead. He walked past his men and pulled his furs from his stallion and threw them at her feet. "Here, sleep on those. 'Tis enough to cover ye."

"My da will come for me."

"I expect he will." Bryce walked over to a tree, sat, leaned against the trunk, and folded his arms over his knees.

"Ye plan to sleep that way?"

"Aye." He let his head drop against the hard bark.

"Ye look uncomfortable." She frowned in his direction. "But, I care not," she assured him. "I'll be home with my family in the comfort of me own bed soon."

Akira brushed aside a few twigs and spread out the furs as best she could with her hands still bound. Then she crawled on top of the furs and brought one end over her. The chill had not bothered her as yet, but the night air promised dropping temperatures. The day had been warm for April and the first time it had not rained in days. It was a good omen for her wedding day—or so she had thought. An image of Gregor appeared in her mind, and sadness closed around her heart. The pain of his rejection hurt more than she cared to think on. She stifled a sob that nearly escaped her throat.

A muffled sound brought Bryce's head up. He studied Akira's feminine form under the moonlight. Her hair sprawled over her arms like silver ribbon. She sighed uncomfortably and shuffled around, restless.

The vision of her face, swollen and blue, made him squirm with regret. He had not meant to hurt her, and he despised his carelessness.

"Blunderin' idiot!" he muttered under his breath.

"Are ye troubled?" The hope in her voice almost made him chuckle as she rolled over on her side and sat up on her elbow. The furs slipped from her shoulder. Akira's silhouetted form shivered against the cool air settling in around them. Bryce looked away and shifted again to ease his discomfort.

"Nay." He dropped his chin on his folded arms.

She continued to stare at him a moment longer before she lay back down to rest.

He let his head fall back against the bark of the tree and looked up at the outline of the branches and leaves above. Footsteps and twigs broke. Balloch plopped down beside him.

"The lady's a beauty, is she not?" Balloch whispered.

"Aye, she is at that. In a few days she'll hate me when she learns the truth." For some reason, that realization bothered him. What should he care of her hatred for him? He wasn't the one destined to wed her, but it bothered him nonetheless. As she prayed aloud for her family, her safety, and a swift return home, guilt plagued him.

When she prayed that God would soften his heart, Bryce could stand no more. He turned to Balloch. "Keep an eye on her. I'll be back."

In one fluid motion he stood and walked away from camp. Safely out of hearing, Bryce looked up at the clear bright stars.

"Lord, Vicar Forbes says to honor yer mother and yer father. I'm only trying to do so." He sighed heavily, wondering if God would hear him after what he had done today. "I really do want peace between our clans. I'm tired of all the bloodshed. Show me how to keep my promise without causing another war."

No answer came from the Almighty. Bryce dropped his head in shame. While he had never been an overly religious man, he had no desire to anger his Maker. Had he gone too far this time?

2

Someone shook her shoulder. Akira wished they would leave her alone. Her head hurt, and she wanted to sleep away the pain.

"Akira, we must ride now."

A man's voice penetrated through her drowsy senses. *His* voice. The horrendous memory of the day before surfaced. A moment of self-pity and dread overwhelmed her. She rolled over, unwilling to face a new day.

"Akira!" Impatience edged his tone.

Wearily, she opened her eyes. The morning was still gray as dawn slowly approached. Bryce must be concerned that her father would be tracking them. The thought gave her renewed strength. She struggled to sit up. During the night she had desperately tried to free her wrists, to no avail. Now she realized that someone had bound her feet as well. She wiggled her feet against the tight leather around her ankles. It might as well have been iron for all she could move them.

Frustrated, she glared up at her captor as he leaned over her with a mischievous smile that did naught to improve her mood.

"I couldn't allow ye to escape, now could I?"

"Aye, ye could," she muttered irritably. "Although, ye shouldn't have taken me at all. I might have wed yer brother willingly if only ye'd asked."

His smile faded, and his eyes glimmered with interest. "Ye were about to pledge yerself to another."

"Perhaps." She looked down before he could see the pain Gregor's rejection had caused.

"So what I did was necessary."

"None of this is necessary." As if to prove her point, Akira shoved her bound feet at him. "Must I hop around all day, or do ye plan to carry me the whole way?"

His gaze dropped from her eyes to her bound feet. "I'll save my strength." He knelt on one knee to remove her bindings. Something else caught his attention and she watched with dread as his mild expression turned to fury. He grabbed both her hands in his and turned over her bloody wrists.

"What is the meaning of this?" His gruff voice faded behind grinding teeth. He would surely have a sore jaw if he didn't soon stop. Akira glanced at the dried blood around her wrists. Her desire to flee had been so great she simply hadn't felt the pain, but she could feel it now as he shook her. The leather tugged against her tattered skin.

"Answer me."

When she only stared back at him, he sighed and shook his head. "I hope ye don't scar. Ye might as well 'ave taken a blade to yerself." He searched her expression as if trying to understand. Bryce lifted his hand and gently rubbed the pad of his thumb against the swollen bruise on her face.

Akira jerked back from his touch. She didn't want his tenderness. It was too much to bear after he had stolen her away from everyone she loved. Her head throbbed, but she would not give him the satisfaction of knowing it.

"One would think I've severely mistreated ye." His soft voice irritated her. His black head dropped to concentrate on her hands. He pulled a knife from his side. She tried not to wince as he tugged the leather to work the knife under it. The blade easily slid through the leather, breaking its hold. In a swift motion, he bent down and did the same to the bindings around her ankles.

"At least ye wore decent soles." He gestured to the small boots laced around her ankles.

Akira had wanted secure footing for an outdoor wedding on a grassy hill. She now recognized the blessing for what it was under the circumstances. She didn't know how long they would be traveling or how much walking she might endure. Someone above must have been looking after her, for she couldn't have possibly known her fate.

Bryce grabbed her by the arm and pulled her up. She stumbled along on stiff legs as he led her to a nearby brook.

"Do that again, and I'll be tempted to strangle ye." He pointed to her bloody wrists.

"Ye canna."

"I can do anything I please. Never doubt it."

"Then my kidnapping would be for naught," she said breathlessly, hurrying to keep up with his anger-driven pace.

"Then I would do the next best thing." He glanced over his shoulder, lowering his voice to a dangerous pitch.

"Which is?" she prompted, determined to ignore her fraying nerves in the face of his anger.

"Don't taunt me, lass." They reached the small brook where Bryce pulled her down to her knees and knelt beside her. He concentrated on cleaning her wounds. "For now ye'll ride unbound, but one trick and I shall make ye sorry."

When he finished, he started to pull her up, but she hesitated. "May I bathe my face?"

Bryce paused. The hope in her expression was hard to ignore, and as the morning sun grew bolder, so did the swelling bruise on her right cheek. Guilt once again tore at his conscience. He nodded, watching as she eagerly splashed cool water on her face. She sighed in contentment. At least he could allow her this one small pleasure.

"'Tis cool." She rewarded him with the first genuine smile on her rosy lips as her long, red-golden hair fell over her shoulders. At the moment her temper was mild, but he had already witnessed the flash of anger that could swell within her at a moment's notice. She glanced in his direction. Her jade eyes sparkled like kindling fire, and her full, round lips curled up. A shudder rippled through him.

"It awakens the sleep in me."

He blinked. "The water?"

She looked at him strangely. "Aye, the cool water. What else could I have meant?"

He grunted, standing to his full height, and wrenched his gaze from her. Watching her had distracted him. If he planned to leave her unbound, he couldn't allow it to happen again, especially with the dangerous direction of his wayward thoughts.

"Hurry, we must ride. Ye delay long enough."

Once again, she rode with Bryce. He stayed in the center of his men. She assumed it was for protection. After a while, her stomach grumbled. Still, she refused to ask for comforts. By mid-morning, clouds gathered in the sky, and she assumed they would continue riding when it began to pour.

Bryce leaned forward, his chest touching her back. "Would ye have willingly wed my brother if I'd asked?"

His warm breath hovered near her ear. She bent her head forward allowing her hair to cover her face to hide her smile. Had he been contemplating her comment until now?

"Would ye?" he insisted.

Her silence must have been too lengthy, for he reached up and pulled her hair back, peering over her shoulder. "Answer me."

Laughter bubbled through her. "Nay, I wouldn't."

He smiled back in spite of himself. "So I thought."

"'Tis not to say ye shouldn't have asked," Akira felt compelled to point out. "It seems that if yer intention was to prevent war between our clans, then ye should have met with the MacKenzie chief. Now ye've provoked my da and brothers—probably the whole clan. 'Twas the wrong action to take."

"No one gives anything for free. I take when I must. Ye forget that ye were promised to Evan first; therefore, ye were his to take."

"Evan didn't take me, did he?" Akira studied his reaction.

He sat motionless for a moment, before answering, "Nay, I took ye in his place."

Tilting her head to the side, she took advantage of the moment. "What is so important that yer brother canna see to his own bride?"

Bryce shrugged. "He's chief of our clan, and therefore a busy man with great responsibilities."

His answer was too vague, and she was not appeased. "My da is chief and a busy man with many of the same responsibilities, yet I've never been neglected."

"Evan doesn't neglect ye. I simply come in his stead."

She did not believe him, but before she could answer, a loud clap of thunder sounded above them and rain began to pour. Akira decided to drop her inquisition for the moment and turned around, keeping her attention focused ahead of them.

They continued their journey in silence, as the rain soaked their clothes and their bodies grew increasingly cold. Lightning threatened the tree branches above them as they rode through the forest. Bryce attempted to cover them with his cloak, and she knew he attempted to shelter her with his body as he leaned close to her. In response, she tried to control her shivers, but they continued. Her teeth chattered, and she gulped to steady her jaw. She crossed her arms, wrapping them around her body to keep the warmth within her.

He tightened his hold and leaned his dark head over her shoulders. "Do ye need rest?"

"Nay, I'm fine." She shook her head, and wet strands of hair stuck together.

"I don't want ye to be ill. If ye need to be out of the rain, tell me."

"I'm in no more danger of getting sick than ye."

"Lass, are ye cold?"

"Nay, no more than the rest of ye."

"We are used to the weather," he said into her ear, to be heard above the downpour.

"Ye're mortal." Another shudder seized her.

It was all he needed to make his decision. "Ye shall rest."

"I need no rest." She tightened her fists in her lap. Why was he so concerned?

He was a MacPhearson and MacPhearsons were barbarians, completely evil, down to their rotten souls. At least that's what she had been taught all her life. Had she been misinformed about the character of the MacPhearsons, or was the good Lord simply looking after her well-being?

"We shall rest." Bryce's tone sliced through her thoughts, daring her to challenge him again. She said naught as he guided his horse away from the line of his men.

"Halt! We shall bed down here!" He raised his voice to be heard above the downpour.

His men exchanged glances. She knew what they were thinking. Her da could be close to them by now. He could have even rallied help from neighboring clans. Was the man daft? Akira felt uncomfortable as some of his men regarded her with expressions filled with hatred and resentment. She refused to lower her head in shame to escape their condemning eyes. She had not asked for special consideration, and she certainly expected none.

Balloch rode over. "What of the MacKenzie clan?"

"I sent two men back. They reported naught. We've taken the chief's daughter, and her life will be in danger if they attack now. He'll think the matter over carefully before he decides how to act. At one time an alliance with us was what he wanted or he wouldn't have signed the betrothal. Perhaps he'll consider the arrangement once again."

Bryce's words were similar to Akira's private thoughts earlier. Her father had signed her betrothal to the MacPhearsons once. What was to prevent him from doing so again? Icy fear twisted in her heart. Would her father sacrifice her to save the whole clan from going to war? In her heart she knew that he would. Although she was his only daughter, she was also only one soul compared to hundreds in her clan. Well, even if her family abandoned her, she felt certain that God would not. She had that one consolation.

"Akira is cold and wet. We shall rest," he informed his men above the patter of the falling rain.

"The lass won't melt!" one of his men grumbled from the back.

Bryce looked up and scanned the faces of his men. "I've taken her to be a bride, not to be a sick burden," Bryce sternly informed all of them. "If ye have anything else to say, speak up now. Otherwise, I will remind ye of the oath ye've sworn to me."

The pouring rain was the only sound around them, as water pellets splashed through the trees. Akira felt the tension in the cold air and despised being the cause of it. "I don't wish to rest." Her voice echoed in the rain.

Bryce's eyes burned, and his jaw tightened. "I said prepare to settle here!" He barked out the order to the man nearest him. They all scattered to do his bidding.

Balloch turned to him. "What shall I do with her?"

"'Tis not what ye shall do with her, but what I shall do with her." He turned back to Akira, who still twisted in her seat to face him. His nose was a mere two inches from hers. They were both soaked and ill at ease. "Ye *will* rest," he ordered sharply.

"I will *not* rest." How could he expect her to sleep in this cold, wet mess? She would rather keep going. At least, they might get there sooner.

"We shall see." He placed both hands on her shoulders and turned her around to face the front. He guided his horse out of the way of his men and dismounted, reaching up to set her down.

She shoved his hands away, determined to dismount on her own. His edgy stallion pranced unsteadily. She turned and reached for the reins to steady his nervous horse.

"Ahern, rise!" he shouted. Without a moment's hesitation the light gray stallion reared back on his hind legs. Bryce must have thought she was trying to escape.

Akira slid backward, landing with an unexpected slosh in the thick, red mud. She could feel the wetness quickly seeping through her wedding gown. Her hands sank at least two inches deep. She tried to stand, but her sodden gown drew her back down. Determined not to be bested, she propelled herself forward, only to lose her balance once more, this time falling forward on her hands and knees. The mud was so thick and slippery, she failed at every attempt.

She glared at Bryce. He couldn't hide his amused grin. His men broke into laughter. Faces turned red, more jests were made, and laughter continued to ring throughout the forest. Bryce managed to stop laughing and bent toward her, extending his hand.

Her lips tightened into a thin line as she considered her options.

Bryce made another move toward her.

"Don't ye dare touch me!"

She might be in an unfavorable position, but she wasn't witless. Drained of energy for the moment, she sank back into the mud to assess the situation further, completely at the center of attention as Bryce's men circled around her. *Let the lot of them rot!*

"Pray tell, what would ye do if I were to touch ye?" Bryce taunted, folding his muscled arms over his broad chest. His men shushed each other to hear her reply.

She smiled sweetly from her mud hole. "The same as ye would," she answered, as if his question were silly.

"Lass, if ye would do as I would, ye wouldn't be smiling at the moment."

She didn't take the bait, and her smile remained plastered across her face. "Ye belittle my intentions. Don't think like a man, but have a wee wit about ye and think like a woman." His men laughed. A few barbed comments reached her ears, but she ignored them, keeping her attention focused on Bryce.

Grinning with interest, Bryce took a step forward and bent. His eyes sparkled. "I believe a lass such as yerself would have the misfortune to imagine herself capable of pulling me down in the mud with her."

Akira's bravery never faltered. She lifted her chin a notch higher for emphasis and looked him straight in the eye. "And I believe a man such as yerself might overestimate his own ability."

His men inched closer, as if straining to hear what Bryce would say next. They would have a while to wait. Before Bryce could come up with a fitting reply, a small fistful of red mud splattered across his face. It hit him so hard his head jerked back to the side.

Amazed at her own reflexes, Akira reached up and covered her mouth, unconsciously smearing a patch of mud on her face. She sat very still, waiting to die. Surely she had pushed him too far?

Fierce gray eyes scorched her. If it were possible, she would have run from him, but she couldn't, so she thought hard to come up with a creative plan. Bryce lunged for her. She scrambled to her knees, pretending to cower before him, bending as low as she could.

Bryce hesitated, surprised by her actions. A second later, he no longer stood.

Akira had sensed his hesitation and chose that moment to lunge at his feet. She pulled and tugged on one of his legs until he came sliding down upon her. She twisted, grabbing two more fistfuls of mud. Knowing time was of the essence and that she might not live to gain any more favors, Akira shoved the mud into his face.

He sat up, trying to wipe the mud away, but his efforts were futile when his hands and every other inch of his body were covered in mud.

"Nay, I didn't use brutal strength to pull ye in. I outwitted ye with yer own conceit, and if that hadn't worked, my gown would surely weigh enough to pull us both in had ye tried to drag me out."

Akira was so engrossed in her pleasure at having bested him in at least one thing that she did not yet realize she was now at his mercy.

"Is that so?"

"Aye, it is." Her smile slowly faded with warranted concern.

"Well, I now have ye right where I want ye."

"Aye," she gulped, acknowledging the truth of his words. His dark eyes peered through his mud-soaked face, roaming over her equally mud-clad features. Her heart started beating rapidly, and she could not calm her racing pulse as he stared at her.

He reached down and smashed a handful of mud in her face. Laughing, he crawled away, watching as she sputtered and spit the gritty mud from her mouth. His men clapped and laughed. They were obviously pleased by his actions.

"Aye, she's a spirited lass. She has a temper to match our Evan's," said a man above the other hearty voices. Akira had heard Bryce call him Kian during their ride.

Bryce glanced over at Akira still sitting in the mud beside him. He held out his hand to her in a gesture that suggested a momentary truce.

Akira hesitated. Should she trust him? If she didn't, she might never get out of this mess. Deciding she could trust him in at least this one thing, Akira placed her hand in his.

He assisted her up. "Reach out to Balloch," Bryce directed. She reached up and strong hands gripped her under the arms, lifting her out of the mud as if she were a small child.

Bryce followed suit on his own, but at a much slower pace.

She stood shivering in the cold rain, blinking as water rushed over her lashes and into her eyes. The rest of the pouring drops washed away some of the mud. Her gown hugged her figure, and she could only imagine the disgraceful sight she must be at the moment. Bryce stopped beside her, allowing his gaze to travel over her. She stiffened, knowing she was being scrutinized once again.

"I wonder if I look as sorry as ye?" Bryce raised a black eyebrow. He cleared his throat and wiped away a thick wad of mud that was about to drop from his ear.

"Aye, ye do," Akira assured him.

Something to the side of her head caught his attention. "Hold still," he ordered, reaching out and pulling a handful of mud from her long hair. He threw it to the ground, and it landed with a thud against the wet ground.

"I suppose now we should concentrate on getting clean." He turned and called over his shoulder, "Balloch, get my soap." Balloch had gone to retrieve Ahern and nodded at the command. Bryce turned back to her. "The rain will not be enough to clean us. We'll go to a nearby loch where we can bathe."

Balloch returned, holding Ahern's reins in one hand and the soap in the other. "Dry out some furs by the fire in the tent. She'll need something warm and dry to wear when we return."

"Aye, Bryce."

"We will go to the loch and bathe. Send someone so we won't be alone. Keep a close watch while we're gone. At the first sign of trouble, alert me." He reached for Akira, easily lifting her onto Ahern's back. Bryce then mounted behind her, reaching his arms around her for the reins and guiding Ahern along the path into the woods.

They rode in silence. The rain slackened to a soft sprinkle. A large clearing came into view. A natural bridge no wider than five feet lay as the only barrier between two lochs. Yellow wildflowers grew along the edges. She marveled at the beauty of this place and wondered how Bryce knew it existed.

"Can ye swim?" His strong voice sounded loud against the droplets of water falling from the trees. He guided Ahern up the grassy ridge between the lochs.

"Nay." She shook her head. "My brothers tried to teach me, but thus far my fear of drowning has proven stronger than my will to learn. I loathe the idea of suffocating to death and that being in over my head would surely bring me to my death."

He chuckled. She gave him a sideways glance. The subject at hand was one she took quite seriously. She didn't appreciate his humor at the moment.

"'Twould appear," Bryce said, as he pulled Ahern's reins to bring him to a halt, "that if ye were to learn how to swim, ye wouldn't be sinking over yer head, but rather floating on top." A mischievous smile toyed at the corners of his mouth and reached into his gleaming eyes.

"'Twould seem," she muttered stiffly.

"It could save yer life." He slid from Ahern's back, and his boots squashed onto the wet ground.

A shiver went through her as he reached up to set her down. She was too weary to protest his assistance this time. Besides, she did not want to provoke him. He might decide to let her drown, instead of having Ahern throw her in a mud puddle.

Taking her hand, he led her to the loch, carrying a bar of soap in his other hand. When they reached the water's edge, he bent to remove his boots and entered the water. Akira sat on the bank to remove her mud-soaked boots. Cautiously, she tipped her feet over the edge, peering intently into the water, trying to measure its depth. Nervously, she glanced at Bryce a short distance away. He stood in waist-deep water, scrubbing mud from his face and neck.

Sighing wearily, Akira stood and stepped into the water, cautiously approaching him. When she reached his side, she smiled triumphantly and held out her hand for the soap.

"Ye'll have to come and get it." His expression was serious, but she could still hear the mischief in his tone. Akira inched forward. He moved backward. The water was now slightly above his waist, but Akira paid no heed. She was too intent on getting the soap.

"Please." She desperately wanted the mud washed from her hair and body. It began to pour again. The rain took her by surprise, and she gasped as the coldness of it beat upon her head and upper body. She took another watchful step toward Bryce. She shivered with goose pimples and imagined her lips must be blue by now. Droplets of muddy rain fell into her eyes, obscuring her view as she crept forward. She splashed her hands in the water to wash the mud off them and wiped her eyes. Bryce appeared to be no more than two or three feet from her. That seemed strange. She thought she had just covered the same distance a moment ago. "Please, give me the soap."

"And I said ye may have it. Ye only have to come and get it."

"Why do ye taunt me? I told ye I canna swim." She splashed her fists into the surface of the water.

"Akira, look at me." He rubbed the soap between his hands, lathering them well. "The water is only up to my chest." He placed a measuring hand across his upper torso. "Ye're a wee bit taller than that. There would be no need to swim." He glanced in her direction while continuing with his task.

It was clear he had no intention of coming to her, and she needed to wash the clinging mud away. Akira scraped her teeth over her bottom lip as she contemplated her next move. He started to whistle. She frowned at him and strode toward him. The water and her skirts slowed her down, but she managed to reach his side and once again held out her hand.

White teeth flashed in the rain as he smiled down at her. "I told ye the water wouldn't be over yer head."

"Nay, I suppose up to my neck wouldn't be uncomfortable to someone who canna swim?" She was near hysterics and even closer to boxing his ears.

He started to hum.

"The soap?" She shoved her empty hand toward him.

"I thought ye might be a wee more comfortable with the water covering ye while ye bathe." He nodded toward one of his men waiting upon the bank. Akira turned, not realizing anyone had followed them. "I intend to be careful with yer reputation. If ye remember, yer to wed my brother."

"I appreciate yer thoughtfulness, but at the moment I'm more concerned about the soap. Would ye please share it?" She was cold and it was his fault she felt so miserable in the first place. When he came to a point in his song, he winked at her. Akira's patience ran out. She lunged at him. He swerved. The slippery soap flew across the water behind him.

Forgetting the water's depth, Akira shuffled after it with a bantering tirade.

"For someone who canna swim, yer not being verra cautious," Bryce called after her—his back to her.

Akira sank deeper and deeper. Her wedding gown and undergarments were so heavy with thick mud, she never had a chance. Rather than waste her strength fighting to stay afloat, she willingly sank to the bottom, trying to release herself from her clothing as the murky depth swallowed her further. The strings were tied too tight. She was running out of air faster than her cold fingers could work the knots. Finally, she worked herself loose from one, but her thoughts began to slip from her. Her lungs screamed for air as she struggled to stay calm and remain sane. She had no energy, and worse, she was losing consciousness.

Lord, help me!

She couldn't do it. Her lungs gave out in spite of her weak attempt to hold in her breath. Akira began choking. She fell to her knees as the water claimed her body. Her hands sank into a cold mushiness, and Akira could only assume she had reached the bottom.

3

*W*hen Akira didn't answer, a flicker of apprehension shuddered through Bryce. All seemed too quiet. He turned and she was nowhere to be found.

"Akira? Akira!"

A cold knot tightened in his stomach. He glanced back at shore, but his man paced with his attention elsewhere and obviously had not seen what had happened. He didn't have enough time to enlist his help.

Bryce took a deep breath and dove under. The rain poured harder, and the dark loch prevented him from seeing underwater. When he thought his lungs would burst, he came up for air. If his lungs were paining him, surely hers would have run out of air by now. With that thought, he dived in after her again.

She could not have gone far, his mind reasoned; she simply hadn't had enough time. He stretched his hands out, reaching for anything within his grasp. His fingers gripped her floating hair. She was already lying on the bottom. *Oh, God!* he prayed. *Please let her live!* He tried to pull her to him, but she was tangled in wild vegetation.

Bryce worked rapidly to release her, realizing that the constricting gown was part of the problem. It felt as if it weighed a ton. He could see how it would have pulled her under and kept her from resurfacing. He should have demanded she strip to her undergarments before entering the water, but he had not wanted to embarrass her. He'd been too busy trying to be conscious of her reputation—and teasing her.

Quickly, he wrapped her in his arms and swam to the top. He dragged Akira's limp body onto the bank and turned her over, pushing on her back. No response. He pushed again and again, until a horrible sound broke through her lips, and she spit up water and dirt. He pushed on her back several more times to get as much water out of her lungs as possible. He hoped Akira would not pay with her life for his carelessness.

"Akira? Akira, answer me," he demanded.

A weak groan escaped her pale mouth.

"Akira, can ye hear me?" He rolled her over on her back. She groaned, catching a deep breath and breaking into hysterical coughs. He realized something must still be lodged in her throat, so he settled her over his lap and pounded on her back. She coughed up more water and dirt.

"Stop hitting me," she struggled to say in the middle of another coughing fit.

In the midst of his fear, he hadn't realized how hard he'd been slapping her back until that moment. He wanted to slam his shaking hands into a rock. Instead, he settled for clenching them into fists.

"Are ye better?"

"How am I . . . supposed to be . . . after nearly drowning?" She gasped for air.

He recognized anger in her weak voice. That was a good sign. The guilty burden in his chest eased. Bryce helped her into a sitting position, but she waved him away. He ignored her, checking her over for signs of other injuries.

Akira pushed at him again with what little strength she had left. Unwilling to let her have her way, he reached for her again, but she evaded his grasp.

"Leave me alone," Akira hissed between chattering teeth. Slowly, she crawled from him and collapsed a few feet from him. She looked completely devoid of strength. Her face contorted with each labored breath as if her lungs pained her. Akira turned on her side and shivered in the cold rain.

Bryce watched her for a moment, but his heart skipped a beat when she lay too still.

"Akira?" He crawled over to her and nudged her shoulder. Her eyes fluttered.

"Sleepy," she murmured.

The area around her mouth looked blue, and the grayish color of her skin wasn't a good sign. He gathered her in his arms.

"My gown," she protested groggily.

He realized she worried about leaving her gown at the bottom of the loch. They didn't have a choice. It was a matter of life and death. Besides, she wore enough undergarments to cover her. "Shush. I know. I'll wrap ye up." He pulled the wet furs from Ahern's back and wrapped her cold body, wishing he had something dry and warm. "It might serve as a covering, but it won't provide any heat." Bryce deposited her on Ahern's back and mounted up behind her. He nudged Ahern into a gallop, needing to get her out of the cold rain—and fast.

Bryce's men had unsuccessfully tried to build a fire. They managed to get a small one going, but it quickly sputtered out before they could draw any warmth from it. The task would be impossible with the ground soaked and a lack of dry wood.

With Akira no longer conscious, Bryce feared for her life. He decided to keep going and ordered his men to pack. If they pushed hard enough, they would be home within a day. Then Akira would be in the finest hands possible, where Finella, his childhood nursemaid, could nurse her back to health.

The thought of returning home brought to mind another unpleasant matter that awaited him at the castle. He'd have to face Evan, his brother. Not looking forward to the meeting, Bryce sighed as the rain continued to pound them. Evan would certainly be displeased that Bryce had taken Akira, but once Evan met her, Bryce felt certain he'd change his mind about not wedding her.

They traveled all night, and it was evident by morning that a fever burned in her body. The rains continued, slacking up here and there, but never enough to allow the sun out for a significant amount of time to dry the land.

He rode his men hard, only allowing short breaks. Akira never completely woke. She thrashed about in her fevered state, calling out names in tormented sobs. Bryce held her against him and tended to her as if she were a wee bairn, dripping water into her mouth and forcing her to swallow.

The long ride provided plenty of time for thoughts as Bryce found himself missing Akira's sharp-witted tongue. He squinted from fatigue and worry to see through the light drizzle. They passed familiar cottages and lodges, marking MacPhearson land. Eager to know that all was well and that the MacKenzie clan had not beaten him home, Bryce increased their pace. He needed to be the first to confess his deeds to Evan.

Things appeared normal. People paused long enough to wave a greeting. Some pointed, curious about the bundle in his arms, while others paid no heed to Akira's hidden form, covered by furs from head to toe. Bryce didn't want anyone to know of her presence among them until he'd spoken to his brother.

The stone fortress came into view. His chest always filled with pride when he saw it. He looked forward to the day it would be completely restored. The castle was at least two hundred years old; the west wing had suffered severe damage from age and weather erosion. The outer wall needed repairs for a better defense, and it would be his main concern now that he'd returned and the promise to his father was nearly complete.

The idea of warm, dry clothes and a full belly appealed to him. His brothers, Evan and Sim, waited in the courtyard. Apparently, they'd been alerted of their return.

As soon as Bryce drew to a halt, Evan marched over, grabbing Ahern's reins. "Is that her? Did ye really take the lass?"

Bryce knew from experience that Evan was on the verge of exploding and sought a more private place to converse. "May I please dismount before ye begin yer assaults?"

"'Tis true then? Ye did bring her? I won't do it, Bryce. I meant it when I said nay before. I'll not wed a MacKenzie. Never." He emphasized the last word with finality, slicing his hand through the air.

"I suppose that means nay," Bryce commented dryly, rolling his eyes as he turned to the other side of Ahern and slid down from his horse. He kept Akira's feverish body close.

Evan was not deterred by his action and strode around to the other side of Ahern. He pointed to the swaddled furs in Bryce's arms.

"What's wrong with her? Did she faint from the rain? I canna believe this. To even think I would consider wedding a MacKenzie . . . and a feeble lass at that."

Bryce felt honor-bound to defend her since it was his fault she was ill. He gave Evan a dark, impatient glare. "Ye know absolutely naught about her or what she had to go through to get here. This lass showed more courage on this trip than ye'll ever see in a lifetime!" His wet hair clung to his neck. He felt tired, hungry, and worried that a fever still blazed in Akira's shivering body.

Evan stepped back from his brother, obviously a little surprised at the vehemence in Bryce's voice. Then he smiled. "Bryce, what did ye do to her?" Evan knew him well enough to know when he harbored some kind of guilt.

Holding his temper, Bryce veiled the irate expression that he knew burned in his eyes. Giving Evan no further time to decipher his feelings, Bryce turned and carried Akira inside.

Akira's hands and arms lashed out in front of her. She thought she fought Bryce, but she could not tell for sure in the darkness. Her own strange voice shouted in the distance, and yet she knew her own voice could not be in the distance.

"Shush, lassie. Yer just havin' a bad dream. 'Tis naught to worry yer wee head 'bout. Shush." The unfamiliar voice of a woman soothed her. A gentle hand wiped a strand of hair from her sweating forehead. The woman's soft voice crooned to her again. Akira slowly calmed. She realized Bryce was not around, but her whereabouts were still unclear. Could her father have come for her after all?

"Da?" She reached out for him.

"Shush. 'Tis all right, lass. Yer da isn't here."

"Did he come for me? Da!" She tried to open her eyes, but as soon as she did, a dizzy spell hit her, and her stomach churned. She groaned, gulping for air, but she couldn't seem to catch her breath. What was wrong with her? Had they poisoned her?

Gentle hands pushed her shoulders back. "There now. Yer not ready to get up yet. Ye haven't the strength."

"Gavin? Where's Gavin? Where's Elliot?"

"Lassie, I dunno who ye speak of."

That comment made her realize she was not at home and that neither her da nor her brothers had come for her. Disappointment assailed her, but her heart still held hope and confidence that it wouldn't be long now before they came for her.

"The Lord won't fail me," she muttered hopefully. "God will send them to me. He won't let them desert me."

"Ye must get yer rest," the woman coaxed. Akira felt a warm hand on her forehead.

Akira didn't want to rest. She wanted to know where she was and why she felt so terribly weak.

Determined to learn more about her surroundings, she opened her eyes and again fought the sick feeling that rose up in her stomach.

Squinting, Akira could see the dark room, lit only by a fire that illuminated an elderly woman bending over her. Her gray hair was pulled back into a tight bun, leaving her face open to view. A slight smile and a missing front tooth made her look more affectionate than unappealing and lifted the wrinkles around her soft brown eyes, giving her a wise countenance.

The woman gently took Akira's hand and tucked it under the furs with the rest of her body.

"Are ye hungry? Ye've not eaten in a few days."

Days? Why had she not eaten in days? "Where am I?"

"Yer in a guest chamber at MacPhearson Castle, but ye're not to leave this room alone. 'Twill be locked."

"May I have some water?" Her throat felt swollen.

"Aye, lassie. Indeed, ye may." The old woman brightened and hustled over to the pitcher, sitting on a nearby dresser. She turned to see Akira struggling to raise her head and rushed back to her patient. "Nay, lass. Don't overdo it the first day." She gently reached behind Akira's neck, supporting her head to drink.

Akira was quite thirsty, more than she had originally thought, and drained the goblet of its contents. Water had never tasted so sweet. "More, please?" She wiped her mouth with the back of her hand. The kind woman hurried to refill her goblet and assisted her again as she drank.

"My name's Finella. I've taken care of ye since they brought ye in."

"Who brought me in?" Akira sighed, handing her the empty goblet, and leaned back to watch her nurse closely.

Finella shrugged, stepping closer. Her figure towered over Akira lying on the bed.

"Lass, do not pretend ye don't know how ye came to be here."

"I only remember Bryce taking me from my family and a flood of some sort."

Finella gasped. "Lass, 'twas no flood. Ye nearly drowned in a loch."

Akira's mind clouded with confusion, and it made her head hurt to think about it. "Aye, 'tis true," she amended, trying to block out the horrifying memory.

"No need to worry. Few know of the incident or that ye're even here," Finella assured her, while fluffing her feather pillows.

"'Tis a secret?"

Finella's smile turned into a frown, and her countenance grew colder than a winter's day. "Isn't my place to tell ye." The woman tucked in Akira snugly and bustled out of the chamber without another word, leaving Akira to her own frustrated thoughts.

Too exhausted to evaluate her situation further, Akira drifted back to sleep.

*

When Akira next opened her eyes there was no one in her chamber to keep her in bed. She ignored her aching head and body as she sat up and tossed the covers aside. The sudden movement made the room spin, and she waited for it to stop. When it did, her surroundings came into focus. The bed she'd slept in looked much smaller than what she was accustomed to and the chamber half the size of hers at home. The dull brown furniture appeared to be cheaply carved from simple wood, not the sort of thing one would expect to find inside the walls of MacPhearson Castle. She noticed one small window across the chamber. Closed shutters barred the morning sunlight, casting dark shadows about her room. Evidence of a fire from the night before singed the air, and dark soot filled the fireplace.

Akira hated darkness. She stood, not realizing she had made the decision to do so, and had to fight a wave of nausea. Determined to bring in some light, she tiptoed in her bare feet across the cold stone floor. Reaching the window, she opened the shutters. Akira squinted as bold rays lit the chamber. When her eyes adjusted to the sunlight, she could see children playing and their parents tending to their daily chores out in the courtyard. A flower garden bordered the castle. At least her view was pleasant, even if her guest chamber was not.

A sudden thought made her pause in horror. What if her abduction was a plan to thwart her clan so that the

MacPhearsons could attack the MacKenzies with ease? Could that be the reason why Bryce had come for her and Evan had not? Evan could have been leading the attack while she was being swept across the countryside. Fear gripped her.

Akira knew her imagination might be getting the better of her, so she did what she had been taught to do in times of trouble. She sank to her knees and bowed her head over the bed.

"Lord, I know I have had some dreadful thoughts about the MacPhearsons. Please forgive me. Right now, I'm scared and I need yer help. Please show me what to do. I admit that my temper is my worst enemy. Help me keep it under control so that life here will not be so unbearable. I pray that ye will help me find a way home. Lord, I pray for peace. Amen."

She glanced at the door to her chamber and wondered if she were locked inside. She looked down at the white nightgown Finella must have dressed her in. If the door was unlocked, she could not very well leave the chamber dressed as she was.

Akira took small, unsteady steps to a nearby dresser, pushing aside her weakness as she slowly made her way. She ignored her parched throat. She wondered how long she'd slept and how little she had actually eaten in the last few days. If she wanted to escape, she would have to wait until her strength returned.

She spotted a brown dress and some undergarments lying on a chest by the dresser. Assuming they were for her, Akira dressed as quickly as her fatigued limbs would allow. In spite of the dizziness still plaguing her, she made it to the wash basin where she splashed cold water on her face and washed her hands and arms. Feeling more awake, Akira grabbed a comb lying on the dresser and brushed the tangles from her hair. With that task completed, she looked at her reflection in the full-length looking glass that stood in the corner of the chamber.

The brown dress resembled nothing she would have chosen for herself. The dull color lacked appeal—more akin to a servant's garment. Not only that, but it was too short and just reached above her ankles. The material stretched across her frame and pulled lower than she preferred. Akira tugged at the cloth to pull the bodice higher. The dress ripped under her arm. Twisting this way and that, she tried to find the hole in the looking glass. Satisfied that it would not show, she stopped pulling on it, for fear of destroying the rest of the garment.

The waistline would cut off her circulation before the day was through. She sucked in her stomach and then let it out again. She didn't have the energy to hold it in place. Akira frowned. She looked like a sick, lowly beggar. Dark circles framed her eyes in contrast to her pale skin. Maybe her unappealing appearance would disgust Evan to the point of changing his mind about their wedding.

Akira smiled with renewed hope. It was a sound plan. For the moment, she had no other recourse. She strode to the door with a confidence she didn't feel. Her hand shook with nervousness as she firmly gripped the knob. To her surprise, it opened. She peeked out into the hallway. Seeing no one, she stepped out to begin her investigation.

"Have ye gone daft? I said I'll not wed the wench!" Evan roared across the library. He paced anxiously in front of the fireplace. A lock of brown hair fell over his eye, and he brought a hand up, impatiently shoving it out of his way. His cheeks were flushed with anger, and his mind seemed to be searching for any excuse that Bryce would accept. "One would think ye're the clan chief around here. Yer meddlin' has got to stop, Bryce. 'Twould serve ye well to return her to her da and forget this foolishness."

"Ye know as well as I do that's now impossible. 'Tis only a matter of time before we hear from him." Bryce sat at his desk in the corner by the window, patiently watching his brother pace back and forth in front of the blazing hearth.

Bryce struggled to control his emotions. Evan knew him well, and with one slip, he would notice Bryce questioning the sanity of his own actions. Bryce rose and leaned against the window sill, paying no heed to the surroundings below. His thoughts were on his present dilemma.

"This union won't save a war between the clans. If anything, 'twill only serve to feed the already festering hate, while Akira and I are caught in the middle of it."

"'Twas arranged by our da. He told me upon his death that he wanted it to be honored. I won't fail him." Bryce balled his fist and shook it at his brother.

"Well, then, he asked the wrong son. 'Twould not be ye who fail him, but me."

Bryce sighed. He was growing weary of the constant arguments over the subject; neither of them had budged an inch. "Evan, please be reasonable about this."

"I'll not waste my life on that wench. And I certainly won't wed her." Evan's voice carried through the library.

"And I wouldn't waste a precious day on a MacPhearson."

Bryce and his brother turned toward the entrance where Akira stood in a weakened state, holding onto the door for support, but her burning eyes were defiant. She had spoken with quiet precision and force.

"I'm relieved to know our feelings are mutual." Evan finally recovered from his shock at being overheard.

"Since we both feel the same, I'm certain we can come to some kind of an agreement." Akira's voice was full of resolve as she prepared to bargain for her freedom.

"Let the negotiations begin," Evan said, rubbing his hands together, eager to escape the trap Bryce had set for him.

"Nay," Bryce cut in, frowning. "The two of ye will honor the betrothal as our fathers deemed appropriate."

"If ye recall, my da was wedding me to Gregor when ye abruptly snatched me away. I wouldn't agree that he still feels this match is necessary."

"Evidently, the love of yer life didn't feel the same way. I've asked this before—where was he when I came? 'Tis him I should have had to hit, not yer brother."

Akira ignored him, determined to steer the conversation back to her escape. "To what lengths would ye go to make me wed Evan? Would ye have me brutalized?" She stepped forward, apparently growing braver by the minute.

"'Twould be no need," Bryce informed her sternly, his gaze slipping down to her bare feet and noticing her delicate toes.

"Would ye use threats?"

Reluctantly, he answered, "Again, there would be no need."

"How then, do ye intend to convince me to agree to the vows?" The frustration in her voice indicated that she couldn't imagine what he planned. She stole a glance at Evan, who appeared to be just as curious as she. He watched Bryce's reaction with interest.

"I'll keep ye both guessing. In the meantime, keep up the effort of yer protests though they be in vain." His gaze darted from Akira to Evan.

"Ye fool!" Akira shouted. Her face turned a bright pink as her anger flared. Both Evan and Bryce were momentarily stunned by her outburst. "Ye're so bent on preventing war, and so daft ye canna see that ye'll be the cause of it." She strode to him, breathing heavily from her anger and weakness. "Because of what ye've done, my father will be forced to take action."

"But not in war. I've a written agreement that he signed yer betrothal. The MacPhearsons had a legal right to stop that wedding. I'm sorry, lass, but he will have to agree to negotiations," Bryce informed her.

"He'll never agree to wed me to a MacPhearson, not when he has a written letter from Evan saying he would not honor the betrothal," she persisted.

"He'll have no choice, for we will agree to naught else." Bryce crossed his arms over his chest and tried not to be distracted by her weakness.

Akira reached out as if seeking support. "How dare—"

Bryce knew the moment she would faint. He reached for her, making sure she fell safely in his arms. He swept her up and carried her from the library. She felt soft and light in his arms as he climbed the stairs. What had she been thinking, rising out of bed so soon? Where was Finella? He gently laid Akira on the small bed in her chamber.

"Will she be all right?" Evan asked behind him. Bryce glanced over his shoulder at his brother's concerned frown, unaware until that moment that Evan had even followed.

"Aye, she's weak from the fever and lack of nourishment. The fool woman knew better than to get out of bed. Where in the world did she get that inappropriate dress? We'll have to see that she's properly attired. She looks like a serving wench in that thing. And shoes? Couldn't Finella at least find her some shoes?"

"I dunno." Evan bent over her, brushing a strand of hair from her face. "Too bad she's a MacKenzie. After meeting her, I kind of like her spirit."

Bryce glared at his brother and turned away. It was what he'd wanted. If Evan grew fond of her, then it would be easier for Bryce to keep his promise to his father and maybe they would finally achieve peace by joining their two families. He glanced at her still form. Akira's face was delicately carved with a depth of strength. Her lush hair framed her face in thick folds on the white, feathered pillow. Her lips were the color of dark rose and fully rounded. When awake her jade eyes were like fire, lighting darkness and drawing one to their warmth. He cleared his mind.

"Have Finella come to her. She'll know what to do with the lass," Bryce suggested.

Evan continued to stare at her sleeping form.

"And for goodness sake, stop gawking over her. She isn't yer wife yet." Bryce stormed from the chamber, unhappy with how well his plans were succeeding.

4

$\mathscr{T}$he following day Bryce plunged himself into his work to keep his mind off Akira. He felt responsible for her near-death experience, as well as for her illness. Frustrated that he couldn't concentrate, Bryce dismissed his men early that afternoon and decided to see how Akira was faring.

As he strolled down the hall, he tried to relax and slow his pace. Her melodious voice echoed in laughter down the hall leading to her bedchamber. Bryce paused outside the open doorway. Her laughter was like a flood of relief and eased the tension in his shoulders.

"A horse? Nay?" She was asking someone in her room.

The lack of verbal response made Bryce suspect that his younger brother Sim entertained her. Deaf and mute, Sim used exaggerated gestures and imitations as his only means of communicating. He liked making people guess at what he tried to say. He enjoyed it as a game.

"Hmm. A mule?" Akira clapped with delight. "I knew it!" She laughed again.

Bryce had meant to leave them undisturbed, but the sound of her laughter tugged at his curiosity even more. It wasn't enough just to hear her. He wanted to see laughter in her eyes and watch how a simple smile could light up her face. His feet seemed to float into the large chamber where he had ordered Finella to move Akira.

Sim stood at the foot of her bed, making funny faces and moving his hands about. Akira hugged her knees in the center of the bed, surrounded by a frame of four intricately carved oak posts. The lad must have noticed Bryce's entrance, for he turned and waved. Akira's gaze followed his attention toward Bryce. Her eyes flickered from joy to disdain, and her beautiful smile melted.

Bryce tried to ignore his mounting disappointment and stepped closer. "I wanted to see if ye were better."

"I roll in happiness away from yer gracious presence. So, ye may take yer leave." Her expression harbored distrust as the corners of her lips curled upward in a sardonic smile.

He chose to ignore her angry words. "I see ye're in good company." He kept his voice light and casual and nodded toward Sim. "The lad is full of wit and good humor, even if he is my brother."

"Yer brother?" Her eyes grew wide in surprise.

"Aye, he's the wee one." Bryce folded his hands behind his back. Her innocence intrigued him. He fought the urge to stare at her as he tried to interpret her stunned reaction.

"Are there more of ye?" Her voice held a hint of contempt, as if the idea of more MacPhearson brothers gave her anxiety.

"Only the three of us." Bryce shook his head.

The tension in her expression eased into relief. She glanced at Sim, and her lips puckered into another frown. "The poor lad. He's so young to be all alone."

Her reflective tone echoed with a trace of pity that Bryce didn't like. He shrugged, slightly offended. "He isn't alone. Evan and I take care of him—sometimes too much."

"Why do ye say that?"

Without answering, Bryce turned to Sim and touched his shoulder to gain his attention. "Evan is going out for a ride if ye'd like to join him."

Reading his lips, the lad eagerly nodded and hastily disappeared from the chamber. Sim popped back in with a good-bye wave to Akira. She waved back, and he disappeared again.

Bryce shook his head, sporting a fatherly expression of pride. "He loves to ride."

Akira cleared her throat. "Did ye forget my question?"

Bryce sighed as he dropped in a chair and scooted closer to her bedside. "Nay, I didn't forget yer question, Akira. 'Tis quite simple. He's at the age when he must begin his training."

"Training for what?"

Bryce paused, wondering if she was as innocent as she obviously wanted him to believe. "To be a warrior. Sim must learn to defend himself. Evan and I have worked with him some, but not to the degree that is necessary. I'll not have him fail in a battle because of my negligence."

She leaned back and gazed into his eyes. "Then train him, but do not send him into battle."

"Soon he will be a man, and I canna deny him the right to do as he wishes."

"He's only a lad. What does he know of the world? Can he even read or write?"

"Ye ask a wee bit much of a lad who canna hear nor speak." Bryce closed his eyes and rubbed his temples. "Reading and writing will not help him keep his home and his land. This world ye speak of, Akira, is built upon survival. The strong conquer and live, while the weak crumble and die."

Abruptly, Bryce scooted his chair back and rose to pace around her chamber. He and Evan had borne the weight of Sim's disabilities for so long that it now seemed of little or no consequence, until he thought of Sim being a man of his own. And Bryce knew that to deny him those basic rights would be like denying him his manhood—his birthright.

He whirled around and bent toward Akira. The smell of lilacs drifted to his senses, calming the frustrated passion coursing through his veins. He took a deep breath as he searched her lovely face for understanding. "Do ye not realize, lass, that there's no limit to what I'd give to hear Sim speak?" Bryce lifted a finger so close to her face that her eyes blinked and her long, dark lashes fluttered. "Even if only one word?" The sincere conviction of his voice portrayed the emotion he fought to hide. He could tell she listened as mixed emotions filled her expression and a new compassion entered her eyes.

"Then let him live and don't even consider the possibility of sending him into battle. Educate him instead. Men like ye will always need someone to keep yer records. And ye need someone ye can trust, someone who won't talk about yer finances or the state of things. Give him a life worth living instead of empty days full of naught save bloodshed."

Bryce stepped back, folding his arms across his chest and shaking his head. "I wouldn't expect a woman to understand the responsibilities of a man."

Her lips tightened into a thin line, and she glared at him with burning, reproachful eyes. "I understand a man's responsibilities well, but I also understand the lad's limitations." She shifted and again hugged her knees to her chest. "I simply believe he deserves a chance at life, which has absolutely naught to do with me being a woman." Her expression glowed with a savage inner fire as she met his gaze with a boldness that many of his men had yet to master. "Bryce MacPhearson, sometimes ye're everything to be despised."

"That's unjust. Ye twist my words into things I don't mean."

"It isn't unjust! Ye claimed a woman couldn't understand the responsibilities of a man, and I simply challenged ye on the matter."

He stepped closer, and recognizing the guarded look in her eyes, dropped his hands to his sides. She feared him and that bothered him. "How long will it take ye to forgive me, lass?"

Something about Akira made his pulse quicken, and he needed to keep his distance to maintain a clear head. He stepped back. Other than Evan, Akira was the only one who had the nerve to challenge his decisions and way of thinking. She made him see different perspectives. Bryce couldn't decide if it was a blessing or a curse. As much as he hated to admit it, her thoughts mattered, and he had no idea why.

Akira visibly stiffened and straightened as if drawing on all her inner strength to maintain his gaze. A flicker of apprehension momentarily crossed her features and then it was gone.

"I am commanded by my Lord to forgive my fellow man." She spoke with quiet, but decisive firmness. "Bryce MacPhearson, ye shall have my forgiveness, but never my trust."

He exhaled a long sigh of relief. Her forgiveness was a step in the right direction, but he wanted more. He also wanted her trust. As a warrior he had been trained to do what was necessary for the good of the clan and to protect his people. A guilty conscience was not an option. It could be the very thing that got a man killed on the battlefield. Yet with Akira, he seemed to be going against the very principal that he had been trained to avoid.

He leaned forward and lowered his voice. "There's softness in ye, Akira, that ye'd prefer to hide. But I remember the way ye cleaned my leg after ye retched all over me."

Her face clouded with uneasiness at the reminder. "I was insane with fright," she said. Akira pulled at a loose string on her blanket, careful to avoid his gaze.

"Ye were as calm as ye are now," he countered. "Ye've changed since yer experience at the loch."

"I've not changed. If ye recall, ye nearly killed me."

"That isn't true and ye know it. If I wanted ye dead, ye would be."

The truth in his words seemed to reverberate against the awkward silence that filled the chamber. Her steady gaze hid her thoughts. An unexpected smile curved her round lips.

"I never did believe half the rumors my clansmen spread about the MacPhearsons, but let no one ever say ye're not a forthright man."

"What rumors?" Bryce raised a dark eyebrow, not bothering to hide the glimmer of interest in his expression.

"That ye are all evil," Akira replied without hesitation.

Bryce crossed his arms over his chest and chuckled, amused by the exaggerated imagination of her clansmen.

"Ye may fence words with me all ye wish," Akira informed him, "but regardless of anything ye say, I am naught more than a simple tool to gain what ye want."

"True." He did not deny it. "But, ye'll become one of us and will be treated and protected as such." The quiet emphasis in his tone left no room for further argument.

"And who'll protect me from ye?" Akira regarded him with a thoughtful gaze.

Bryce grew silent as he considered her question. For a brief moment, he couldn't help wondering if she referred to her experience at the loch or something deeper. Could she sense the growing attraction he felt for her? If so, he would simply have to do a better job of rejecting it. She would be his brother's wife. He would do naught to interfere with their union, especially after he had risked so much to see them wed.

"Ye need no protection from me. Ye've my word on it," he assured her. "I'll take my leave now. Finella will soon bring up yer meal." He turned and strode from her chamber.

☙

"Sim, what do ye think about this scheme of our brother's?" Evan rode his mount hard, giving his destrier the exercise he needed. Sim followed close behind on his own mount. Evan knew Sim couldn't hear him, and it was just as well. Talking aloud helped him sort through his scattered thoughts.

It wasn't that Evan disliked the lass. He didn't know her. She carried MacKenzie blood and bore the name. As far as he was concerned, that alone justified not wedding her. What kind of suffering had his father endured to ask Bryce to do such a foolish thing? Evan snapped his fingers. Aye, that had to be it. The loss of blood and the severity of his father's wounds must have been too much. He couldn't have been thinking clearly. His father hadn't really intended for him to wed the MacKenzie lass.

Evan slowed his mount as he brooded over his troubles. He leaned forward and patted the animal on the neck. The sound of neighing horses pulled Evan from his thoughts. Two men rode out from a wide hedge and charged toward them. Sim's horse reared on its hind legs in fear. Evan couldn't help Sim as his own mount pawed the air. Both brothers struggled to maintain control as their chargers shot forward and raced through the woods. Their pursuers surged after them.

Evan stole a glance behind and recognized their MacKenzie plaids. Anger flared through him. There could only be one reason MacKenzie warriors were on MacPhearson land—retaliation for Bryce's abduction of Akira. When he got out of this mess, he would strangle Bryce for causing such a tangled web. Right now he needed to protect Sim. Evan dodged low-lying tree limbs, shifting his weight to the right and then to the left.

Sim turned and missed seeing a sturdy tree limb in his path. Hard pine slammed against his chest, nearly knocking the breath from him. His horse flew out from beneath him as he tumbled to the ground. Evan glanced back. His brother lay on the ground in a dazed stupor as one of the attackers slowed, dismounted, and headed toward him.

Evan's pursuer gained speed. He had two choices. He could keep going and hope to rescue Sim with help later, or face his challengers now. Taking a deep breath, Evan slowed and unsheathed his sword. He couldn't risk what might happen to Sim if left at the mercy of MacKenzie warriors.

His opponent also unsheathed his sword. They rode toward one another, both yelling the ancient battle cries of their ancestors. The sound of steel crashing against steel echoed through the dense forest. The effort drove each man sideways in his saddle. Their arms locked into opposing positions. Evan used as much force as he could muster to hold back his attacker's sword. The man grunted as he shoved against Evan's defensive hold.

Both men fell, hitting the hard earth and rolling to their feet. They turned to face each other, circling around in a fighting stance. Each man carefully assessed the other, waiting to see who would make the next move.

"Gregor, this one is just a lad and he carries no weapon. I'll bind him and hope he talks," said the man bending over Sim.

"He canna talk." Evan tried to divert their attention from Sim to himself. "But I do!"

The man named Gregor continued to circle with him, his sword poised, ready to strike. "Ye must be Evan MacPhearson." He tilted his head in a questioning gaze. His blond hair fell in layers above his shoulders. Cold, brown eyes penetrated Evan's concentration.

The other man turned from his struggle with Sim. "Gregor, no sparring. Remember why we're here. We need to talk to them."

"Ye attacked me on MacPhearson land. My sword can do the talking for me." Evan swung a wide arc, and Gregor matched him. Their swords clashed again.

The other warrior finally secured Sim's bindings and stood. "I'm Elliot MacKenzie, and I came to see about my sister."

Evan kept his gaze on the blond warrior before him. "Are ye a MacKenzie as well, here to see my bride?"

"My name's Gregor Matheson, and yer mistaken, I am the man who will slay ye this day!" The next time their swords met a spark flared between the two sharp blades.

"Stop the sparring before ye regret it. Dead men canna talk." Elliot strode toward them.

Gregor jabbed his sword at Evan, who stepped on pebbles and slid. His balance faltered, and he couldn't block Gregor's sword. The blade slid sideways into his chest between his ribs. Momentum forced Evan's arm down in an arc slicing into Gregor's throat. Both men slid to the ground with their life's blood rapidly staining the earth.

Elliot ran the rest of the way to Gregor's side. Too late. The wound in his neck had nearly beheaded him, killing him instantly. Elliot turned to see Evan's skin turning milky white. His eyes were open and glazed with pain, watching and waiting for Elliot to finish him.

Instead, Elliot pulled the heavy sword from Evan's chest and wrapped his own plaid tight around him. "I only wanted to talk to ye. Gregor always let his temper get the best of him. Although I'll most likely lose my head, I'll not leave ye here to die. MacPhearson Castle is the closest place, so I'll take ye home and hope I might survive in the effort."

Elliot bent and untied Sim's feet and hands. "Guess I'll have to take the chance that ye'd rather save yer brother's life over avenging him." He pointed toward Evan. "He needs help." The lad looked at him with a dazed and fearful expression. His gaze followed the direction of Elliot's finger. His eyes met and held Evan's. Tears gathered in Sim's brown eyes. The lad looked away, struggling to control his emotion.

"He's deaf . . . and mute." Evan spoke with short gasps of pain.

"We have to get help," Elliot said again, grabbing Sim's shoulders and forcing the lad to pay close attention to what he said. "Show me the way home." Sim nodded, obediently scrambling to his feet.

Elliot moved back to Evan and carefully lifted him in his arms. Evan groaned.

"I know 'tis painful, but I must get ye back so ye can be saved. I've done all I can out here in the wilderness." He grunted under Evan's weight.

"Who . . . is Gregor?"

"He was betrothed to my sister, Akira." Elliot balanced the burden of Evan's weight.

"I . . . was . . . betrothed to . . . her."

"Aye, ye were. He was to wed Akira after we received yer letter denouncing the betrothal. We couldn't understand why ye would refuse Akira and then steal her away. My father is considering the circumstances and weighing our options and the consequences of our actions. 'Tis the only reason he waits to retaliate."

"Not . . . me." It was all Evan managed to say before he lost consciousness.

Bryce lunged at his opponent with his sword. He personally assisted in the training of each new warrior. The lad's slow response could cost him his life. He needed to build his strength to wield the heavy sword more accurately.

He looked up and saw Balloch and Kian approaching. Their grim expressions didn't bode well. He ordered one of his men to take his place and strode to where they waited. He wiped his sweating brow with his sleeve. "What is it?"

"Evan is severely wounded. Someone reported seeing a MacKenzie, carrying Evan through the village. I doubt they would have let him through the gates if Sim had not been with him."

"Gather the men together. No one is to harm the MacKenzie until we know the circumstances." He turned to Balloch. "I need ye to guard Akira. Do not let her leave her chamber under any circumstances. If she discovers a MacKenzie is here, she'll attempt to get to him in some way. Kian, get the physician and bring him to Evan's chamber."

By the time Bryce left the fields and entered the courtyard, Sim shoved the side door open, and a man hauled Evan's limp body into the castle. Bryce rushed to meet them, his chest pivoting into tension. "I don't know if he'll make it." The man spoke in a tone of sympathy.

"He'd better." Bryce's clipped tone sounded full of worry, expressing no appreciation or accusation. He looked into the eyes of the man carrying his brother. "I don't want to jar him. I'll show ye where to lay him, and be quick about it," he snapped, already moving in another direction, expecting the MacKenzie warrior to follow.

The man laid Evan down as gently as possible, and the waiting physician came forward. Bryce turned to Kian and two of his men outside the doorway.

"Escort him to the library and guard him there until I return, no matter how long it takes."

Kian nodded and reached for the man's arm, but he jerked away. "I wouldn't have brought him here if I intended to be trouble." He turned and gave Bryce a level stare. "Ye could at least treat me with courtesy for bringing him to ye."

Kian waited, raising an eyebrow toward Bryce.

Bryce nodded. "Go then, with Kian. But I will want answers after my physician has seen to my brother."

Angus Cullum, the MacPhearson physician, tore through Evan's clothes and ordered hot water and cloths. After he cleaned the wound as best he could, he stood back and shook his head. "'Tis not good. The wound is verra deep, no doubt piercing a lung. It barely missed his heart. His lungs are hardly holding on, and he's lost too much blood already. Ye'd better call Vicar Forbes."

A flash of lightning stole Bryce's mind from the present into the past. As a lad, Bryce had bent cradling his father's head as he suffered from a wound similar to Evan's. The same feeling of helplessness filled him now as a grown man. His mind cleared as Angus continued painting a grim picture that offered no hope. In a mad rage, Bryce grabbed him by the neck and shoved him against the wall. The physician started choking until Bryce loosened his hold.

"I am not God. I canna perform the impossible." Angus gasped for air.

"Bryce! Put him down. Ye're not helping Evan." Akira appeared, pulling on his arm.

"I thought I told Balloch to keep ye in yer room?" He glared at Balloch standing at the entrance. Balloch looked down awkwardly, staring at his feet to avoid Bryce's outrage.

"Ye did, but after he told me about Evan's wound, I convinced him I might be of some help." She went over to Evan.

"Angus says he'll not live." Bryce's voice sounded gruff and foreign, even to his own ears. What had come over him? He looked at Angus apologetically and dropped him to his feet. "I'm sorry," he muttered to the middle-aged physician, who rubbed his throat where Bryce's handprint still lay.

Angus edged away from Bryce. "It isn't wise to murder the only physician in yer village." He glared up at Bryce. "Would ye rather I lie to ye, lad?"

Bryce shook his head and glanced at Akira, who turned to him with a bold calmness he hadn't anticipated. She reached out and firmly gripped his arm. Something in her gentle expression gave him a peace he couldn't explain.

"Ye canna give up hope when that is all ye have."

ℒ❤

Finella made a special healing salve for Evan's wound, and Akira applied it. She talked to him while she worked and couldn't help wondering if he actually heard her. After a while his lack of response made her concern grow. She turned in frustration and tightly closed her eyes.

Lord, please let him live. Too many lives have been lost from this terrible feud between our clans. Heal our families. Amen. Akira whispered the silent prayer in her heart, careful not to disturb Bryce.

She opened her eyes. Bryce stood alone in the shadows. He wore a grim expression and prowled the quiet chamber like a caged animal. His broad shoulders slumped forward as if they carried the weight of the world. She thought of the bond she shared with her own brothers and then it was clear. She knew what Evan would fight for.

With a new purpose Akira leaned toward Evan. Her golden-red hair spilled over her shoulders as she bent to whisper in his ear. "Evan, Bryce is here to see ye. Evan, ye must fight to live. Sim needs ye." She stole a glance at Bryce. He still stood in the shadows, but his posture had straightened, and she could feel his intense gaze upon her. She sensed the tension in his shoulders as they rose a little. She could almost feel the hope rise within him. "Bryce is waiting for ye," she continued. "Ye're a MacPhearson. Ye must stay alive to lead yer clan as ye were born to do. Ye're the chieftain and yer people depend on ye for direction."

Akira talked to Evan with encouragement, hoping something would come of it. She grew weary and her back ached at bending in the same position for so long. Evan's head moved. At first she thought she imagined it, but then his eyes fluttered open. He stared at the ceiling.

"Bryce, he's coming to," she whispered with excitement. Evan tried to take a deep breath and choked as if gasping for air.

"Evan?" Bryce moved beside her. "Evan, I'm here."

"Aye." Evan's eyes half closed. "I . . . hear her too." His voice sounded strained.

Akira straightened. She glanced at Bryce, wondering if he would want her to leave now that Evan was awake. But Bryce paid her no heed, watching his brother for signs of recovery.

Evan had been so set against wedding her and bitter against her clan that she feared he would distress himself at the mere sight of her.

"Akira . . . I was . . . wrong . . . about . . . ye," he managed to say with great effort.

Her brows wrinkled in a frown. "Shhh," she whispered. "Ye need yer rest."

"Yer . . . voice . . . sounds like . . . angel," he muttered weakly, letting his eyes close again. He lifted his hand and not knowing what else to do, she slipped hers in his.

"Wit-ness . . . my . . . words." He paused to swallow and winced, his face wrinkling in pain. "I name . . . Bryce . . . as my . . . successor."

"Ye're clan chief." The command in Bryce's voice startled her since he had been so quiet, but the fear in his voice was undeniable. Akira risked glancing at him. His dark eyes were full of concern. She wanted to deny the feelings of sympathy stirring inside her. His black hair fell in disarray where he had been combing his fingers through it. And the circles under his eyes carried the weight of his burdens worse than his strong shoulders.

"The Coun-cil . . . w-will . . . vote for ye. Do . . . right . . . by the . . . lass." He paused for a long time, and it was as if she and Bryce were both holding their breaths. "I . . . want . . . to pray."

Akira had whispered several prayers for God to have mercy and save Evan's life. Now she was eager to say those prayers more boldly. She took his cold hand in hers and tried not to think about how stiff it felt.

"God, please . . . forgive me," Evan's raspy voice muttered between breaths. His tense body shook as his lips parted, and he released his last breath. Evan's body lay still.

Akira's heart squeezed in anguish as comprehension dawned. She covered her mouth and closed her eyes. It didn't matter that he was the enemy and that she would have been forced to wed him. Compassion touched her soul, and for a moment, fear of her situation faded into a reverent grief. Tears threatened to slip from beneath her tired lids.

A disheartened silence filled the chamber. With no warning Bryce raised his fists and faced the stone ceiling above. "Naaaaay!"

The agonizing cry took her breath away. Tears stung her eyes. The cry came again. She looked down, her eyes too blurry to see. Akira barely knew Bryce, and yet she could feel his pain. She refused to fight the feelings now. What harm could it do to comfort him? He had no one except for Sim, who could offer no words of comfort and who would need the same solace as Bryce. She took a step toward him, but he swerved away and stormed from the chamber.

Finella had been standing quietly in a corner. Unable to control her emotions any longer, the old nurse burst into sobs and fled as well. Sim had been waiting patiently outside the chamber so as not to get in the way, but when he saw Bryce and Finella, he rushed in. He came to a halt a few feet away from the bed. Akira watched as the lad began to shake and would step no closer. Tears slowly crawled down his face, and she wondered what he would say if he could speak. Talking things out would never be an option for him.

Akira felt pity and walked around the bed toward him and opened her arms. Unlike his elder brother, Sim willingly went to her. She would stand there and comfort Sim for as long as he needed her.

Her mind wandered to Bryce, who now carried so much responsibility. Soon he would no doubt be elected as the new chieftain of the MacPhearson clan. How would this change of events affect her future? No wedding with Evan would take place. Akira should have felt relieved, but no joy would come while the child in her arms trembled and suffered with such grief.

She turned and led Sim from the chamber. So much would have to be tended to, and for the first time, Akira wondered how it had all come about. Who had wounded Evan and why?

She would not ask Bryce and could not ask Sim. Perhaps Finella or Angus would know.

5

Akira left Sim asleep in his chamber and went in search of Bryce. It occurred to her that now would be the perfect opportunity to make her escape, but in the midst of so much grief she couldn't attempt it. Perhaps she would later regret being such a sensitive fool, but for now she'd stay and hope and pray that God would later make a way for her release.

As she neared the library, Bryce's voice echoed into the hallway. "Let me understand this correctly. Ye didn't attack my brothers? Ye merely wanted to ask them questions about Akira?" Acute disbelief laced his tone. Akira paused and listened. "Ye expect me to believe that under the circumstances?"

"We rode out of the brush, and they thought we were attacking them. We had no choice but to defend ourselves. I didn't have to bring him here. I could have left him to die." Alarm sliced through Akira as she recognized Elliot's voice. What did Elliot have to do with Evan's death? Akira backed against the wall, seeking support for her weakening knees. *Oh Lord, give me strength,* she silently prayed. How could her brother be linked to the death of the MacPhearson chieftain? It was enough that Evan had been laird over his own lands, but as the clan chief, he resided over all the other MacPhearson lairds. If Elliot was indeed involved in Evan's death, his involvement could cause the MacPhearsons to rally against her father in an all-out war.

"He died anyway." Bryce's voice hardened with pain.

An awkward silence ensued. "I'm truly sorry. I didn't mean for him to die or for any of this to happen. As I told ye before, I was tending to Sim when the other two pulled out their swords."

Bryce scoffed. "Ye mean ye were binding my brother while yer friend was slaying my other brother." Bryce laughed sarcastically. "When a man draws his sword, his intentions are quite clear."

"Yer brother slew Gregor Matheson first. His corpse still lies in the woods."

Akira gasped, tears stinging her eyes. She rushed into the library to make her presence known. "Gregor is dead?" Her voice sounded hollow in the cold room filled with tension.

Elliot turned, and Akira hardly noticed the surprised relief cross his face. She stopped a few feet away, wringing her hands in distress. "Gregor is dead?" She repeated the question, searching her brother's expression for a truthful answer.

Elliot reluctantly nodded. "Aye, lass, he is dead." He bent his head to avoid her eyes.

She grabbed her stomach with one hand and leaned over a nearby chair with the other. "Oh." She could feel the blood drain from her head as dizziness claimed her senses.

"Akira?" Elliot seemed concerned for her.

A few moments ago, she would have run into her brother's arms, thankful that he'd come for her, but now two men, one from each clan, lay dead. Reality settled in her mind like thick mud. Elliot took a step toward her and she lifted a hand, giving him and Bryce a meaningful glare.

"I grow weary of death, and now I fear that more lives will be lost. Neither of ye can prove the deaths of these two men were accidents. People will be hurt and angry and they will seek revenge."

Her mind paced in time with her feet. Tears welled in her weary eyes, and she rapidly blinked them back.

"Bryce, what were ye thinking when ye took me? True, I didn't want to wed yer brother, but neither did I wish his death. Where is the good from what ye've both done? And where can we go from here without ending more lives?" She looked from one to the other, hoping for an excuse to calm the panic gripping her insides.

"Men." She clenched her fists at her side and ground her teeth. "I pity yer love for war and death, but most of all, I pity the women who must be used in yer evil deeds and suffer from yer actions. For that is my role in all of this. Without me ye would not have been so successful in creating such a mess."

She turned and ran from the library, hoping to gain some privacy with the Lord. She needed strength and comfort. People often failed her, but the Lord, He always gave her exactly what she needed.

Both men looked down at their feet in an awkward silence as if accepting her parting words as proper chastisement for whatever role they had played in the chaos.

Bryce cleared his throat, swallowing his own remorse. "Akira has a way of expressing her mind, I've noticed."

Elliot nodded, still looking down as if deep in thought. "Aye, she always has." Sadness lingered in his voice.

Bryce turned to Elliot. "I'll provide ye safe passage home. In the meantime, I'll have Finella prepare a chamber for ye. For now, I must tend to my brother's burial. And our Council will meet to elect the new chieftain. Until then, ye and Akira will be watched closely. I don't care to have the two of ye plotting my death nor anyone else around here plotting yers."

Elliot smiled as if in a melancholy mood. "At the moment, I'm not sure she wishes to return home with me."

Bryce looked up and gave Elliot a level stare, returning the same smile of sadness. "Nor, I fear, does she wish to remain here, but she must come to terms with it. For I will not let her go." His determined voice issued a clear warning of his intentions.

Elliot rose defensively, taking his words as a direct challenge. "She was betrothed to Evan and he's no longer here."

Bryce exercised great self-control. "Thank ye for bluntly reminding me of my brother's death. As it is, I am now the MacPhearson laird, and while it remains to be seen if I will be elected as clan chief, as laird I will wed Akira. 'Twas the last request Evan made of me, and seeing as how I failed to protect his life and carry out my father's dying wish, I'll not fail now. I want to unite the two clans, and if possible, prevent war. Tensions were strained before, but now that all this has happened, something must be done and quickly. Birk MacKenzie is less likely to wage war against his only daughter."

"Yer a fool." Elliot's brown eyes burned like coals, and his face was so intense he looked as if the veins in his head would soon burst.

"Then so be it." Bryce thought back to the arguments he and Evan had had over Akira. Bryce had called Evan a fool for not wanting to wed her. How ironic to have the same words thrown back at him for wanting to wed her. Akira was right. If he had not taken her, then Elliot and Gregor would not have attacked Evan and Sim, and of course, Evan would still be alive. Guilt consumed his tortured soul.

The truth of the matter was that he had wanted Akira while he sought her for Evan. For the first time in his life, he had actually envied his brother's birthright. The realization gripped him in its iron clutches. How could he look upon Akira without feeling the pain of his brother's death?

"Akira doesn't deserve the strife she would have to face here as yer wife."

As if knowing the path of his thoughts, Elliot's words hit him with a reckoning force. Bryce shook his head to clear his mind. An image of Akira's pain-filled eyes haunted him. He turned from Elliot, pretending to look out the library window. He needed a moment to regain his composure. As he grew up without a mother most of his life, his father had been hard on them as lads. Emotion was a sign of weakness, and he had learned not to show weakness in front of his father. Bryce cleared his throat.

"'Twill grow easier with time. I know how to deal with my people."

"Ye're not convincing yerself. And ye're definitely not convincing me," Elliot said through clenched teeth, pointing a finger in Bryce's direction.

An aching emptiness rose in Bryce. He longed to find relief and fill the void with something that would make him happy and complete. The thought of letting Akira go only made him feel worse. He turned to face Elliot, determined to defend his position on the matter.

"I need not convince ye. 'Twill be as I said." Bryce kept his voice low as he crossed his arms over his chest.

"'Tis naught to do with yer sense of honor for yer brother and father. I think ye want her and will stop at naught to have her. Leave my sister be." Elliot challenged his motives.

Bryce's jaw tightened, and he took a deep breath to calm himself. "If ye were not her brother and soon to be mine also, I would make ye sorry for those words." He spoke every syllable slow and clear.

"Bryce!" Finella called in distress.

Sighing, Bryce pointed a finger at Elliot. "We'll finish this later."

"The lady is gone from her chamber. I know not how long. I checked on her earlier, and she was comforting Sim." Finella rushed in looking near to hysterics, wringing her hands.

"Finella, she was just in here with us. She couldn't have gone far." Bryce laid a hand on Finella's shoulder to reassure her.

Elliot tilted his head. "Well, that depends. Akira ran out of here upset, and ever since she was a wee lass, she's had the habit of disappearing when she's upset."

Bryce felt the first stirrings of concern. He patted Finella's back to let her know he didn't hold her responsible. "Finella, we'll find her. Don't worry." He strode to the door shouting for Balloch. Boots echoed down the hall as Balloch answered the summons. "Watch Elliot MacKenzie until I return. Feed him if he wishes, but do not let him out of yer sight."

He turned to Finella and overlooked the nervous twitch she had of biting her lower lip when distressed. "Prepare a guest chamber for Elliot MacKenzie and show him to it when it's ready. I'll search for Akira myself."

In the courtyard Bryce stopped to reflect. Akira had been upset when she fled the library; most likely she wanted time alone. He placed his hands on his hips and looked around. The tall steeple looming over the stone wall of the courtyard looked inviting. In the short time he'd known her, the lass seemed to pray often. Perhaps she sought refuge in the small village chapel.

Thoughts of Evan's death, the burial preparation, the upcoming Council election for the new clan chief, and the dilemma of Elliot MacKenzie alternated in his mind.

"I do not have time for this," he muttered angrily as he strode to the village chapel. The heavy burden he now carried, coupled with the raging grief inside him, moved him into a brooding mood. The last thing he needed was for Akira to cause trouble.

He stepped over the threshold of the chapel door and all the pent-up anger he had felt evaporated into unwanted compassion. The heavy door groaned to a close behind him, and he heard her weeping. She was bent over the altar on her knees, rocking back and forth in her grief. Her long, golden-red hair spilled across her back like silky waves.

Vicar Forbes stood and turned to Bryce, motioning him forward. Awkwardly, Bryce moved down the aisle between the rows of wooden pews as if he was a lad about to be reprimanded. Forbes met him in the middle and whispered, "Ye need to go to the lass. Ye've entered into the house of the Lord, and ye must do what is right."

Evan's last words, *do right by the lass*, rang in his ears. He swallowed with difficulty and looked at Vicar Forbes.

"Me?" Bryce shrugged his large frame and raised an eyebrow. "What can I do? I know naught of weeping women."

Father Forbes stepped back and swept a hand toward Akira. "Ask the lass what ails her."

Bryce stifled a sigh and rubbed his weary eyes. "I have a burial to prepare for and a war to prevent. Comforting a weeping woman isn't a priority right now."

Vicar Forbes gave him a rebuking glare. "Well, it had better be." He pointed in Akira's direction. "That innocent, weeping woman could be the key to preventing a war."

Bryce started to argue, but then thought better of it. What exactly was the vicar referring to? His father had often sought the vicar's council, but lately, he and Evan had avoided him. Cedric MacPhearson had been a man of respect, someone to revere, and known to be wise. Perhaps it was time for Bryce to follow his father's example. He crossed his arms and planted his feet.

"I'm listening."

"Lad, I realize ye have a lot on yer shoulders and ye're grieving over Evan, but ye can only solve one problem at a time." He nodded toward Akira. "Ye created this problem with the lass, and yer the one to fix it."

"How do ye figure that?" Bryce held on to his patience.

"'Twas ye who took her from her family and brought her here, were ye not?" Without waiting for an answer, the vicar continued, "The lass has been torn from her home and all she's ever known. While ye grieve for Evan, she grieves for a whole family." Vicar Forbes paused, letting his words sink in. "If ye intend to keep her here, 'twould be wise to make her a friend ye can trust and not a bitter enemy under yer roof."

Father Forbes had a way of speaking that made a man want to atone for all his misdeeds.

Bryce let out a slow breath. "Aye, I am guilty of what ye claim, but there's no undoing it. What do ye suggest I do now?"

The priest laid a gentle hand upon Bryce's shoulder. "Make yer penance to the Lord and do the right thing by Akira."

"I will not let her go. I have made a promise, and I intend to keep it." Bryce's whispered tone grew sharp with determination.

"Look into yer heart and ask yerself what God would have ye do." The small priest patted his shoulder one more time in a fatherly gesture and walked away, giving Bryce privacy with Akira.

Bryce scoffed at the priest's suggestion. Look into his heart, indeed. His so-called heart was what had gotten him into this mess. Bryce's heart had broken at the thought of not keeping a promise he should have never made in the first place. He had only been a lad, but even then he knew the stubborn streak his elder brother possessed and the difficult road that lay ahead if he intended to keep his word. Bryce was a man who honored his word. He despised a double-minded man and had no intention of being one.

Akira sniffed, looked up at the wooden cross hanging against the stone wall behind the altar. She made the sign of the cross from her forehead and over her chest and turned.

Their gazes locked. The puffy red skin around her swollen eyes made them look like glistening orbs. His breath caught in his throat, and a nervous ripple fluttered through his stomach. No woman had ever taken his breath away. He regretted the deep sadness in her soul and longed to help her overcome her grief, but he didn't know how.

Akira clasped her hands together in front of her, waiting.

"I forgive ye . . . again," Akira said with as reasonable a voice as she could manage, unsure of what to expect now that Bryce had tracked her down in the chapel. Was she to have no place of privacy where she could be alone? She had thought the sanctuary of the chapel would be safe from someone like Bryce, who seemed determined to cause war and mayhem with every decision he made. He didn't strike her as the type of man who frequented the chapel, seeking the Lord with prayers and petitions.

His expression changed from sympathy to utter amazement. "Pray tell, lass, what new sin have I committed against ye this day?"

Akira searched his face. An unfamiliar shadow of a beard etched his jaw. Beneath his intense gaze lay a grief too strong and fierce to hide. Weary pain showed in his dark eyes as he looked at her with a mixture of distrust and concern. Something in the core of her heart stirred as she realized how difficult the day's events had been for him. After all, he had lost a brother, while she had only lost a dear friend in Gregor.

"I came here to ask God's help to forgive ye of what ye've already done. I'm not aware of any new sins."

At first Bryce blinked and continued to stare at her as if he couldn't believe his ears. Then he chuckled, shaking his head as if to clear his mind. He crossed his arms over his chest and gave her a level stare. "Lass, ye continue to amaze me. I never know what to expect ye to say."

"Expect the truth. I have naught to gain in lying to ye. It isn't in my nature."

"Aye, but truth be told, I expected ye to wail at me for some new wrong I've done," he confessed. "Ye did say ye forgive me *again*."

She tilted her head in concession. "Aye, I did. I've tried to forgive ye before. I have to keep asking the Lord for His help. When next ye wrong me, I canna deny that I won't express my feelings on the matter. I've always struggled to hide what I feel."

Akira looked up at him, hoping he would deny any new wrong against her, but no such promise came forth. Instead, Bryce lowered his gaze and turned from her. He paced with his arms folded across his chest and one hand cupped under his chin in thoughtful concentration.

"If I've committed no new sin against ye, then why were ye weeping as if yer world is falling apart?" He asked the question without looking at her. "Did ye love the man Gregor that much?"

Akira shook her head, wondering how he could be so blind. Her world *was* falling apart, and Gregor's death only contributed to a portion of it. So much had happened in the last couple of weeks, and she feared what would happen next.

"Nay, Gregor was a dear friend of mine, and I cared deeply for him, but I am grieved by how he and Evan died. 'Twill cause more pain and anger between our clans. I fear more people will demand revenge and retribution." Akira paused, searching for the right words to make him understand. "I fear more bloodshed. This time 'twas yer brother. Next time it could be mine." She walked toward him and laid a hand upon his right arm. His strong muscle tensed beneath her touch and then relaxed. "M'lord, when will this feuding ever stop?" Her voice broke into a whisper.

Bryce laid a comforting hand upon hers and looked up at the ceiling. "I don't know, lass, but I do have a plan that I hope will be the beginning of reconciliation." His voice softened.

"What is it?"

He shook his head and looked down at her. "Now is not the time to speak of it. I prefer to wait until after Evan's burial and then I will explain it to ye." Gently he moved her hand from his arm and held it between his. He lightly caressed her fingers with his thumb. Her sensitive skin tingled. Akira marveled that this MacPhearson warrior could exhibit such tenderness.

"Ye didn't love this Gregor then?" Bryce asked as if he needed to be reassured, his eyebrow arching.

Akira bit her bottom lip and shook her head. "Nay, not in the way a woman should love her husband, but I had hoped that perhaps in time I would."

"Why were ye about to wed him then?"

Akira didn't know him well enough to lay open her heart, yet neither would she lie to hide her inner feelings. Her being here at MacPhearson Castle and the feud between their clans was not of her doing. She had no more power over her circumstances than she had over what Bryce would choose to do with the knowledge of her true feelings. The only thing she could do was tell the truth as God's Word commanded and trust in the Lord to protect her. With a confidence she didn't feel, Akira looked up and boldly gazed into his eyes.

"I had known I was betrothed to yer brother since I was a wee lass, but over the years the stories I had heard of the MacPhearsons were horrible. While I knew that many of them were greatly exaggerated, I still feared wedding into a clan that bore so much hatred for my people."

Akira searched his face for some sign that he understood, but Bryce's expression remained unreadable—full of scrutiny. She took a deep breath and continued.

"I am but a woman. A man has the right to do as he wishes with his wife. I imagined all sorts of possibilities. What if my new husband beat me? Starved me? Rejected me? Hated me just because I was born a MacKenzie?" She paused, giving him time to digest her words. "Can ye see where my imagination might have run away with me?"

At first he didn't respond and then his expression changed to a semblance of regret. "Aye. They shouldn't have filled yer head with so many lies. They should have given more caution to yer sensitive feelings."

Akira jerked her hand from his hold and stepped back. "I didn't tell ye this so ye'd have more of a reason to rant and rave against my clan." She felt raw disappointment that he would use her words in such a way. "I'm well aware of the tales I shouldn't have heard, but I am also thankful that they didn't try to protect me from the truth."

Bryce folded his arms across his chest. "And what is that truth, lass?"

"That our clans have fought for two lifetimes, and there is so much bitterness and hatred between them that one union isn't likely to dissolve it. There's too much betrayal, distrust, superstition, and lies for me to have a joyful marriage to a MacPhearson."

"So ye decided to wed Gregor."

Akira momentarily closed her eyes, trying to regain her composure before she answered. "I had prepared myself to accept Evan MacPhearson as my husband if that was to be God's will, but I saw no harm in praying for God to inter-vene on my behalf." She clasped her hands in front of her. "When we received Evan's letter saying he had no intention of honoring the betrothal, I believed God had answered my prayer."

Bryce ran a hand down his face and stroked his chin in thoughtful silence. "Aye, I can see where ye would feel that way," he finally admitted. "For all his wit and bravery, my brother wasn't always a level-headed one. He had his reser-vations over wedding a MacKenzie lass as much as ye did a MacPhearson. And rightly so."

Akira cleared her throat. "My father was angry over the letter. He saw it as a final insult to our clan. Although the raids continued after yer father passed away, he continued to hope for a peaceful truce between our clans. He thought that perhaps with a little more age, Evan would come to see the wisdom in yer father's betrothal agreement. But each year as my birthday rolled around, my father became more anxious that I not grow beyond a suitable age for marriage. So he sent Evan a letter inquiring after his intentions."

Bryce gazed into her eyes as if he could determine her unspoken thoughts. "What happened next?" he urged in a lower, huskier tone.

Deeply affected by his presence, Akira suddenly felt very aware of his nearness. With the exception of Sim, Bryce was the only one in his clan who truly made her feel safe, in spite of the fact that his presence distracted her and sent her mind spinning. What was it about him that made her heart beat faster and her pulse quicken?

"So, lass, how did ye become betrothed to Gregor?"

Bryce bent his head toward her as if inclining his ear to better hear her response. A faint scent of lye soap drifted to her nose. She stared at his bent head, wondering why her relationship with Gregor seemed to be of so much importance.

"My father came to me and told me I was free to choose a husband from our clan. Gregor and I were close friends growing up. I knew him well, and I trusted him to take care of me. There was never a soul more loyal to my father. I confided in him of my concerns, and he suggested that we wed. We decided it would be a marriage of convenience and naught more, although we both hoped that in time we would come to love and desire one another."

"Then why would he desert ye?"

Bryce moved fisted hands to his sides and looked back at her with a clouded expression she couldn't fathom. Why would he care that she had been deserted upon her wedding day?

The reminder brought a sad countenance upon her, and she turned from him to hide her discomfort. Even though they were never in love, Gregor's rejection in front of the whole clan had brought shame upon her and their family. She had always valued his friendship, and she felt like she had lost a close friend. Deep down she had known things would never be the same between them again, but she had not anticipated his death.

Bryce stepped forward, and all the tension in his body seemed to fade as he gently cupped her chin so he could see her face more clearly. "I'm sorry, lass. I didn't mean to hurt yer feelings." She could hear the sincerity in his apology.

Akira sighed and allowed her gaze to travel from his unshaven face, over the firm set of his lips, to his perfectly sculpted nose, and finally rested on the gray eyes staring back at her. Was it her imagination or did she see tenderness in his expression?

"Ye did naught to hurt me, m'lord. 'Tis only the memory of my shame that day."

"Lass, I didn't mean to cause unwanted memories. If ye don't wish to speak further on it, I won't ask ye."

Akira shook her head. "Nay, I've a need to speak of it. Ye came before I was able to finish my explanation to everyone. I've not had a chance to talk about it."

"I'm listening." Bryce dropped his hand from her face and waited.

"Gregor had every intention of going through with our wedding, but the night before he had a dream that changed his mind. He knew I would understand because of all the dreams I've had over the years."

"Why would a dream make such a difference on the man's decision to wed ye? Nearly all my dreams of the night make little sense. If I were to base such a huge decision on a dream, everyone would think me demented." Bryce scowled at her with his forehead wrinkled in confusion. "Do ye mock me, lass?"

His reaction infuriated her, and she struggled to calm the rising flames within her.

"M'lord, how could I be mocking ye when this isn't about ye, but me?" Akira pointed at her chest as her voice rose a notch. "Have ye never had a dream that made ye break out in cold sweats or yer heart beat faster until ye wished ye would have never had it?" Akira rose to her tiptoes. "What about a dream that was so pleasant ye wished it would never end?" Her voice broke above a whisper.

She knew the moment her words connected with a memory he had long forgotten or pushed aside. An emotion so raw and potent flickered in his expression. Just as quickly he brought his composure back under control, to create the façade he obviously wanted to present to her.

"Perhaps," he reluctantly admitted.

Akira felt a kinship developing between them. "Ye do understand what I mean, don't ye?"

She had told him so much of her feelings; couldn't he at least share one thing with her? She laid a hand over his arm. At the contact, Bryce looked down at her hand and then back into her eyes.

"Aye, lass. When I was a lad, I was there when my da died. He made me promise that I would see Evan honor the betrothal between him and yer father." Bryce reached out and gently caressed her cheek with his knuckles. His tenderness made her resolve against him melt for the moment. "A murderer had run a sword through him, and I remember how he gasped for air as pain ripped through his body. Sweat poured from his brow as he struggled for that last promise from me."

Bryce dropped his hand, and Akira felt the cold air upon her cheek from the absence of his warm fingers.

He sighed. "After that I had nightmares about his death for years to come. Many of them ended with me not keeping my promise to him and the bitter disappointment on his face. If I ever get a chance to see him again in the afterlife, I never want to see him look at me like that."

His voice carried such contained grief. Akira could hear the pain of a lad still caged inside of a man who had grown into a fearsome warrior.

Akira reached for both of his hands. "I'm so sorry. I didn't mean to cause ye pain anymore than ye intended to wound me."

Their gazes met and something deeper than understanding began to stir between them. Akira wasn't sure what it was, but she didn't want the moment to end. For the first time, she felt a measure of peace and truth between them. Was it possible?

The warmth in his smile turned her stomach upside-down and she felt a heady sensation course through her.

"Lass, ye aren't to blame for something that has been happening to me for years."

"Ye seemed so against believing that a dream could have such a strong impact that it could change a man's mind regarding marriage. I only wanted to make ye understand the truth of what I was trying to say."

"I understand, lass," Bryce assured her. "Tell me. What did he dream?" Bryce looked down at her with open curiosity and a smile that gave her hope.

"An angel came to Gregor in his dream and told him he wasn't to wed me. I was meant for another. I'm not one to argue with the Lord, but I was so stunned by this news, I didn't know what to think. When ye took me I thought that perhaps I was meant to be a MacPhearson bride, but now Evan is gone. I guess God has something else planned. Far be it from me to know what it is."

Bryce seemed to pale, and he let go of her hands and stepped back from her.

"M'lord, whatever is wrong? Have I said something?"

"Nay." He turned and kneeled before the altar. He bowed his head and seemed to be whispering a prayer of thanksgiving.

Akira couldn't hear everything he said, but she patiently waited. When he made the sign of the cross and stood to his feet, she said, "M'lord, ye're acting a wee bit strange."

"Ye were always meant to be a MacPhearson bride, Akira."

"What are ye talking about?" Her stomach began to clench in tight spasms. As gently as she could, Akira reminded him, "Evan is gone, m'lord." Was he so grief-stricken that he would deny his brother's death?

"Ye weren't meant to be Evan's bride."

"M'lord, ye're not making any sense. Pray tell, what are ye talking about?" Akira pleaded.

"Ye were meant to be a MacPhearson bride. Ye were meant to be *my* bride."

6

With the hole in the earth dug and prayers said, Akira tried to block out the weeping women who stood all around her, but her heart wouldn't allow it. Several times she clenched her teeth and bit hard to avoid tears. She didn't want to feel for these people. They were her enemies, and she was forced to be here among them. Those she had met were not overly friendly, or they ignored her completely, as if the mere sight of her disgusted them.

Akira had not wanted to attend Evan's burial. She didn't feel that she or Elliot belonged, but Bryce had insisted. He said he would feel better knowing they were both in sight rather than worrying that they might be attacked. As predicted, his people were angry and hurt, and they wanted revenge. They wanted MacKenzie blood. Elliot and Akira were both easy targets. Since Bryce wanted to promote peace and forgiveness, he had to walk as an example before them as their newly elected chieftain. Locking Elliot and Akira up for their protection wouldn't give his clan the impression he had in mind.

Determined to keep from responding to the grief around her, Akira turned her mind in a different direction. She looked across the gravesite at Bryce. He stood beside Sim in a warrior's stance, his face a mask of stone, his tense hands folded in front of him. Only Akira noticed the slight twitch in his eye and the way his jaw muscles locked each time he swallowed. His stormy eyes portrayed the emotion swirling within him like a volcano before the eruption. She wanted to hate him, and yet, the recent tenderness she had seen beneath his rough exterior tugged at her heart.

Beside her, Elliot reached for her hand, locking fingers with hers. Akira clung to him for comfort. Growing up she had depended upon her other brother, Gavin, for most of her emotional support, but Gavin wasn't here; Elliot was. His presence reminded her of home. Elliot squeezed her hand as if reading her thoughts and gave her a wink with a reassuring smile.

Bryce had not allowed them much time together, but they managed to steal moments of conversation here and there. Elliot had given her a bit of news from home. As she had expected, her mother was frantic with worry and her father was unusually quiet. He refused to make a rash decision concerning Akira's plight, always having to consider what was best for the whole clan.

Elliot and Gregor, impatient with his caution, ventured onto MacPhearson land without Birk MacKenzie's knowledge. Gavin was restless, but content to wait on Birk's direction, and so they had not included him in their plan. Elliot claimed they had not intended to attack anyone from the MacPhearson clan. They only wanted to confirm that she was not being mistreated.

Akira's gaze rose to the distant sky as more wailing reached her ears. The afternoon sun began to set, and a light pink shade slowly dissolved the magnificent blue of the sky. Soon it would be dark, and she wished it would come quickly. She felt uncomfortable and completely exhausted. The thought of retiring from the day brought a refreshing reprieve.

Vicar Forbes made the sign of the cross and ended his prayer. Four men moved forward and filled the dirt in Evan's grave, a sign that the whole ordeal would soon be over. Her chest lightened with relief while people came forward and placed handpicked flowers at the foot of the grave.

A weak groan caught her attention. Sim's chin shook as he tried to control his grief. Bryce offered him no comfort, while he accepted expressions of sorrow from members of their clan in his role as head of the family. Sim needed someone, and surely it couldn't hurt if she went to him. Finella stood further back in the crowd with her own family and couldn't see Sim. Another groan slipped from his lips, and without another thought, Akira broke from Elliot's hold.

Sim saw her coming and didn't bother hiding his relief as he wrapped his arms about her. He looked up and fresh tears swam in his eyes, seeking comfort and strength from her as he would from his mother. Deeply touched, Akira's throat constricted as she fought the onslaught of tears . . . and lost. She rubbed his bony shoulders. It mattered not that he was a MacPhearson. He was God's child.

Akira knew her simple act of compassion would be scrutinized by all the MacPhearsons, but what did she care? None of them seemed to like her anyway. It seemed as if there was naught she could do to gain their favor. If they cared so much for Bryce's family, shouldn't someone have come forward to console the lad?

She could feel many watching her from a distance, unsure of her motives, some with interest and hope, others with more hatred burning in their hearts than ever before. One pair of eyes in particular made the hair on Akira's nape prickle and her skin crawl with an eerie feeling. A breeze brushed against her skin. She sensed someone moving toward her and looked up from comforting Sim.

A beautiful woman approached; her flowing blond hair seemed to silhouette her upper body in a golden halo. Her blue eyes were cold with open disdain, as she strode purposely toward Akira. Her arms moved back and forth; her hips swayed. Clothed in the MacPhearson plaid, her beauty drew attention as she stopped in front of Akira.

Her gaze perused Akira from head to toe as if the sight disgusted her. Ruby lips twisted, drawing out the contrasting blue of her eyes embedded in a creamy white face so completely flawless that Akira wondered if she could even be real. She spat in Akira's face, leaving her to wonder no more.

The woman turned and walked away, while Akira used her sleeve to wipe away the offending spittle. Straightening her posture and rolling back her shoulders, Akira set her face like flint, determined not to let them drag down her spirit. She lifted her chin and focused on the vicar while they watched her. Sensing Bryce's attention upon her, Akira resisted looking in his direction. The satisfaction she would see lurking in his eyes would snap her control and send her into a roaring rage.

Vicar Forbes took his calling to heart and proceeded as planned. "Bryce." His authoritative voice claimed the clan's attention as he motioned for Bryce to come forward. "'Tis time."

Bryce nodded and, with a commanding glance, waited for Sim to follow. For the next half-hour the two MacPhearson brothers accepted words of sympathy and comfort, while Akira stood alone, awkwardly avoiding Elliot's accusing gaze. She knew her brother's opinion of what she had done. He'd be angry that she had left his side to comfort a MacPhearson— even a lad.

Akira stared at the flowers on the fresh grave as if she were in a trance.

"Lass, 'twas kind of ye to tend to Sim."

The sound of another woman's voice addressing Akira made her tense. Were her ears deceiving her, or had someone actually spoken kind words? Akira's gaze rose to a tall, thin woman who stood before her holding a small lad's hand. The top of his brown head reached just above her hip.

"The lad needs a lovin' touch every now and then, and God knows he's lacked plenty of it in his life. His brothers have always tried their best, but 'tis not the same as a woman's touch." Akira realized she referred to Sim. The woman wore her brown hair pulled in a tight bun, and her pale complexion glowed in a heartwarming smile. Her gaze hesitantly drifted to an impatient man motioning to her. "I must be goin'. My husband Tavis is waiting." She turned, paused, and glanced back. "My name is Vika."

"Thank ye," Akira said, noticing Bryce staring directly at her, his gaze cold and unreadable. She shivered. Aye, meeting Vika was a comfort. A friendly face might well mean an ally in this place filled with stares of animosity for anyone with ties to the MacKenzie clan.

Tavis and Vika were the last to express their condolences. Kian and Balloch escorted Elliot, while Bryce firmly gripped Akira. Sim eagerly grabbed her other elbow.

"We will now have our evening meal," Bryce announced.

They walked back to the castle in silence.

During their meal Bryce seemed quiet, and the whole atmosphere held a bit of melancholy. His profound silence disturbed her more than she would like to admit. She welcomed the distraction from Sim as he sat by her side, trying his best to communicate with hand signals.

She lifted her goblet and drank her wine. Low conversation buzzed around her as she set down the goblet. Feeling uneasy, her gaze slipped in Bryce's direction and their eyes met. Breaking eye contact, Akira shifted in her seat and reached for a block of crowdie from the platter. She could still feel him watching her as she chewed her food and wished he would forget her existence, at least for the moment, so she could eat in peace.

"Akira can hold her own with a sword against any man," Elliot said across the table to Kian, "except for the fact that she lacks the strength of a man, but not the skill." He grinned impishly and winked at her.

Akira frowned. "Elliot, please. This isn't the time or place to speak of such things."

"Elliot, do not give her reason to test her skill," Bryce's rumbling voice interjected. All conversation momentarily paused as everyone exchanged glances.

Elliot shrugged, grinning mischievously. "I merely speak the truth. I have no need to lie of my sister's skill."

Bryce leaned forward as he took a swallow from his goblet before replying. "Even so, Akira will be my wife and will conduct herself as such. Her life as a MacKenzie is over. I protect what is mine, and I intend for her to have no need of that skill." Akira twisted in Bryce's direction, a fervent denial on the tip of her tongue, but Elliot's angry voice sliced through the air.

"Are ye implying that the MacKenzie clan doesn't protect their women?"

She watched as something shifted across her brother's features. A feeling of dread plummeted in her stomach. She knew him well enough to know that he was extremely offended by Bryce's words. Her gaze shifted back to Bryce, hoping he would dismiss her brother's careless question.

Bryce seemed to be considering his words carefully. "I am only saying what I will do as her husband. Surely, ye'd want yer sister to have a husband who would willingly protect her with his own life?" Bryce's dark eyebrows lifted as he raised a chunk of crowdie to his lips.

The response served as a direct challenge that Akira knew Elliot hadn't expected. When put so valiantly, he could hardly deny it, or appear to not care for Akira.

"Yer correct, indeed." Elliot's lips twisted. "But, Akira was betrothed to Evan, not ye." Elliot picked up his goblet and watched Bryce's reaction as he drained its contents.

Akira glowed with satisfaction as she waited for Bryce's reply. Elliot had said exactly what she would have said, if Elliot hadn't been creating such a spectacle of himself. She wisely reserved her comments in case she must plead Elliot's cause later. Her brother's presence gave Bryce something to use against her, and the knowledge of that power scared her. She would do anything to protect her brother, as Bryce, no doubt, knew.

Bryce pushed his plate to the side and linked his fingers on the table. "Elliot, I understand and respect yer point, but take a moment to view it my way. The signed agreement stained with my father's blood says she will wed the MacPhearson chief, not Evan MacPhearson. Therefore, Akira was, and is, betrothed to the MacPhearson chief, and that is me."

A sharp pain spiraled through Akira's chest. She had never seen the written agreement her father had protectively guarded all these years. If what Bryce said was true, then he would have a legitimate claim to her.

Hushed whispers and soft gasps rippled through the great hall as people realized the impact of Bryce's words. He simply rested his chin upon his knuckles and looked at her. His eyes mocked, daring her to deny the fateful trap he'd set for her.

Elliot's response brought a smile to her face. "I'm afraid that's an issue ye'll have to take up with the MacKenzie chief."

Akira's heart filled with love for her brother; at least he still defended her. Elliot went back to eating his food, knowing there was no need for Bryce to reply. Akira could feel the lingering tension and finished her meal in silence as conversations began to stir again.

Desperate to escape, Akira asked to be excused. Bryce nodded and stood, assisting her. Akira's stomach twisted into knots as he led her from the table. She had hoped to be allowed the privacy of her own chamber, but she should have known better. As they passed by, she gave Elliot a reassuring nod to keep him seated at the table and out of trouble.

"I would like to walk," Akira said, removing his hand from her arm once they were out of sight.

"As ye wish, but I canna afford to give ye the luxury of being alone."

He led her to the courtyard where Akira could smell the sweet night air as the balmy breeze stirred her senses. It had been a long day. With Evan's burial followed by the tension at the evening meal, she felt drained of energy. How she wished to be safe at home in her father's keep, away from this uninviting place. She missed her father terribly. She even missed her mother's nagging objections to her unladylike behavior. Suddenly, she realized that the things she used to complain about were her most cherished memories.

The sound of running water caught her attention, and she followed it to a fountain filling a small, round pool of water encased in a bed of stone. Akira sat on the edge and lifted her head to the stars.

"Ye must be wishing ye were far from here." Bryce spoke softly behind her, sending small shivers up her spine and tickling her neck. She sensed he was only a whisper away by the heat of his breath upon her neck. Akira shut her eyes, wondering what she should do.

"Ah, my guess must be correct. Ye close yer eyes as if ye wish I would disappear." She neither confirmed nor denied his statement, opening her eyes once again to gaze into the night sky.

"I, too, wish I were far from here." He paused a moment. "I've been left with a great deal of responsibility. I don't wish to fail my people and many question my reasons for upholding the betrothal."

"In that regard I am not much different from them." She wanted to be civil in case there might be a chance of reasoning with him, but Akira couldn't hide the biting edge in her tone.

"I made a promise, Akira." His firm voice sounded as if he'd made up his mind.

"Yer promise is not my burden to bear."

"That is where ye're wrong. Ye happen to be the only daughter of the MacKenzie chief, and I will see my promise carried out."

"Ye made a promise for Evan. 'Tisn't fair for ye to expect me to spend the rest of my life keeping yer promise." She shook her head in denial. "M'lord, ye ask too much." She tried to control the rising anger as she fully turned to him, searching by the light of the moon for answers in a face of stone.

Bryce paced, rubbing the knotted muscles in his neck as he considered her words. "I only told ye a small portion of the story in the chapel. I'll tell ye the rest now. Ye deserve that much.

" 'Twas upon his return from meeting the MacKenzie chief and signing the betrothal that my da was mortally wounded by a MacKenzie warrior. Evan and I knew he should have returned, but rather than alert the clan of our worries, we went in search of him. We split up, and I was the one who found him. He still had the agreement and was insistent that I see the betrothal through. I couldn't deny him his dying wish."

Akira thought back to the evening meal when Bryce had said that the agreement was stained in his father's blood. MacKenzie warriors killed both his father and his brother. She couldn't knowingly commit herself to a marriage where she would most likely be a constant reminder of so much pain and loss. Too much of a legacy of hate existed between them, a lifetime built solely on one man's promise with no foundation of love or loyalty to even bind them together. If only she knew God's will. She was but one woman and Bryce one man. How could their union bring an end to decades of hate and bitterness between so many families among their clans? It would take a lot more than the two of them—a miracle.

"I understand the need to honor yer promise, but I canna willingly commit myself to a marriage neither of us want. What kind of life would that be? Yer people hate me. I couldn't stand to be here for the rest of my life. Surely, ye understand that?"

Bryce stopped pacing and stood in front of her, his large shadow lurking over her in the moonlight. "Akira, I didn't tell ye this to win yer agreement. I felt ye should know the reason for my actions."

"I do. It makes sense now why ye took me and not Evan."

"That's not what I'm referring to, lass. I intend to wed ye, and wed ye I will."

Akira shook her head in denial, fear rising to the back of her throat. "Nay. Ye'll blame me for everything the MacKenzies have ever done. We should forget the betrothal."

Akira rested her shaking palms against the rough stone where she sat. She took a deep breath, trying to calm her escalating nerves.

"I never break a promise, Akira. I'll not lie to a dead man, especially my da." He slowly approached.

Fear suffocated her like fingers crawling around her throat. She needed to be free of him, if only long enough to gain control of her swirling emotions.

Praying she could make it past him, Akira bit her bottom lip and broke into a run. Bryce lunged to the side and reached out a heavy arm, blocking her path from escape. He pulled her to him and tossed her over his shoulder, locking his arms around her legs like iron chains. Akira scrambled to breathe as his hard shoulder pushed the breath from her lungs. Taking a moment to recover, she managed a few grateful breaths and continued to struggle.

"Bryce, put me down." Akira beat her fists upon his back.

He hauled her through the courtyard with only a few lit torches and the half-moon for light. She tried to ignore the discomfort in her stomach as she bounced on his shoulder. His brisk pace was much worse than being hauled over Ahern's back. The corded muscle of his shoulder dug into her soft body.

They approached the tall towers near the gates to the castle. Hearing a sudden sound from the shadows, Akira clutched the back of Bryce's shirt in her fists. A feminine giggle reached her ears. Akira relaxed, certain they were not in danger of being ambushed.

"Just a couple having a bit of sport," Bryce coaxed, noticing her reaction.

"I'm not afraid," Akira declared. "Merely cautious."

A woman laughed, running from the shadows and looking behind her to make sure her lover followed. Bryce had no time to step aside. He lost his balance as she plunged into them. Bryce maneuvered Akira from his shoulder to cradle her in his arms as his large frame broke their fall. Akira remained unharmed, but she suspected Bryce's hip would surely be sore by morning.

He uttered a string of incoherent words as he moved to a sitting position, glaring at the woman peering down at them with interest. "Mirana, if ye were a man, ye'd be feeling the brunt of my ire about now."

"Aye, Bryce. As if ye've not made that promise before." Her silky voice oozed with self-confidence.

Curious at the familiar voice, Akira pushed her nose from Bryce's chest and turned to see the woman. Akira froze in sudden anger. It was the woman who had spit at her during Evan's funeral. Akira started to rise, but Bryce gripped her arm and held her still.

"Akira, are ye all right?" His pretense of concern only heightened Mirana's anger.

"Since when did ye become concerned about the welfare of a MacKenzie, Bryce?" Mirana interrupted, shrugging her lover's hand off her arm when the warrior tried to pull her away.

Instead of answering, Bryce directed his attention to the warrior beside her. "Rae, take her away before I lose my temper."

He nodded and grabbed her hand, but Mirana jerked away from him. "I have one last thing to say." She stepped forward and spat on Akira again.

Appalled, Akira gasped and rose before Bryce could restrain her and slapped the wench as hard as she could. "That is the last time ye spit on me, ye foul—"

Bryce reached around Akira's waist and pulled her from Mirana with such force that she had no choice but comply.

"I've had enough of her!" Akira warned through clenched teeth. "She spat on me at Evan's funeral, and I'll not tolerate someone treating me like that again."

"Rae. Take her away—now," Bryce ordered in a demanding tone.

"Aye, Bryce." He scooped a whining Mirana up into his arms and carted her off in the opposite direction from whence they had come.

Akira shoved away from Bryce, but he wouldn't let her go. "That isn't how I would imagine my future husband taking up for me. This silly notion ye have of us wedding will not work and I refuse. Her spitting on me and her contempt is exactly what I was referring to earlier."

"Ah, lass." He shook his head from side to side and made a tsk-tsk noise. "Ye still don't understand, do ye? Ye have no choice in the matter. I am the chief, and I command ye to wed me. As for Mirana, I'll see that she's justly punished. Her behavior at Evan's funeral did not escape my notice."

She stopped struggling against him and grew pensive. "Ye're not *my* chief." She kept her voice calm, but firm.

"I have a promise to fulfill, and ye will wed me." His hands gripped her arms above her elbows and for a moment she thought he would throttle her. Instead, he searched her gaze in the moonlight. "Lass, don't fight me on this. Yer efforts are futile."

"Ye can drag me to the vicar all ye want, but I'll not agree to any wedding vows." Akira refused to yield on the matter.

He let go of her and stepped back. "If ye don't wish to be present at yer own wedding, that's fine by me. I'll wed ye by proxy and be done with it." He waved his hand in the air as if to dismiss her.

"Ye jest." A chill slithered up her spine to her neck.

"I assure ye, lass, I wouldn't jest about such a thing. Proxy weddings are perfectly legal. I'll find another woman to stand in yer place if ye aren't there in person. I'll have the vicar prepare the papers in yer name and the woman who stands in for ye will sign yer name. I have your father's seal on the document signed by yer father, stating that ye're betrothed to the MacPhearson chief."

Akira straightened her shoulders and lifted her chin in defiance. "I'll not allow ye to intimidate me."

"Then don't."

Unsure how to respond, Akira yawned, covering her mouth with her hand, and stretched her back. "I'm tired. I wish to retire for the night."

His white teeth flashed against the shadow of his face in a rakish grin. Before she realized his intent, Bryce leaned forward and his lips touched her forehead. He paused, his mouth smooth and gentle against her skin, and then slowly pulled away from her.

Akira felt something stir inside her as he whispered, "Goodnight, and sweet dreams, my lady."

❧

The next morning someone slipped a document under Akira's chamber door. The shuffle noise caught her attention, and she bent to retrieve it. She turned it over and read her name beside Bryce's on an agreement of matrimony. Last night when he had threatened to wed her by proxy, she didn't actually believe he would go through with it, but now she held the proof in her hand. Bryce's bold signature leaped out at her. Vicar Forbes had signed the parchment as well. She looked at her own name in unfamiliar round letters and wondered who had signed on her behalf.

Fury burned inside of Akira like a bonfire. Who would believe her against the word of the MacPhearson chieftain and Vicar Forbes? She had begun her morning devotions, but now she felt too angry and distracted to continue her daily routine. Even the clergy had sided with Bryce by signing the marriage agreement. She felt betrayed and abandoned.

Lord, why are ye allowing this to happen to me?

Akira clutched the thick paper in her hand and stormed from her chamber in search of Bryce. Her mind filled with worry as she flew down the flight of stairs. She bumped into Finella as she rounded a corner, nearly knocking her over.

"Oh!" Finella wrestled with the bundle of dirty linen in her arms and toppled from side to side to keep her balance.

Horrified, Akira took a moment to help steady her. "I'm so sorry, Finella."

Finella turned an exasperated expression in Akira's direction, which instantly turned to surprise. "Lass, ye left yer bedchamber in yer nightgown?" Finella eyed her in the white material cascading down to her bare toes, protruding beneath the hem. Her eyebrows rose in concerned suspicion.

Akira ignored her attire and raised the document in her fist, shaking it. "Do ye know what Bryce has done?"

Finella adopted a dazed look as she searched her mind for some outrageous deed the lad might have committed.

"I canna think of anything," she answered honestly, and then brightened. "He hasn't slept in his bed. Has he left on another adventure then?"

Akira hesitated with that bit of news and then decided to tell her anyway. "I awoke this morn' to find a written document under my door that says Bryce wed me by proxy last night. Even the vicar signed it." She waved the paper in front of Finella's nose. "And I don't know how to get out of it."

She clamped her jaw, barely holding back tears of frustration. Sighing, Akira lowered the document in despair. It wasn't Finella's fault. Ranting at the poor woman would do no good.

Finella looked sympathetic, her bottom lip puckering in an understanding frown. "Lass, I don't think he intends for ye to get out of it," she said, patting Akira's hand as if she were a small child.

Not wanting to hurt her feelings, Akira pasted on a smile and moved past her without another comment. When she reached the door to the library, she looked down at the signed document, mustering the courage to face Bryce. A loud crash sounded behind the door. Akira's head jerked up. Could someone be hurt? She turned the knob and pushed open the door.

Shattered glass fell from the wall above the hearth.

"Who dares disturb me?"

Akira's gaze shifted from the wall to the man towering in the middle of the room. He shoved a hand through his disheveled hair as he turned, clearly annoyed by the intrusion. His eyes burned like ashes, and his black brows were knit in a tight frown. She allowed her gaze to roam over his wrinkled attire.

Grief lurked in the gray depths staring back at her with a raw and primitive threat. She realized Bryce had picked up the glass goblet from a nearby tray and thrown it. Hardening her heart, Akira held up the marriage agreement in her hand.

"I don't suppose ye might be losing any sleep over this?" She held herself rigid as she waited for a response.

"Come hither."

His smoldering gaze took in her appearance in the long white nightgown and how her hair hung loose about her shoulders and down her back. Akira hesitated. Perhaps this wasn't such a good idea after all. Hauling herself to the library in a mad rage wouldn't likely change his mind. Discomfort gripped her as an afterthought and shame rose through her alert senses.

"Don't make me repeat myself. I'm in no mood for games," Bryce snapped, crooking his finger, beckoning her to him.

Akira clasped her nervous hands in front of her, still holding the wedding agreement. She took a deep breath and stepped forward, pausing nearly three feet from him.

"Closer," he commanded.

She took another step.

"Closer," he demanded again.

Akira met his gaze, ready to deny him, when he gave her a warning look meant to intimidate her. Determined not to give him the satisfaction of seeing her cower before him, Akira stepped forward until she was only inches away.

"I want to see yer every expression in the glowing firelight."

No sunlight filtered through the library windows as it neared dawn.

"Yer eyes give yer thoughts away, Akira." He circled around her as she stood still. "Ye feel sympathy for me because of Evan's death, and yet, ye fear me."

"Grief must be hard to bear. I've been fortunate in that I've never had to face it. But ye overestimate yer power, Bryce. I don't fear ye."

His lips twisted. "Ye didn't believe I'd do it, did ye?" He gestured toward the marriage agreement in her hand. "Ye forced my hand, Akira."

She whirled on him in anger. "I forced no such thing. Ye do as ye wish, with no regard to others."

Bryce stopped pacing. "Everything I've done is for the sake of others." His restrained voice severed the air.

"Nay." She shook her head. "Ye did it because of a promise."

"'Twas only one of the reasons."

"Release me from this commitment. Please?" She would beg if she thought it would do any good.

"Nay." His voice was firm as he looked away from her. "I thought ye said ye wouldn't honor the marriage, so why should it matter if I release ye?"

Tears threatened to storm her cloudy eyes, but she contained them. "Ye know I have no other recourse but yer mercy if I'm to return home. My da hasn't come for me," she admitted, hating the familiar pain rising in her chest. "No one will defend me against the vicar's signature on this document. Women are married off to unhappy marriages every day; 'tis a fact of life. But, ye have a choice. Ye don't have to do this."

He shook his head, glaring at his booted feet. "Ye refuse to understand, Akira. I had no other choice."

Akira threw the document at him. "Ye stubborn, ignorant beast. How dare ye do this to me?"

"Akira, ye're Birk MacKenzie's only daughter. I have no other choice."

"If this marriage brings any harm to my family, I will betray ye to yer enemies, and that is *my* promise."

In spite of her vow not to cry in front of him, tears of frustration slipped past her lids, but she wouldn't let it hold her back. "This marriage isn't real. 'Tis in name only." She wiped her eyes. "Since ye wed me by proxy, ye must live by proxy. I'll have naught to do with ye. I'll not willingly consummate this marriage, and there will be no bairns."

Akira turned and ran from the library, hoping to reach her chamber before anyone else saw her.

7

*U*nable to stand the sight of the box at the rear of their traveling party, Akira focused ahead as she rode the mount Bryce had provided. Shortly after Evan's burial and a brief ceremony accepting Bryce as the new clan chief, they set out for MacKenzie holdings. Bryce intended to see Gregor's corpse home in time for burial, which meant they would have to travel light and make haste. He also planned to present her as his wife and speak to her father about a peaceful truce between their clans.

Akira had no doubt that her father would agree to peaceful negotiations and approve their marriage. It had always been his wish to avoid more bloodshed, and the fact that he had not come for her proved it. In her heart, she had hoped her father loved her enough to find a way to negotiate peace with the MacPhearsons without using her as the bargaining price. As the days turned into a fortnight, her hopes became futile. The harsh reality of her situation became increasingly clear.

Akira continued to pray for her family and for God to give her father wisdom, but of late her prayers had taken on a new focus. She needed God to help her accept her fate, as hard as it was to swallow. She prayed for the Lord to guard her heart from the vile bitterness threatening to take root in her. It pained her that the one man she had loved and highly respected all her life—the man who had sired her—would desert her.

She lifted a delicate hand to shield her eyes from the sun and squinted, scanning the view ahead. Elliot rode several yards away, surrounded on all sides by MacPhearson warriors. After he had learned of Akira's marriage to Bryce, Elliot would not even look at her, much less speak to her. He knew naught of how she had been forced into the union by proxy. He considered her outward acceptance of her marriage to Bryce as a betrayal of their clan, yet what could she have done to prevent it? She considered telling Elliot the truth, but Bryce had cautioned her of the lives at stake if others thought her marriage an unwanted sacrifice, particularly in light of the recent deaths of Gregor and Evan. Grudgingly, Akira kept silent, tolerating Elliot's scornful behavior, making her plight even harder to bear.

Akira's heart beat more rapidly when Bryce rode to the front of their traveling party. He no longer looked as fierce as she once thought, but rather handsome as he sat astride his mount in a comfortable and straight posture as befit a king. His broad, muscular shoulders were quite capable as he held the reins, scrutinizing his men, ensuring that all was in order. He looked as if he would ride by a second time, but a peculiar expression crossed his face, and instead, he pulled up beside her.

"M'lady, ye look upset. Is something amiss?" His gaze captured hers as he analyzed her reaction in what appeared to be sincere concern.

In light of her circumstances, everything was wrong, and yet his nearness gave her comfort. Abandoned by her family and hated by his clan, Bryce felt more like an ally than her enemy with each passing day. Her feelings felt like betrayal. How could she continue to resist him when he seemed so intent on winning her affections with more kindness and thoughtfulness than she ever thought him capable?

Akira shifted in her saddle. She wasn't used to riding for such long periods, but she wouldn't waste precious time by complaining. It was imperative that they carry Gregor's body home for burial before he decayed even more. She shook her head.

"Nay, I'm fine."

Not satisfied with her answer, Bryce turned to Balloch riding beside her. "Balloch, see that she rests when she needs it. I've noticed the lass is a wee bit stubborn at times and won't tell ye if she's tired."

"Aye, Bryce. I'll take care of m'lady." Balloch snapped to attention.

Bryce started to move on.

"M'lord!"

Her voice caused him to stop.

She shielded her eyes from the blaring sun. "Who will take care of Sim? His grief is still so strong."

"Finella will care for him." He watched her with a guarded expression, as if assessing her every thought.

"'Tis not the same. What I mean is . . ." Words failed her. She didn't want to insinuate Finella was incapable of caring for Sim. After all, Finella had cared for her when she first arrived. Akira knew Finella would care for Sim's physical needs, but what about his emotional needs? Grief could be such a terrible thing to overcome, especially for one so young. He had seemed so depressed as he watched them leave.

"Have ye appointed yerself as Sim's caretaker?" A smile curved Bryce's lips, obviously pleased by her concern. "Is it possible ye've come to care for a MacPhearson?"

He made her sound like an enemy to herself. Akira needed time to adjust to the changes in her life and wouldn't be coaxed before she was ready. She sent a challenging gaze in his direction.

"Sim cannot help what family he was born into."

Bryce stared at her and then chuckled with a triumphant gleam in his eyes. "My sweet, I would have ye remember that neither could I. Wear yer new name with pride. For we MacPhearsons could not help the faults of those before us, but we are to blame for what we do today."

He rode away, leaving her no chance to reply.

✑❦

Hours later they stopped riding. Balloch stood before Akira, smiling up at her with crooked and stained teeth. For all his brawn and unappealing looks, Balloch seemed to have a gentle nature about him. At the moment, he appeared to recognize her discomfort.

"I'll carry ye, m'lady."

She stifled another yawn, shaking her head with a wave of her other hand. Poor Balloch had endured her ceaseless chatter throughout the day, and when Bryce announced they would make camp for the night, Balloch hadn't missed her weary yawns. He dismounted and hustled over to her before she could even consider sliding from her mount.

"Nay, don't protest. It does me good every now and then to have a comely lass like yerself in my arms," he teased, lifting her as if she were fragile and could possibly crumble in his large, awkward hands.

"I didn't know ye could be so chivalric, Balloch," she said with a fond smile, clasping her arms about his neck.

"Usually, he isn't." Bryce appeared with a raised eyebrow in Balloch's direction.

Balloch seemed startled as if Bryce were scolding him like a child. Akira watched the two men with interest.

"Balloch was being chivalric," Akira informed her new husband.

"I'm sure he was," Bryce mumbled, stepping forward and holding out his arms. "Balloch, I need ye to oversee the men as they prepare camp. I'll take Akira."

Balloch practically dumped her into Bryce's arms, despite her protests. Her husband did not set her down as she expected. Instead, his arms tightened around her, and he called for Ahern. The stallion obeyed at once. Bryce started to lift her up onto his back when Akira clutched his arm and refused to let go.

"I prefer to walk."

"What's wrong?" Bryce paused, looking at her quizzically.

"I've been riding all day, and I'd like to walk a bit to stretch my legs."

"Nonsense, I was going to take ye to the river to wash up before we eat, and I know ye wouldn't want to walk that distance."

He started to place her on Ahern's back again when her arms flew around his neck and she again refused.

"Don't put me back on another beastly animal until the morrow," she hissed in his ear.

"As ye wish."

He set her down and her numb legs hit the ground. She grabbed for Bryce and managed to seize his arm just as he turned from her.

"Don't leave . . . please."

Akira tried to take a step forward on a wobbly leg and almost lost her balance. She rarely rode astride an animal, but in order to keep up with their pace she had chosen to do so. Now she wished she had ridden side-saddle.

Understanding dawned on Bryce, and he reached for her elbow as she took another step toward the river.

"How shall I punish ye for not resting as ye should have?" His strained tone almost sounded like a growl.

"I believe I'm being punished quite enough at the moment," Akira grudgingly pointed out.

She stumbled, and he reached out to steady her. "Ye fool woman—"

"I believe Balloch certainly has more chivalry than my new husband," Akira interrupted. "He at least would have carried me out of sight so no one would be the wiser, but nay, ye have to let me waddle out of camp like a sore duck."

Bryce chuckled, trying hard to suppress the grin spreading across his face. "Ye deserve it."

Maybe she did, but he could at least be more understanding. "I didn't want to slow ye down. Not so long ago I could ride a horse as many hours as ye and never suffer a sore muscle, but within the year Mither took it into her head that it was time I rode like a lady."

"Yer too stubborn and full of pride for a female." He bent and swung her up into his arms.

At the water's edge, Akira bent her knees and dipped her hands in the cool water. She leaned forward with the intention of splashing cool water on her face, but Bryce jerked her back so hard she could barely catch her breath. She gasped and turned to see him gripping her skirt by the waist.

"Bryce, what are ye thinking?"

"Not again." He breathed heavy. "I won't let ye fall in again."

"Bryce, ye've got to let go. Yer hurting me."

"Not this time, Akira. I won't be so foolish again. I've learned my lesson." Bryce still clutched her skirt from behind.

"I promise I won't fall in again. Now let go." She leaned forward. He jerked her back. Akira twisted out of his grasp and slapped his hands away. He caught hold of her. "Let go." She tugged on her skirt. "Bryce, ye're holding me so tight, I canna even reach the water."

He must have realized she spoke the truth, for he loosened his hold.

She stepped forward, and he moved with her. Akira started to bend her knees again, but Bryce jerked her back. She landed on her backside. Akira clutched her stomach to catch her breath. Bryce leaned over to help her, but Akira shoved him away. His foot slid and his knees bent into her back as he fought to maintain his balance.

"I'm not in danger of suffocating from the river; rather 'twould be from ye." Suddenly, the whole situation seemed humorous and she laughed. "Since I've met ye, how many times have ye nearly killed me?"

Bryce frowned as he settled his hands on his hips. "I've done naught of the sort," he said. "If anything, I've tried to save ye from further mishaps." A fierce determination glittered in his smoky eyes as he took her hand in his. "Lass, ye're my wife. 'Tis my duty to protect ye."

She stared at him. "I've always been able to protect myself. I had my da and brothers, but I never needed their protection. Now, however, I find myself in great need of protection."

He sighed heavily. "Lass, I would protect ye with my life. I spoke my vows before God and the vicar and other witnesses. I will honor my words."

"And how would I know what ye've pledged to me?" Akira demanded in an accusing voice that stabbed the air around them with tension. "Since I wasn't there to witness my—"

Akira broke off, her voice breaking in raw bitterness. "That's twice now I've been cheated of my own wedding." She wrapped her arms around her middle.

Bryce avoided her gaze and rose to his feet, turning from her. "If ye recall, I asked ye to wed me willingly."

Akira rose, standing behind him. "If ye'd only given me a wee bit of time I might have considered it!" She took a deep breath, determined to make him understand her point of view. "Do ye think I've enjoyed our clans feuding and shedding the blood of innocents? I needed some time to know ye."

Akira's chin trembled, but she forced the emotion back, hoping he wouldn't turn around and see her momentary weakness.

Bryce looked up at the sky, beginning to darken into dusk. "Akira, there wasn't more time. We needed to bring Gregor's body home for burial, and I could not bring ye back to yer family unless we were wed. The risk would have been too great." He folded his arms over his chest and looked down at the ground. "The risk is still great. I pray yer father will honor the betrothal and not demand an annulment." He sighed. "I know I don't deserve yer loyalty and there hasn't been sufficient time to earn yer trust and win ye over." He paused, as if uncertain if he should continue. He poked at the dirt with the toe of his boot. "I fear I may be in danger of losing ye to yer family again."

Akira closed her eyes. *Lord, is it too soon to hope that he might care?* Akira's heart ached with confusion and hope. She had to face the fact that her father had made his choice by not coming for her. Did it matter that Bryce wanted her to keep a promise to prevent war? Theirs wouldn't exactly be a love match. She had been willing to marry Gregor, and she didn't love him either. Bryce wasn't the evil barbarian she once thought. Beneath his fierce exterior beat the heart of a gentle man who cared for and loved his people. She even enjoyed his company when they weren't arguing, and she couldn't deny that she had some feelings for him. Proxy wedding or not, by law she and Bryce were wed, and she owed her loyalty to her husband.

Akira rubbed her eyebrows and blinked as she straightened her shoulders. She approached him from behind, laying a hand upon his shoulder. "I've been taught to hate ye and to never, ever trust a MacPhearson, but now ye're my husband, and I am a MacPhearson. Although I wasn't given the consideration to pledge my own vows, I willingly give them to ye now."

For a moment Bryce didn't move and she waited, giving him time to consider her offer of trust, a sacrifice she wasn't certain she should give. Aware of the heat emanating from him, Akira wondered if she were losing her mind. Something about his presence drew her to him like the undercurrent of the sea.

After a few more moments, Bryce turned to her. His dark gaze assessed her intently. "What are ye saying, lass?"

Her heart pounded rapidly against her ribcage. She swallowed, knowing the importance of her next words. *Lord, help me*, she thought. *Help me to keep this pledge I give him and help him not to take advantage of me.*

"While I soon return home to the family that I was born into, I return as a MacPhearson and as yer wife. I'll not betray my MacKenzie family, but my loyalty belongs to ye. I give it willingly and with the trust that ye'll honor me as yer wife."

"Do ye truly mean it, lass? Are ye really giving me yer pledge of these promised blessings?" Bryce asked hopefully.

Akira nodded. "Aye. I won't lie to ye. I feel that my father betrayed me when he chose to protect the clan over his own daughter." She paused, giving herself a moment to control her rising emotions. Admitting her feelings aloud sliced her wounded heart even deeper. "If ye truly want me, I am yers with one simple request."

"Aye?" He eyed her cautiously.

"Give me time to know ye better before we consummate our union." Akira felt her nails digging into her palms as she waited for an answer.

"And in return ye give me yer loyalty?"

"Aye." She nodded.

"How much time do ye need, lass?"

Akira shrugged and looked away to avoid his gaze. "I know not the length of time. I'll just know in my spirit." She pointed to her chest.

Suspicion rose in his gray eyes. "How do I know ye won't change yer mind and go against me once yer anger with yer father subsides?"

She linked her hands in front of her. "I've naught to give ye but my word. We're both highlanders and ye know how important a highlander's word is to any man or woman." Her insides shook, but she squared her shoulders and boldly met his eyes. "I give ye the honor of my word as a highlander and a Christian."

His gaze traveled over her face and searched her eyes. He reached out and gently touched her lashes with his finger, letting the moisture of a tear soak his skin. She caught her breath, and his gaze slipped to her mouth as his lips lowered to hers. At first Akira stood like a statue, afraid to move, and then his warmth melted her defenses. She leaned into him.

He pulled back, staring at her with blazing eyes. Akira now understood the look smoldering in his eyes. While it could never be a substitute for true love, perhaps with God's help and in time, it could be a beginning. Holy matrimony would be a lifetime commitment, and she had no wish to be with someone who didn't love her. Akira had no choice but to trust in God for something more to develop between them.

He leaned his forehead against hers. "Lass, ye give me a test in asking me to wait before I make ye completely mine." He cupped her face between his hands and gazed into her eyes. "But I promise we'll wait until ye're ready. I give ye my word as a highlander. I'd give my word as a Christian, but I'm not for certain how the Lord feels about me right now."

"Do ye believe in God?"

"Aye."

She smiled with relief. "Then ye give me something to work with."

His grin widened. "Does that mean I'm not a hopeless cause then?"

She nodded against him. "Aye."

"I find it hard to concentrate on my responsibilities with ye around, and that could be dangerous to a man about to walk into enemy territory. 'Twill be like walking on the edge of fire the whole time we're at yer family's holdings." He traced a lock of hair down the side of her face with a gentle finger. "Lass, yer pledge of loyalty may be harder to keep than ye think once yer back home." Doubt filled his voice with a mixture of concern.

Akira understood his confusion and doubt all too well. "Are ye sorry ye've wed me then?"

He cupped her cheek in his hand. "Nay." He shook his head. "On the contrary, I worry our clans will try and pull us apart."

A warm fire blazed as Akira pulled a piece of venison from the portion Bryce offered her fresh from the flames. "Careful. 'Tis hot."

She blew on the meat and tried to ignore her burning fingers as she looked up across the camp. Elliot sat alone with his back against the trunk of a tree. He refused to eat everything they offered him. Disappointment tugged at her heart. Would he never forgive her? She sighed sadly and bit into the tender meat.

"Mmm." She could taste the tender juice from the flames, and it tasted delicious, much better than she expected without her mother's spices.

"Balloch is the best hunter. We'll never go hungry as long as he's around," Bryce said beside her.

"Aye, when a man's hungry, he does what he must," Balloch chimed in.

"That is why I refuse to travel without Balloch." Kian walked up behind Balloch, giving him a brotherly slap across the back and swiping a piece of meat from Balloch's hands. How he managed to reach around Balloch's large frame, Akira would never know. She watched as Balloch looked at his empty hands for a moment and then at her, debating whether to keep his manners in front of her or abandon all caution and attack his friend.

"Balloch, I believe ye might have to catch another deer." She laughed.

"Nay, m'lady. I might have to squash me a bug." He went after Kian, who took off running in the opposite direction.

"Never steal a hungry man's food," Kian called back. They ran by Elliot and again Akira's attention lingered on her brother. She could not enjoy her meal while he sat in hungry stubbornness. Maybe he would eat something if she were to offer it to him instead of Bryce's men.

Akira stood and ignored the stares as she walked to Elliot. She sat at an angle so she could still see everyone else by the fire.

"I brought ye something to eat." She held out a chunk of meat. He turned away from her. "I thought ye might be hungry." Still, he ignored her. She reached out to turn his face to her, but he shoved her hand away.

"Talk to me, Elliot. Why are ye doing this? I can understand why ye won't speak to them, but why do ye refuse to speak to me?" She fought the confusing feelings his behavior toward her conjured inside her. "Please don't do this." She reached for his hand and once again he shoved her away. The meat fell to the ground. "What did ye do that for? Ye're acting like a spoiled bairn."

Never one to accept criticism too graciously, Elliot finally faced her. "Ye've changed, Akira." His tone sounded like an accusation. "Ye always loathed the idea of wedding Evan MacPhearson. When he died ye should have run with yer freedom. Instead, ye willingly gave yerself to him." Elliot pointed in Bryce's direction, not bothering to hide his contempt. "Yer betrothal was with Evan, not Bryce. Ye've betrayed yer family and yer clan."

Akira closed her eyes, allowing hot tears to trail down her cheeks. "The betrothal did not specifically name Evan. It stated the heir to the MacPhearson chieftainship."

"That's what *he* claims," Elliot growled, nodding in Bryce's direction. "Ye make me sick the way ye pine after him as if ye're already besotted with him."

Akira hastily wiped her cheeks. "He is now my husband, and I'll treat him with the respect God's law commands. Besides, he isn't the barbarian ye've always made him out to be. He's treated ye with nothing but kindness, while yer manners leave much to be desired."

Elliot waved her away. "Go on, Akira." Elliot crossed his arms over his chest and turned from her. "I'll not listen to ye defend him."

Akira shivered. Would the rest of her family treat her like this? Out of the corner of her eye she noticed Bryce moving to stand as he watched them a short distance away. The last thing she needed was her husband's interference. She knew her brother well, and he would earn himself a good beating from Bryce and his men if provoked.

Bryce strode from the fire. "I thought I heard him raise his voice to ye, lass." Bryce looked from Akira to Elliot.

Akira scrambled to her feet, stepping in front of Elliot. "Nay, 'tis only a family quarrel."

"I'm yer family now," Bryce said, his voice low, but firm.

"Aye, and so is he, whether he wants to admit it or not." She held onto Bryce's arm. The rest of his men stood watching by the fire.

Akira turned to her brother. "I'm still the same, Elliot. I only have a new name."

"A name I will always loathe."

She bent forward with her hands on her hips. "And what would ye've had me do, pray tell?"

He looked up at her with a hatred that pierced her heart. "Anything," he spat out. "Anything before sacrificing yerself to a MacPhearson. Where is yer loyalty, Akira? Yer pride? Ye betrayed us. We're yer family."

Akira's chin trembled as she straightened. His words echoed deep in her heart. "I made no sacrifice, Elliot. I made the only peaceful decision that would ensure my survival when the MacKenzies abandoned me to the MacPhearsons. Why be bitter and angry at me if I'm now content? Mayhap this is what the Lord intended all along—for me to take the MacPhearson name and stand in the gap for peace. If this is God's will, then so be it. I'll not call it a sacrifice. I owe no man a higher allegiance than I owe my God."

Akira turned from her brother and faced her husband in the moonlight. "Please do not hurt him," she whispered so Elliot wouldn't hear. "Hopefully, he'll come to his senses in the morn'. I'm ready to retire." She moved past Bryce and walked away.

Bryce looked up at the stars, hardly able to stand the sight of Elliot without wanting to take revenge for the pain he caused Akira. At the same time he hadn't been able to meet his wife's gaze and see the hurt that lurked in her eyes.

Having spent little time in the company of women, Bryce was unaccustomed to their tender feelings and had no idea how to comfort her. Hadn't he promised he would protect her? How did a husband go about protecting a wife's tender feelings? For the first time in his life he felt inept. He disliked seeing Akira upset, but he didn't know what to do about it, for he suspected if he punished Elliot appropriately, his wife would grow even more upset.

He turned to watch Akira. Her shoulders sagged under the emotional pressure that he imagined she felt right now. He wanted to go to her and comfort her somehow, but he doubted she would welcome him. She probably even blamed him for Elliot's hatred. He glanced at the uneaten food lying on the ground and knew she would not eat another bite tonight.

He waited until she disappeared inside their tent and turned toward Elliot. "She doesn't deserve yer anger. If ye want someone to blame, blame me. Akira has done naught." Bryce clenched his fists at his sides when Elliot didn't respond.

Leaving Akira's brother to his mistaken thoughts, Bryce walked back toward the fire. He had to pass by their tent, and her muffled sniffles clutched at his chest. He paused in midstride. He hardly knew her. How could she possibly have the ability to affect him so deeply? Bryce closed his eyes and shook his head. He might not know the answers to his own questions, but he knew he wanted to make her feel better if he could—if she would let him. He half turned to the tent in thoughtful silence, unaware that his men still watched him. The low sound of her weeping tugged at his heart and lured him forward until he stood before the tent. He took a deep breath for courage and lifted the flap, bending to crouch inside.

Akira shifted, sitting up. He couldn't see her expression in the dark, only the silhouette of her body as she moved, breathing deeply.

His throat constricted as he crawled on his knees toward her. He opened his mouth to speak, but his tongue stalled and his mind went blank. An unfamiliar fear struck him. It wasn't the kind that he was used to facing in battle. This kind of fear left him feeling awkward and uncertain. He wanted her to let him comfort her, even if he didn't know how. Bryce hated the thought of being rejected.

She sniffed. He paused, reaching out to her. His unsteady fingers tangled in her hair. "Akira, I . . . " About to apologize, the words died on his tongue. He couldn't apologize. He wanted to feel her hair between his fingers.

She lifted her head. "Bryce, I want to thank ye." She spoke in a hoarse whisper.

Relieved that she didn't order him out, he swallowed hard and continued to stroke her hair where it lay over her shoulder and down her back. "For what?"

For a moment she remained silent, and he wondered if she would answer. Then she took a deep breath and cleared her throat. "For not killing Elliot. I can see how he's pushed yer limits these last few days. I'll be forever grateful."

"Akira." He leaned his forehead against hers, drawing in a ragged breath. "While I'll admit it's been tempting at times, I couldn't hurt him, lass. My goal is to prevent war, not start it." He cupped her cheek. "Although, I'll not tolerate him mistreating ye, even if he is yer brother."

She turned her face into his hand. Her soft skin begged for kisses, but he managed to keep himself still, hoping to do naught but comfort her. This woman had some kind of pull on him that he didn't quite understand. Evan had hated her for being a MacKenzie, but Bryce could not. He closed his eyes as he contemplated the words she had spoken to Elliot. Mayhap her being a MacPhearson was the Lord's will. The day Bryce fetched her from the chapel, he had a strong feeling that Akira was never meant for Evan, but for him. Bent over the altar and on his knees, he felt both regretful that his brother's life had ended, and grateful that Akira would be his.

Was Evan right? Could a MacKenzie never be trusted? Tomorrow she would be back among her people where she would no doubt feel pressured to resist him. What if Birk MacKenzie demanded an annulment? Bryce's heart nearly stopped at the thought. Bryce felt a great urge to wrap his arms around her and crush her to him, but he held back. He had come in here to comfort her, not scare her.

Akira laid her hand against his chest as if sensing something. "Bryce, ye trembled. Why?" His pulse quickened. "Yer heart is racing."

"Aye, lass, ye seem to have that effect on me." He wiped away the last of her remaining tears with his thumb. "Don't weep, Akira." Even though he couldn't see her expression, he tilted her chin up to ensure he had her full attention. "Elliot didn't mean those things he said. He's just angry and probably blaming himself for not saving ye as he came to do."

She gulped, nodding in understanding. On impulse, he gripped her trembling shoulders, and pulled her to him. "Shush." Bryce clenched his teeth and swallowed in spite of the tightening at the back of his throat. "Don't weep, lass." He stroked her silky hair and closed his eyes, reveling in her lilac scent.

"Why can ye not be the barbarian ye're supposed to be, so I can hate ye right and proper?" Her voice trembled.

A smile tugged at his lips. "Maybe because I don't want ye to hate me right and proper."

She chuckled, and the weight of his heart lifted.

Now that she seemed to be calming, Bryce rubbed his tired eyes, realizing that this husband and wife thing might not be so easy after all.

"Bryce?"

"Aye?"

"Must ye take me back?"

He shifted to a more comfortable position so he could stretch out his long legs. "I thought ye'd like nothing more than to see yer family again."

"I would, but—"

"But, what?"

"I'm not sure." She sighed heavily and moved away from him.

He could not let her leave him hanging like that. He leaned over and grasped her chin, forcing her to face his direction. He wished for light. At that moment he wanted very much to see her eyes.

"I don't wish to know if they hate me the way Elliot does. I would rather remember my life as it was."

Deep inside, his chest shook like an earthquake mixing with the tides of guilt. "They wouldn't feel that way, Akira.

Elliot allows his hatred to burn out everything else that is good within him." He tried to put her fears to rest.

"I suppose ye're right. Elliot is quite different from the rest," she said pensively.

Bryce felt the weight of her trust more than any other responsibility he had ever carried in his life. He wouldn't want to be the cause of hurting her more. As the MacKenzie chieftain, her father had been forced to make decisions that wounded her tender heart. How would he act as the chief of his clan without doing the same? Already he'd tricked her into marrying him, and as a result she had suffered Mirana's wrath and Elliot's scorn, not to mention other slights. He wished his father were here. Had his mother meant more than the land and clan? Where should a man's loyalties lie if he happened to be the clan chieftain?

It shouldn't matter, he decided. After all, he had married her to fulfill a promise and gain peace, and Lord willing, he intended to have it.

8

$\mathcal{A}$kira finished her morning prayers and looked up. The gray sky dissolved into bright orange with the awakening of dawn, while distant treetops of the forest outlined the sky in an uneven symmetry. The lake below shimmered from the morning glory, and she welcomed the beautiful display of God's creative wonder. She strolled to the water's edge and sat with her knees bent up, wrapping her arms around them. Here was the perfect spot to watch the sunrise. Akira closed her eyes and listened to the singing of the birds that flocked together in the neighboring forest. The musical interlude brought the peace she had longed for in the last few days.

"I awoke this morn' to find my fair lady missing." Sleep lingered in Bryce's voice. He settled next to her. "I worried something might have happened to ye."

While they shared the same tent to keep down the gossip, Bryce had kept his word and slept a few feet away from her. Akira gazed into his eyes, realizing she now trusted him more.

"Nay, I'm fine." She flashed him a reassuring smile. "I enjoy rising at dawn, spending time with the Lord and enjoying His beautiful creation."

He laid an arm across her shoulders and surveyed the magnificent scenery before them. They sat in silence for a while, and then he turned to her.

"Lass, I've enjoyed this time together, but we must get an early start."

He rose and held out a hand. Akira accepted him, and together they made their way back to the others.

As they traveled through the day, Bryce stopped twice, and each time he made certain she walked around to stretch her legs. By late afternoon, two of Bryce's men charged toward them on their war horses. She couldn't hear what they were saying as she watched Bryce nod and briefly look in her direction. His men gathered around him, except the ones guarding Elliot.

Slowly, she eased her horse over to their group, careful not to be noticed, but hoping to get close enough to listen. "How many are there?" Bryce asked.

"At least fifty, possibly sixty. 'Tis hard to tell. They're moving rather quickly and have no women among them," Tavis answered.

"How much time do we have before we meet?" Bryce wanted to know.

"Fifteen minutes, maybe less."

Bryce rubbed his temple as he gathered his thoughts. "If at all possible, I want a peaceful greeting. They are probably angry, and with good reason. Neither Gregor nor Elliot have yet returned. We must not give them any reason to pick a fight. It sounds as if they outnumber us two to one, and I'll not battle my own family."

"They're not yer family," Kian said, his eyes blazing in rare defiance.

Bryce looked up, and Akira could tell by his expression that Kian's comment had angered him.

"They are Akira's family, and therefore, mine. Under no circumstances will we rise against them, except in self-defense. If anyone here disobeys me in this, he will be putting his own life at risk. Is that understood?"

None of them looked happy, but they nodded in consent. Kian turned away in disgust.

Bryce looked beyond his men toward her. "Akira, we shall welcome yer da a day early." Bryce looked around at his men with a challenging gaze.

"Why?" She frowned in confusion.

"It appears that he is riding this way—toward MacPhearson land."

He searched her features, probably looking for some sign that she would break her word to him. She kept her gaze steady, while her heart lifted at the thought of seeing her kinsmen again.

Akira clutched the reins tight in her hand as Bryce turned, giving her no time to question him further. He edged away, leading Balloch, Kian, and Tavis. Unexpected pride overwhelmed her. He looked powerful and confident as he rode Ahern, and at that moment, Akira realized she wanted peace more than anything.

Riders appeared over the horizon. At first they looked like small specks moving in the wind, but as they grew closer, Akira could make out the sight of the MacKenzie plaid. Four men broke from her father's riding party to meet Bryce, and although the distance prevented her from seeing him clearly, she knew her father led them.

Akira felt as restless as the horse beneath her. She tried to calm the animal while she watched the two chiefs greet each other. She prayed in a soft whisper, not allowing herself to think of the consequences if things did not fare well.

The men talked. No swords were drawn. Surely, that was a good sign. She hated not being able to hear their conversation, and she hated even more not being able to see their faces. The urge to disobey her husband and ride after them grew within her, but she dared not. This moment was too critical. For once in her life, she would have to be patient and wait.

Bryce and his trusted warriors halted only a few feet from the MacKenzies who rode out to meet them. He knew Akira's father instantly. The chief of the MacKenzie clan commanded respect with a quiet disposition and an observant eye. As a lad, Bryce had seen him in battle against his father. He knew the speed, wisdom, and power Birk MacKenzie possessed. Bryce also knew he craved peace for his people.

Making the first move, Bryce nodded to Birk MacKenzie, and then the others. "I bid ye a friendly welcome, for we are on our way to visit yer holdings."

A flicker of interest sparkled in Birk's eyes. He remained quiet, however.

"Yer son rides with us up the hill yon," Bryce continued.

Birk raised his hand to shield his eyes from the sun and skimmed the row of riders, waiting patiently upon the hill. He looked back at Bryce and waited.

Bryce felt compelled to continue, but he would not be dominated by this man's silence, so he also waited.

After what seemed like an eternity, Birk finally took a deep breath. "Where is yer brother? He is chief of the MacPhearson clan, and yet, it is ye who always seem to carry his responsibilities." Birk spoke in a deep voice that Bryce imagined shook his men into action when giving orders.

Bryce wanted to defend his dead brother, but he refused to take offense. Many of the MacKenzie and MacPhearson clansmen alike shared this view. "Evan is dead." He hated the words even as he said them. Swallowing back his grief, Bryce concentrated on ignoring the anger threatening to surface at the unintentional reminder. He had no wish for the tension to unfurl at such a delicate moment.

"We're bringing Gregor Matheson's body home. I wanted to see ye personally and express my condolences."

One of Birk's men snorted in disgust, and Birk released a fiery scowl upon him.

Bryce ignored the man. His own men remained quiet and expressionless, which pleased him.

"Yer son is perfectly healthy and has been treated well. Before my wedding, he behaved with exceptional decorum, but has managed to be quite a nuisance since then." Bryce paused. "During this journey he has been anything but civil to my wife."

Birk glanced behind Bryce to the hill above. "Ye brought yer wife?" He sounded astonished that Bryce would do such a thing.

"Aye, I thought she might like to see her family."

"Akira," Birk whispered, realizing the situation.

"I'll not have her mistreated, not even by her own brother." Bryce could not mistake the emotion in the man's eyes at the mention of his only daughter. Surprised that Birk MacKenzie allowed such a relieved expression to show, Bryce gave him a moment. It was a weakness that Bryce, as her husband, could certainly use against him. "Elliot seems to resent Akira for wedding me."

"Did she have a choice?" the older man asked suspiciously.

Bryce did not answer. Instead, he decided to let Akira answer for herself. "Why not ask her?"

"I believe I will. I wish to see her. Now."

Bryce nodded and guided his horse around, waiting for Birk to follow his lead. They rode up the hill side by side, leaving the others with no choice but to follow. Bryce's men trailed a good ten feet away from Birk's men, both clans scowling as hard as they could.

"They're coming!" In the midst of her excitement, Akira forgot her anger with her father. She spurred her mare forward, slipping past her guards before they could stop her.

"Da!" she called to him even before he could possibly hear her.

Birk increased his stallion's pace, leaving Bryce and reaching his daughter as she hastily descended her mare. Birk easily leaped down and gathered her in his arms reminding her of the greetings he used to give her when she was a child. Akira marveled the moment she felt his embrace, realizing she had feared never feeling it again.

He pulled back and examined her closely. "Were ye forced to wed?" He asked the question as Bryce and the others caught up with them. His expression changed to a serious and protective nature.

Akira did not falter. She looked him straight in the eye. "I have accepted my marriage in the hope of peace." In a sense, it was true. She'd willingly given Bryce her pledge by the creek that day.

A mixture of emotions alternated across Birk's face, and her heart lurched, but there was naught she could do. She had made her decision and what had been done was done.

She remained silent as he placed both hands on her shoulders and looked up at the clear blue sky, closing his eyes as if in pain, and then he slowly looked back down at her.

"Then 'tis over. There will now be peace among us." He turned, and for the first time, Akira noticed her brother Gavin, but she would have no time to go to him. "Gavin, go summon the rest of the men," her father ordered.

"Aye." He nodded and turned to do their father's bidding.

Moments later, the MacKenzies gathered on the south side and the MacPhearsons gathered on the north side, facing each other as both clan chiefs stood between them. Birk threw his sword. It sank into the ground with the handle facing the sky. Bryce did likewise.

"I pledge peace between the MacPhearsons and the MacKenzies," Birk MacKenzie shouted loud enough for all to hear. "There will be no more bloodshed or death from wars between us as long as I am alive and MacKenzie clan chief. I give my allegiance and my word on my honor to Bryce MacPhearson. I shall, from hereforth, never rise against ye again without just cause." He looked at Bryce. "Ye're my family. Ye've wed my daughter, and ye'll have wee bairns from both clans, uniting us not only in friendship and marriage, but in blood."

He looked around at all of his men and pointed to his sword. "If there be one of ye to disagree with this peace of alliance, take my sword and challenge me now."

Akira held her breath. No one moved. Most had dazed looks upon their faces, and she knew they had trouble accepting peace when they had known only years of hate. Her father waited a while longer and still no one moved to challenge him. Just as her shoulders began to relax, she tensed at the sound of Bryce's voice.

"I pledge my allegiance to Birk MacKenzie. I, too, pledge my loyalty, honor, and friendship to Birk MacKenzie. Any man who would challenge me, take up my sword against me now."

She glanced nervously at each man's face. Akira breathed a sigh when enough time had passed and no one stepped forward. Both men bent down to retrieve their weapons.

Akira watched her husband and father. Both men possessed qualities alike—honor, loyalty, courage—and they both cared about their people. That was why they were born leaders. Suddenly, it struck her that she would not have been content with anyone but Bryce. She and Gregor were never really suited.

With a bright smile, Gavin dismounted and strode toward her. They embraced.

"I thought ye would hate me," she confessed quietly in his ear.

He stiffened and pulled back for a better look at his little sister. "Why, Akira?"

"For being a MacPhearson. Elliot is still so upset with me that he will hardly even speak to me."

Gavin rolled his eyes in mild irritation. "He'll come 'round. He only needs time, and ye need a little patience." He touched his finger to her nose as he used to do. The simple gesture brought a warm feeling, and she threw her arms around his neck, silently thanking the Lord for reuniting them once more.

"Oh, Gavin, I've missed ye so."

He squeezed her tight. "Akira, I thought we had lost ye for good. I'm so relieved to know ye're fine."

"I love ye, Gavin." He did not answer. Instead, she felt his large hands on her head, and before she could stop him, he tousled her hair in a huge mess. It was a game they always played. He knew she hated it when he messed up her hair, and that is why he did it. She flipped her head back and brushed her fingers through the long strands. "That is not something I've missed," she teased.

While Elliot's dark mood lifted with the presence of the MacKenzies, Akira spent most of her time with Gavin. She could remember many childhood instances when Gavin had defended her against Elliot.

"How is Mither?" Akira couldn't resist asking.

Gavin's smile faded a bit. "The same."

Akira looked down at her feet. "I know we've had our differences, but I've missed her so. I could have used her advice in the last fortnight."

"Aye," Gavin nodded, glancing over at Bryce talking to Birk. "I'm sure ye could have. Does he treat ye well?"

Akira nodded. "Aye, better than I could have ever imagined." She held her breath and then decided to confide in Gavin. "I didn't know Evan verra well, but I truly believe the Lord intended for me to wed Bryce all along."

"Well, Akira, if there's one thing I've learned in my short years it's that there is naught that catches God by surprise. He always has a plan, even when we don't."

❧

Akira looked happy to be home, and Bryce enjoyed her radiant smile. She swung by on her father's arm, gazing up at Birk as if he were the only man in the world. They were outside under the stars, circling around to the far side of the fire. Bryce sat facing the MacKenzie Castle, staring at her over the dancing flames. Everything about his wife fascinated him as he learned of her childhood and all about her family and clan.

Upon their arrival, they had quickly buried Gregor. Akira had stood beside Bryce, weeping with her kinsmen. Since then she had been quiet and withdrawn until tonight. Bryce sensed a distance growing between them, and he disliked it. He kept reminding himself of her personal vows to him and renewed his commitment to trust her daily.

Bryce allowed her free rein and undertook the task of leading his men in civil conversation with the MacKenzie clan. They were visibly uncomfortable, and so were MacKenzie's men. They mostly avoided talking to each other, sitting together in an unsettling silence. Bryce could see doubt forming on the faces of his clansmen.

Too often, Bryce knew Akira occupied his thoughts where he should have been concentrating on his men and the situation at hand. A familiar form sat beside him, but Bryce paid no heed, intent on watching his wife's delight as Elliot brought her a harp to play.

"The men are getting restless." Kian's deep voice broke his concentration.

"Aye," Bryce sighed with a nod.

"A month ago I would have laughed at any man who might have said that Bryce MacPhearson would become a besotted fool over a female, but I'm the fool. Ye've proven me wrong. Ye've become lovesick, my friend."

Kian's voice sounded so disgusted that Bryce turned, giving his clansman his full attention. He surveyed his friend with a thoughtful expression.

"She canna be trusted," Kian continued, shaking his head. "I don't care to see ye hurt. Betrayal is the worst kind of pain for a man to endure, especially where a woman is concerned."

Bryce smiled and patted Kian on the back. "Yer loyalty means a great deal to me, Kian. We've been friends too long for me to be angered by your concern. I want ye to know, I intend to give Akira a chance before I assume the worst in her. And as besotted as ye think I may be, I'm still watchful. I observe her. As ye've pointed out, I canna afford not to. Too much faith on my part could prove to be fatal. Many people are depending on me, and I canna act foolishly. Ye've naught to fear." He leaned forward turning at an angle to view Kian. "But at the same time, I would have ye remember that she's now a MacPhearson as if she's always been a MacPhearson."

"Aye, in name, but a name doesn't bring loyalty. As a friend, I ask ye to remain careful and remember those who have proven themselves to ye." Kian stood and strode over to Balloch, leaving Bryce to mull over his words.

Bryce disliked Kian's tone, but his mind reverted to another direction when Akira's melodious voice hypnotized the air and the ears of both clans. She sat between her two brothers, Gavin and Elliot, while her younger brother Leith sat at her feet. She played the stringed instrument as if it was born from her very fingers, and her voice carried ballads from his memory to new heights.

He had never heard a more beautiful voice, and evidently, neither had his men. They crept closer, mesmerized. For the first time since their arrival, both clans were immersed into one another, drawn by his wife's sweet voice.

Bryce watched her, absorbing every word. While he liked the idea of spending the rest of his days watching her, he now knew he could just as easily spend them listening to her.

"Ye didn't know about her music, did ye?" a woman's voice spoke beside him.

He turned to see Akira's mother, Nara, the lady who had wept for hours when they first arrived. But now she wore a pensive smile of pride as she enjoyed her daughter's performance. Bryce understood the feeling all too well. Even though he'd only just discovered Akira's musical talent, the beauty of her voice and her skill with a harp pleased him immensely.

Bryce shook his head. "'Twould appear I'll never know enough about her." He crossed his arms over his chest, hoping Akira would share more of herself in the future.

The timid lady beside him placed her hand on his arm. "My daughter will come 'round. We are different in nature, but I know her. Ye'll have to be a patient man."

Bryce looked down at her with curiosity, wondering why she had approached him this way. Familiar jade eyes stared back at him. Her image reminded him of an older, wiser glimpse of his wife in the future. A feeling of longing slapped him in the face.

"I'm learning to be patient."

Her eyes lit up, and a smile curled her lips upward. He couldn't decipher her.

"Then yer marriage will succeed. Once Akira makes up her mind to love ye as her husband, ye'll never find a more devoted woman as long as ye live."

Hope rose within him, but as he caught a glimpse of his clansmen's sour expressions and wary gazes toward their old enemies, it dashed to ashes. He looked away, afraid to hope too much.

"I fear she loved another." He wanted to bite his tongue, wondering what possessed him to say that.

"Nay." Nara shook her head. "She and Gregor were only childhood friends."

Nara's words were similar to what Akira had said earlier, but he'd thought little about them then.

"She's tried to hide it," Bryce said, "but I believe she grieves deeply for him. I canna imagine her not loving him more strongly than a friend. It's torture to be jealous of a dead man. I wouldn't wish that fate on anyone." He paused, scraping his teeth over his bottom lip. "We know so little about each other. I've no idea what she likes or dislikes. I know nothing about her past. We canna share or talk about childhood memories. She would have had all of that with Gregor."

"But that wouldn't have been enough." Nara patted the top of his hand. "Trust me on this. Akira doesn't know about ye, either. The two of ye have the fun of exploring these things about each other. Believe me, in time, ye'll make her happy." Nara sounded more confident than he felt. "Underneath all her bravery, Akira's heart is soft." Nara first pointed to him and then herself. "And between us, that's why I'm glad she's wed to ye and not Gregor."

Her words stunned him. Everyone else seemed to be of a different opinion. Gregor's burial had been tense and extremely uncomfortable for him and his men. While Akira had wept with her kinsmen, she had spurned Bryce's consolation. Her coldness had hurt, but he couldn't blame her. He was partially responsible for Gregor's death. If he had not taken Akira, then Gregor and Evan would not have lost their lives. He looked at Nara.

"Why do ye prefer she wed me over Gregor?"

"'Tis better. A mother knows." She clapped with the others at the end of Akira's ballad. Akira took another request and began singing again. Bryce lapsed into thoughtful silence as he listened. He mulled over the conversation with Nara and could find no reason why she would lie to him. Her words brought confidence and hope. He'd found none from anyone else since the day he took Akira as his wife. Both clans were against their marriage.

Bryce glanced over at Nara, realizing how much he missed his own mother, and that thought brought Sim to mind. He hoped his younger brother fared well and smothered a longing for home. In that moment, he knew how his wife felt and vowed to bring her back to MacKenzie Castle more often.

❧

"Akira, sing our favorite!" Leith bounced to his knees beside her, shifting from one leg to the other. The sight of Leith reminded Akira of Sim. He was a little shorter than Sim and two years younger, but they were alike in so many ways. Akira turned her full attention to Leith as his sharp eyes beamed up at her.

"And what might that be, wee one?" She bent toward him, ruffling his hair.

Normally, he would have gotten annoyed with her, but not this time. She'd been away far too long. The child had obviously missed her the way he had followed her around since her return.

"Couthie pree!" Leith announced in excitement.

"Nay, not that one." Akira shook her head, while all the others nodded and murmured their enthusiasm.

"Why not, Akira?" Fergus wanted to know, not bothering to hide his disappointment. "Teach us all about the *Loving Kiss.* We've not heard it since the last time ye sang it."

"Akira, ye'll be leaving soon; honor their request." Nara's voice broke through their grumbling.

Akira looked at her mother now standing beside her father. In all her memory, she could not remember her mother ever requesting her to sing a particular song. This request she could not, and would not, deny. No matter how many times she knew her eyes would betray her and roam over to Bryce, she would sing it for her mother.

She turned to Elliot. "Please bring the bagpipes." A gleam entered his eye, and the two exchanged a smile.

"You're going to play the bagpipes with that song?" Fergus asked with disbelief, squinting in concern.

"Aye, Fergus. 'Twas a combination Elliot and I were working on before." She turned to Leith. "Go retrieve yer cuisle. We will need the flute with this one." She smiled as he beamed and dashed off to retrieve it.

A moment later Elliot and Leith returned. Gavin sat nearby with his hand drum, and the four of them began to play. The combination sounded beautiful. Everyone doubted the bagpipes would blend with such a romantic song, but they made a beautiful melody. That night the MacPhearsons learned that the bagpipes were meant for more than war. They contained a unique, refreshing softness.

Akira's voice floated through the air, and all the outside sounds around them dissolved. Even the creatures in the surrounding forest seemed to grow quiet. Akira managed to hit every pitch perfectly, and she never faltered with a single low key, which sometimes plagued her to a fault. This song remained her favorite, and the passion with which she sang it captivated them all.

As she sang about the fair lady who sacrificed her life to save her true love, Akira's gaze strayed toward her husband. Unable to help it, she sang for him. For the first time in her life, she actually had someone to sing this song to, and he would never know its significance to her. Their gazes met, and for a moment she forgot about their fighting clans, the history of hate, and the embellished lies. Only a promise of hope for their future together seemed to exist in the gap between them.

"His fair lady used the last o'her strength to give him one final blessin', a loving kiss. 'Couthie pree,' she whispered, as she closed her eyes and breathed her last."

Akira's voice ended the lyrics, but her gaze met with Bryce's until others looked back and forth between them. Silence ensued. One person coughed, and a couple of sniffles followed.

"What next?" Elliot grew impatient and grabbed her arm, glaring at Bryce.

Dazed and shaken, she looked down at her instrument, not ready to meet Elliot's gaze. She knew the condemning eyes she would see. "I believe I'm through for the evening. My throat is sore, and I'm weary."

"But, the night is still young, Akira," Elliot protested.

"Would ye like to walk, Akira?" Gavin leaned over her, holding out a hand. Akira smiled. Dear, sweet Gavin had once again come to her aid.

She sighed with relief and looked up at him graciously. "Aye, Gavin." She turned to Elliot. "Would ye put away the instruments?" Without waiting for a reply she accepted Gavin's hand, and he led her away.

9

Akira and Gavin strolled through the woods with the moonlight peeking through the tree branches. They walked on a familiar path that led around MacKenzie Castle. She and Gavin had taken many strolls along this path. As the heir to the MacKenzie chieftainship, Gavin had always been the level-headed brother, who had a way of calming her fears and teaching her wisdom. Elliot, on the other hand, was the mischievous brother, who exhibited impatience and a lack of tolerance for rules. Growing up he had always teased and taunted her until she lashed out at him.

She held Gavin's arm and noticed that there seemed to be more layers of muscle above his elbow than she remembered.

"Have ye been practicing with the sword?" Akira squeezed his arm for emphasis.

Gavin gave her a sidelong glance and chuckled. "Aye, that I have." Gavin rubbed his jaw thoughtfully. "Bryce gave me a hard punch on the day he took ye, and I've been preparing for our next meeting." He patted her hand on his arm. "But, once I discovered ye were wed and Da intended to seek peace through yer union, I decided 'twould be best to befriend my new brother."

Akira sighed sadly. "I knew that unlike Elliot ye would never defy Da's decision."

"Things have a way of working themselves out, Akira. I've been watching Bryce." Gavin shook his head. "I can tell he's taken a real interest in ye by the way he looks at ye."

Gavin's statement took Akira by surprise. A warm glow flowed through her at the thought.

"If for no other reason, I truly believe the Lord intended us to wed so we could build a bridge of peace between our clans. I pray that there will one day be love in our marriage."

"Well, judging by his actions, I would say there is the distinct possibility he is falling in love with ye, if he hasn't already."

Akira had been guarding a flicker of hope in her heart, but Gavin's words ignited a burning torch in her soul. Gavin had always given her sound advice, and she trusted his opinions implicitly. She squeezed Gavin's arm in her excitement and smiled up at her brother.

"Oh, Gavin, I pray ye're right. At first I didn't know if I could trust Bryce, and at times I still wonder if I am wise to trust him now."

"I'm sure he struggles with trusting ye as well. There's no rule that says attraction warrants trust. If that were the case, then more wedded couples would be happier."

"I want to have a happy marriage like our parents."

To her surprise, Gavin laughed. "Akira, lass, ye've a lot to learn. Where have ye been all these years? The two of them can barely manage to spend more than a few minutes together without arguing."

She looked up at Gavin in the moonlight, but his unreadable expression concentrated on the path ahead of them. Akira turned away, occupied with her thoughts. She wasn't aware of any problems between her parents. Her mother cried a great deal, but she'd always been overly sentimental and melodramatic. It had always been like that. It didn't mean that her father was at fault or that they didn't love each other.

"Ye jest, Gavin," Akira said, looking up at him. "They're completely happy with each other. Mither is only sentimental at times."

"Have ye ever wondered why Mither is like that, Akira?"

She didn't have a ready answer. Truth be known, her mother's antics often annoyed her. Akira had never bothered to consider that there might be an underlying cause. She dropped her head as shame crept into her cheeks.

Gavin ignored her silence. "Well, I can remember a time when she was verra different. Before ye were ever born, when she first came to us, Nara was more like the way ye are now. She became unhappy when she realized Da wouldn't forget my mither's memory. He even refused to store away her clothes. For the first year of their marriage my mither's clothes remained in their chamber."

Akira imagined another woman's wardrobe in the chamber she shared with Bryce. She shivered at the discomforting thought. It was one thing to respect the dead, and another to reject and ignore the feelings of the living.

"Surely, Da wouldn't do such a thing?"

"I have no reason to lie. I loved my mither, but Nara is a good woman and the best step-mither I could have ever had outside of my own. I hated to see her so unhappy."

"Why did she stay?"

"Ye know as well as I that women have few choices." Gavin shrugged. "I suppose she could have gone back to her family, but she says she loves him."

Akira grew pensive trying to sort in her mind all that Gavin had told her. Images of Bryce came to mind.

"My situation with Bryce is different, but if I didn't think my husband returned my love, I wouldn't live with him."

"Why is yer situation different, Akira?" Gavin shoved a heavy branch out of their path.

"Because I didn't wed Bryce expecting him to love me."

"And neither did yer mither."

"What do ye mean?"

"I was old enough to remember. Nara was young, and it was a pre-arranged marriage between her parents and Da. He thought Elliot and I needed a mither."

Arranged? Akira knew arranged marriages were common practice, but she'd never contemplated how her parents met. She had never thought to ask. Memories of her childhood were full of people doting on her, and Akira grew up basking in all the attention. As the only daughter of the MacKenzie chieftain, she had been quite spoiled. The realization of her self-absorption brought a mixture of shame and regret. A new, humbling realization made her want to hie herself off to the nearest chapel.

They walked in silence for a while until Akira began to wonder about her situation with the MacPhearsons. She worked up the courage to ask Gavin about it.

"Why did Da not come for me when Bryce took me? He could have at least inquired of my safety."

Gavin sighed.

A feeling of foreboding came over her. His reluctance told her more than any words could have.

"Lass, ye have to understand that he felt the marriage might prove to be a valuable alliance for the two clans."

"More valuable than his only daughter?" Her voice cracked, knowing that her fears were true. Her lips trembled. For all the spoiling and pampering she'd received all these years, she still meant no more to her father than a pawn to be used in negotiations. Aside from fulfilling a promise to his father, Bryce had thought to use their marriage the same way. "I wish I were never born female," she said bitterly.

Gavin gave her a sharp look for her tone. In the past it would have reprimanded her; now it only infuriated her. "Don't give me that look, Gavin. Ye know as well as I do that everyone has used me."

She walked away from him, needing to be alone to vent her frustration. He started after her, grabbing her arm.

"Since when is possibly saving hundreds of lives something to be ashamed of and bitter about?"

She yanked her arm free. "I want my life to matter beyond what's best for the clan." She backed away from him. "Is that so much to ask?"

Gavin dropped his arms and looked at her, lowering his voice. "Are ye that unhappy, lass? I've seen Bryce treat ye with kindness and respect. Mayhap in time, ye'll both come to love one another the way God intended between a husband and wife."

Akira bit her bottom lip as confusion swirled through her mind. "Ye don't understand, Gavin."

Gavin raised his hands to his sides and towered over her small figure. "Lass, I want ye to think on this. Sometimes God makes better choices for us than we could have ever made for ourselves."

The dawn air felt cooler than usual. A slight shiver coursed through Akira, and she wrapped the ends of the long plaid tighter around her slender frame. She finished sewing the two clan colors into one plaid. Her reflection rippled across the water in silent motion. The garment seemed to glow around her image like a mystical rainbow. Her lips curled into a smile, savoring the feel of God's creation all around her.

A loose piece of hair slipped from its gathered knot at her nape and flew into her eyes, making her blink. She reached up to brush it away when more strands softly brushed against her neck, tickling her. It reminded her of Bryce's tender touch. Another shiver seized her, and this time it wasn't due to the cool air. Just the mere thought of him made a flush rise to her cheeks. She looked out across the loch, remembering the day it had rained, and she had nearly drowned.

"Ye look at the loch as if ye fear the water might form a tidal wave that could reach out and grab ye."

Akira recognized her husband's familiar voice as he drew closer. She turned to see granite eyes swirled in a cloud of worry, surveying her. His tanned features grew tight.

"When I woke this morn' and ye were gone—" He paused as if he wasn't sure if he wanted to continue, and then shrugged. "I missed ye." He backed up a step. "I hope I'm not intruding on yer solitude."

Akira shook her head. "I was only wishing I could swim." She risked sharing her private thoughts and held her breath to see his reaction to her secret longing.

He nodded. "Aye, I wish ye could swim as well."

"Teach me." Her stomach tightened in alarming fear. What could have made her ask him that? The last time she entered a loch with him, she nearly drowned. Images came to mind of Bryce taunting her over the soap. That day she had witnessed a gentle, playful side to her husband's personality, and she didn't want him to suppress it. Mayhap if she were to show him that she still trusted him, it would ease his discomfort.

"Teach ye?" Bryce raised an eyebrow as if he didn't hear her correctly.

Her brothers had no patience when it came to teaching her to swim, and somehow she sensed Bryce would be different. "Aye, I don't wish to drown." It was her worst fear of all.

"Ye trust me?"

"I'm willing to try." She lifted her chin and met his gaze, refusing to lie.

"Ye canna have a teacher ye distrust." He crossed his arms over his chest, waiting.

"'Twill be reason to learn more quickly."

"That is one way of looking at it." He chewed on his bottom lip, contemplating the matter.

"Will ye do it?"

"'Twould redeem me from my blunder the last time we were in a loch together. If naught else, mayhap my guilt would be relinquished." A grin spread across his face as he bent closer. "'Twill give us a reason to spend the morn' together." He lowered his voice toward her ear.

Relief washed through her. She returned his contagious smile. "I'm ready when ye are."

"At least we won't have to fight the heavy material of a wedding gown this time," Bryce said, his eyes dropping over her dark green day gown. It hugged her curved frame with a gold belt cord at the waist. The long sleeves widened at her wrists.

Akira slipped the garment over her head and gracefully let it fall to the ground in a heap at her heels. She still wore a white chemise and underskirt that covered her figure. Bryce's gaze lingered on something that caught his attention behind her. He squinted, his eyes narrowing in concentration.

"Have ye been wearing a MacPhearson plaid?" he asked with hope lighting his expression. Akira hid a smile. She had never worn his plaid before. He bent, retrieving the material from beneath her discarded gown. His eyes grew wide in surprise as he held up both ends, surveying the two plaids sewn together with a critical eye. His black brows knit together in question.

She didn't know how to decipher his thoughts. She licked her bottom lip in worry. It hadn't occurred to her that he might be displeased. "I sewed them together this morning—before dawn." He continued to stare at it with the oddest expression. "It symbolizes our marriage and the children we will one day share." In that moment he looked at her with longing and something else.

Bryce reached out and pulled her hand to his lips. His smoldering gray eyes held her gaze. "I'm beginning to see that God has graced me with the finest gift ever bestowed to any man."

Akira tilted her head in confusion. "And that is?"

"Ye."

Akira self-consciously lifted her fingers and brushed them through her damp and matted hair. Bryce had worked with her in the loch, but it soon became clear that teaching her to swim would require a longer commitment. They had enjoyed their time together and afterwards lay on the bank in the sun to let their clothes dry to damp. Akira felt so relaxed that she fell asleep. Bryce woke her later, fearing her fair skin would burn in the sun.

They walked back to the castle hand in hand, but as they drew closer, a disturbing noise echoed over the castle wall. Unconsciously, Akira squeezed her husband's hand with worry. It sounded like war had broken out as men screamed and yelled on the other side.

"What is going on?" Akira wondered aloud.

Bryce called to the guard to lower the bridge. At first no one appeared. Bryce called again. Finally, a guard leaned over the gate and stared down at them. Running out of patience, Bryce yelled, "Mon, open the gate!"

The drawbridge slowly lowered, and Bryce and Akira couldn't believe the sight before them. Her heart beat rapidly as Bryce protectively pulled her through the chaos. Men everywhere were fighting. Akira's heart nearly sank to her knees. The MacKenzies and the MacPhearsons were brawling.

"How could this happen?" she exclaimed, jumping out of harm's way as a man went flying by her.

"I don't know, but stay close to my side. I've got to get ye inside the castle where it's safe."

Bryce pulled her along as they weaved in and out of the fighting men. One man rammed his head into another, and they headed in Akira's direction. Bryce grabbed her shoulders and pulled her back just in time.

Bryce groaned as another man stepped back and landed on his foot. He pushed the man away and swiftly bent, lifting Akira in his arms. Dodging this way and that, he ran, carrying her toward the stone steps leading into the castle. Akira wrapped her arms around his neck and held on tight as his jarring movements bounced her against him. He deposited her on the steps and ordered her into the castle.

She hesitated, worried for his safety. Then she noticed that none of them fought with weapons. Where were their weapons? They were fist fighting. Akira stepped down to follow Bryce. He turned and held up a hand, halting her.

"Woman, are ye mad? Ye canna go out there in the middle of a brawl. Ye could get hurt!"

"Bryce, they're not fighting with weapons." She pointed over his shoulder behind him. "Mayhap the damage won't be too much and 'tisn't too late to stop this madness."

"Akira, go back inside," Bryce ordered again.

"We've got to do something! I don't want all of our efforts to be for naught. What about the purpose of our marriage? We're supposed to be uniting the clans, and they're at war in my father's courtyard."

"Akira, I could tend to that duty if I didn't have to worry about yer safety as well." His jaw locked in anger, and his pulse raced through a vein in his muscled neck. "I told ye to get inside where it's safe. I'll do my best to stop this nonsense, but I need to know that ye'll do as I ask."

He arched a black brow in question, waiting for a reply, while his steely eyes burned deep into hers.

Akira nodded. "Aye, Bryce. I'll do as ye ask. Just stop them."

She turned and stomped up the stone steps to the castle entrance. A loud roar nearby caused her to glance over her shoulder as she reached the threshold. A MacKenzie attacked her husband from behind. Akira screamed a warning, but it was too late. Bryce took the brunt of the blow in the back of his head. She started to run to him, but Bryce recovered in time to block the man's next punch. Remembering her promise, she leaned against the doorframe for support, praying for the strength not to intervene. She watched her husband fight until the man finally fell in defeat.

Her father appeared in the midst of the chaos and led Bryce to the stables. They disappeared, and a few minutes later reappeared upon their stallions. Birk took his sword and handed Bryce a sword. The two of them rode through the brawling men as a united front and called their clan members to halt or face charges of disobedience. One by one, the brawling men ceased their actions.

Akira turned and fled inside as Bryce had ordered. The main floor lay in shambles, littered with small statues and collectibles that had been shattered. Her mother's drapes were ripped, and she gasped at the sight of a huge pile of swords carelessly discarded on the floor. Akira stepped through the rubble on the marble floor and made her way to the winding staircase to the right.

She went to her chamber and prayed that their efforts had not been in vain, and that peace would prevail. After an hour of pacing and praying, Akira wandered over to her chamber window to gaze out over the courtyard. She recognized her husband's dark head as he strode over to the well and wound the handle, lowering the bucket for water. When the wooden container reappeared, he reached a long, thick arm out and pulled it to him.

A young woman sauntered toward him. Bryce dipped his hands, splashed water on his face, and then paused to gaze at her approach. Akira wondered who she was and what she wanted. Leaning further out the window, Akira squinted, raising her hands to shield her eyes from the sun's rays. At such a distance she couldn't see the woman's face, but the long blond hair hanging down to her waist gave away her identity: Odara MacKenzie.

Akira knew that her cousin Odara had tried to steal Gregor from her, and she would never know for sure if Odara was the real reason Gregor rejected her. He gave Akira other reasons such as the dream, but she couldn't help suspecting Odara as a possible culprit. Gregor always melted in Odara's presence, and Akira learned to recognize the smitten look he wore when the other woman came around.

Fierce anger flared through her. Akira felt her skin heat like the flames of a fire when Odara lifted a corner of her plaid, dipped it into the water, and raised it to Bryce's face to clean his wounds. Akira slammed her fists on the windowsill, thankful that no one would likely see her spying from so high.

Bryce allowed that woman to touch him? How dare he let her near him! Akira whirled from the open view and strode from the chamber. Outside, she bounded down the stone steps where Bryce had ordered her to safety earlier.

As Akira approached, Odara wiped at the blood staining the skin around Bryce's left eye, so swollen Akira could not see the gray she knew lurked beneath.

"Odara!" Akira called with more force and contempt than she intended. The other woman's hand stilled. Bryce jerked. Akira felt temporary satisfaction at startling them both, but their guilty reaction only served to elevate her temperature even higher.

Without a trace of guilt or discomfort, bright blue eyes gazed at Akira, as Odara greeted her with a knowing smile. Familiar scorn lurched in Akira's chest.

"There will be no further need of yer services," Akira informed her, not bothering to hide the warning in her tone.

Odara stood as if she were trying to decide whether or not Akira meant it. Her lips curled in an odd smile, and she dropped her hand from Bryce. His bruised face hid any expression he might have worn and any thoughts he might have had.

"Ye always were more of the servant type than I." Sarcasm laced her cousin's voice, but Akira didn't allow it to disarm her thoughts. She was used to Odara's goading words.

Akira straightened and matched her cousin's smiling gaze with a determined force of her own. "As his wife, 'tis my pleasure to care for him."

"I doubt that," Odara scoffed, stepping away and turning on her heel.

Akira closed her eyes and swallowed, thankful to be rid of her cousin so quickly. When next she opened her lids, she concentrated on her husband. The swelling bruises on his face looked painful. She picked up the wet cloth and touched his tortured skin. He winced.

"Ye took a good beating." She dabbed at the corner of his lip.

He gave her a lopsided grin as his swollen lip refused to move with the rest of his face. "Are ye just a wee bit jealous?"

Instead of answering, Akira scrubbed at a piece of dried blood on the side of his bruised face.

"Arggh!" Bryce groaned, jerking back and looking at her as if he didn't trust her to continue.

"Ye don't know her like I do. Odara is my cousin, and she thrives on irritating me. Ever since we were children, she has been a thorn in my flesh. Why would ye let her touch ye like that?"

"Ye're jealous," he teased.

Akira paused and gazed into the one eye that wasn't swollen. Jealous? She was hurt. A sense of betrayal throbbed deep inside, and she hated how it felt. She clenched her teeth, throwing the cloth back into the bucket. With her hands on her hips, she stood facing him.

"If that's all ye can say, then I've naught to say either." Akira left him to tend to himself.

10

*B*ryce stared at the empty seat across the table as a servant placed his meal in front of him. The roast lamb and vegetables smelled heavenly. His stomach rumbled. All afternoon he had looked forward to seeing his wife at the evening meal. She made herself scarce after she stormed away earlier in the day. Bryce thought of going after her, but his body ached all over. He hadn't realized his bonny wife could be so sensitive or he would have never teased her.

For the first time since the MacPhearsons' arrival, the great hall buzzed with conversation. Men from both clans talked rather than sitting quietly across from one another in stone silence. Genuine laughter rang through the hall and moods seemed amiable enough. Although their faces were various shades of black and blue, a great deal of tension had eased among them. Lopsided smiles lifted swollen faces with puffy lips, while heartfelt jokes scattered around the two long tables.

After Birk and Bryce disbanded the earlier brawl, several men had approached asking how the feud between the two clans began over a century ago. Apparently, some of them were fighting over the issue, and each clan blamed the other. Birk and Bryce had looked at each other with blank expressions. It seemed that no one really knew. Over the years verbal history between families didn't agree. Misplaced blame and accusations fostered bitterness, and it escalated out of hand.

Bryce met with Birk and Father Mike in the library to discuss a realistic strategy that would encourage amiable camaraderie. Weapons were returned to those who agreed to seek peaceful solutions with opposing clan members and gave their honorable word that they would not attack on the offensive. No man wanted to give up his weapons, so they all gave their individual promises to their clan chief.

Father Mike then suggested that each warrior visit the chapel to pay their proper respects to the Lord and offer prayers of repentance. After receiving their weapons, they all made their way to the chapel, with the exception of three men.

Bryce took this time to offer up his own prayers. He needed guidance on how to be a good husband and a wise leader to his people. Guilt over taking Akira from her family still plagued him. As a result, he decided to let her stay and spend as much time with them as possible, until they had to return home. Gregor had been buried days ago and peace settlements with Birk MacKenzie negotiated.

"Ye're not eating, Bryce. Are ye not hungry?" Nara watched him from across the table.

He looked up at his mother-in-law, and the resemblance to his wife struck a deep chord.

"Akira's late." He nodded to her empty seat.

Nara awarded him a sympathetic smile. "I doubt Akira will come. She's declared silence and finds that easier to do if she's not—" Nara's gaze turned toward the front of the hall. "Well, apparently, she's changed her mind."

In mid-reach for his goblet, Bryce paused to follow Nara's gaze toward the opposite end of the table. Akira walked into the hall with her shoulders squared and her chin set at a defiant angle. She paused to stand with her hands folded in front of her and looked around the sea of faces. Her gaze rested on Bryce.

She cleared her throat. "I have an announcement to make." Akira's voice echoed over the surrounding conversations. She waited.

Startled, Bryce lowered his drink and gave her his complete focus. Conversations slowly died as all eyes turned in her direction. Akira calmly paced a parallel line at the end of the two tables as the silence lengthened. Her long, silky hair bounced down her back with each step. The hunter green dress she wore accentuated her golden-red hair. She stopped pacing and paused between the two tables. Her serious expression stilled. Bryce knew in that moment that whatever she would announce meant double for him. He sensed other gazes moving from his face to hers, but he ignored everyone else and kept his attention upon his wife.

"I daresay, ye all look a poor sight; certainly not a handsome lot, but then, I love ye neither for yer comely looks nor for yer thoughtfulness." She swept her gaze among them.

"The MacKenzies I love because they are my family—people I've known all my life. They raised me, and I am their flesh and blood." She looked directly at Bryce. "And now I find the MacPhearsons are my family as well." She stopped speaking a moment, scraped her teeth across her bottom lip and on a sigh continued. "I tried to hate my new family. I thought I could, for they were the enemy, but 'tis impossible. When I look at Bryce's younger brother, still a child, an innocent, I ask myself, how can a child be an enemy?" She glanced at Elliot. "And that does not make me a betrayer. It only makes me human.

"Ye've all been itching to sink yer fist in the face of someone from the opposite clan." She tilted her head to the side. "How did it feel? Did it change aught?" Some of them lowered their eyes. Others crossed their arms and stared at the table. "I only thank God that yer weapons were taken from ye before someone died.

"Yer senseless brawling changed one thing for me." Akira pointed to her chest. "It showed me how vulnerable I've become and that I couldn't bear more war between our clans." Her voice trembled. She took a moment to collect her emotions. "If ye fight, ye betray the union Bryce and I have committed to the Lord, and the bairns we'll one day have." Akira paused, folding her arms. "I've spent a great deal of time in reflection. I just left the chapel where Father Mike helped me see something new. He showed me in the Latin Bible where it says in the book of Mathew, 'What God has joined together, let no man put asunder.'"

The great hall remained quiet as her words penetrated their minds. A shiver rode up Bryce's spine, and he involuntarily trembled. This woman he'd married was no ordinary woman. She had courage to stand up to the warriors of two clans. Akira understood the nature of men, probably more so than the female gender. She knew a man's pride and the loyalty he demanded from family, friends, and clansmen. With wisdom beyond her age, she spoke of the bonds of family, the bitterness of betraying those bonds, and then appealed to their honor. Yet she felt with the emotions of a woman's heart. Such a dangerous combination gave her the power and the knowledge to strike a man with his own weakness—pride.

Elliot's eyes blazed with hatred, but he managed to keep silent as he abruptly stood, scraping his wooden chair across the stone floor, and stomped out of the hall. Akira watched his retreating back. Her chin quivered slightly, but she clenched her jaw and gave them a look of fortitude. Her unbending resolve in spite of the rejection tore at Bryce's conscience as he held his breath, waiting to see what she would say next.

Her hair fell in a beautiful silhouette over her shoulders, folding over her arms in intricate waves. Her cheeks glowed like rose petals and her eyes sparkled with sensitivity. All afternoon Bryce had set his mind to apologize, but after such a bold and courageous speech, he would publicly give his wife the respect she deserved.

Bryce stood and bowed to her. "My dear wife, I've no words that could be more noble or more worthy than those which ye've spoken tonight. Please forgive me for teasing ye earlier today."

Akira's eyes grew wide in utter surprise. She clasped her hands tightly in front of her. Bryce stepped from his place at the table and ambled toward her, his gaze steady upon her as he slowly approached. When he reached her, he gently pulled her trembling hands into his own and raised them to his lips.

Bryce straightened, still holding her hands in his. She licked her dry lips before speaking. "Yer forgiven," she whispered in a hoarse voice.

The sound of a chair shifted across the floor. Birk MacKenzie stood. "I propose a toast to my daughter's wise council. The Lord has indeed joined Akira and Bryce together, and in doing so, has also joined our two clans. What God has joined together, let no man put asunder."

"Here! Here!" Gavin rose.

Fergus, who outranked all the other MacKenzie warriors, leaped to his feet. "Aye," he bellowed.

Other than her husband, Balloch was the first to stand from the MacPhearson clan. Tavis then followed, and then a few others. Kian finally rose. The hall became a loud noise of chairs moving and sliding against the stone floor.

As Bryce watched the scene unfold, he wondered if he'd just witnessed his first miracle.

✒

Akira requested a warm bath be brought to her chamber. She sat in a tub of hot water and leaned her head back. Shadows danced across the ceiling from the flames of the fire in the hearth and the three candles on each side of her chamber. The hot water soothed her aching muscles and helped her relax. She reluctantly left the water as it began to grow cold. Sarah, her mother's servant, assisted her into a warm dressing gown that had been toasting by the fire. She brushed Akira's long hair and called for the tub to be carried out.

Akira crawled into bed, knowing that Bryce would stay up late with her father discussing important matters. She yawned and wearily recited her nightly prayers. She drifted to sleep and soon dreamed.

> *A small lad with brown hair walked alone in a dark forest. She could sense his anxiety as she drew closer to him. His bright eyes gleamed with a hint of hazel, and she drew in a sharp breath, realizing the lad was her younger brother, Leith.*
>
> *He began to cry. She tried to reach out to him. He walked toward her, but then his image changed. He grew a little larger, and his hair darker along with his eyes. His tears continued, and his chin began to shake. Was he now Sim?*
>
> *The lad reached out to her, but they were too far apart. The forest changed to an open field with a meadow of green grass. Sim's body lay upon the ground by a huge, gray rock at least two feet tall and three feet wide. His eyes were now closed, and*

he no longer moved. Somehow she knew that he wasn't sleeping peacefully. A feeling of dread and sorrow clutched her, and it grew heavier when she called his name and still he did not stir.

"Sim!" A splatter of something dark red dripped down the large rock. Akira screamed in horror, realizing it was blood, and that his head had struck the large boulder. His face looked pale. A raw and primitive grief overwhelmed her. Tears slid from her eyes and she turned, wiping her face against the surface of her feather pillow.

Bryce leaned on his elbow and rubbed her back with his free hand. "Akira?" He brushed her long hair back from her face and peered toward her in the dark. "Are ye all right, lass?"

Akira's breath caught in her throat before she could answer. She swallowed and breathed deeply. "Bryce, it's time we go home."

"Lass, while I'm thrilled to hear ye call MacPhearson Castle home, I canna help but wonder why ye're telling me this in the wee hours of the morn' after ye obviously had a bad dream."

She didn't want to talk about her dream. Bryce had just lost one brother. The thought of something happening to Sim would cause him unnecessary worry. Over the years, Akira had experienced dreams that she considered divine warnings from the Lord, but many of her dreams came to naught. This one seemed so real, and the threat of imminent danger lingered with her spirit still.

Akira sat up and swung her legs over the side of the bed. With her insides trembling and her mind so preoccupied she knew that sleep would evade her from this point on. She sighed and slid her feet on the cold stone floor. Most likely dawn would be rising soon.

"Aye, I had a bad dream," she admitted. "I'm sorry I woke ye. I'm afraid I canna go back to sleep."

Bryce sat up and stretched his muscled arms over his head and yawned. He rubbed his eyes and then opened them more clearly. "It wouldn't hurt for me to get an early start this morn' as well."

"Can we leave this day?" She stood and walked to the window, pulling back the drapes to reveal a pink-orange cast beyond the horizon.

"Ye're serious, aren't ye?" Bryce raised black eyebrows.

"Aye," she nodded, moving toward her armoire. She opened it to peruse her wardrobe. "I think I shall bring some of my clothes back with me. I've missed my belongings." She pulled out her gowns one by one and tossed them on the bed.

"Before I agree, I'd like to know about yer dream." He leaned against the headboard and folded his arms, waiting.

Should she tell him? Akira gathered her plaid tight in her fingers and gazed into her husband's eyes. "There are times when I have dreams that I believe are warnings from the Lord. Some of them have come to pass. I don't always understand them, but I've learned to trust my intuition, to know the difference between a divine warning from the Lord, or a simple dream that means naught."

He tilted his head forward as he watched her carefully. "And the dream ye just had, was it a divine warning?"

Akira looked down and tossed her plaid on her other dresses. "I believe it could be," she mumbled truthfully.

Bryce breathed deeply, and Akira turned back to her armoire, feeling uncomfortable with where she knew this line of questioning would lead.

"And why would this dream make ye want to go home so suddenly?" His smooth voice remained persistent.

She grabbed the rest of her clothes and slowly turned to face him with a resolute expression. "I dreamed that something happened to Sim, and it upset me."

At first, he didn't move or speak. After he had a few minutes to digest her words, he stroked his chin and gave her a concerned look. "I want ye to tell me about it."

She told him all that she could remember. He sat and listened in silence, asking questions to clarify his understanding. When she finished, he pondered upon his thoughts, rising to pace across their chamber. Uncertainty and myriad emotions flashed across his face. He turned toward the window, then suddenly whirled to face her. A stab of guilt pierced her chest as his eyes darkened with pain.

"If ye know of some treachery the MacKenzies are planning against me and my family, tell me the truth, now. I'll not allow ye to conjure up this dream thing to warn me. Speak plainly, woman!" His voice sounded rough with anxiety.

Akira gazed at him in despair, the spark of hope that he would understand slowly extinguished. "I know of no one plotting against ye. I spoke true of this dream. I'm concerned for Sim. Please believe me." Akira struggled to hold onto her already thin fiber of nerves that threatened to unravel.

Indecision flashed across his face, and he looked away from her, rubbing his eyes with his fingers as if he fought the onset of a headache. "I've never heard of anyone having dreams that come true. While I may not be an overly religious man, I'll have naught to do with sorcery, not even from my own wife. I believe in God, and I do not wish His wrath to come down upon me and my household."

It was like a knife twisting in her gut for him to attack her faith, even if out of ignorance. "It hurts that ye would even suggest such a thing when I love the Lord so dearly." Tears welled in her eyes, and she stubbornly clamped down on her jaw until she could trust herself to speak again. "In all the time that ye've known me, have I ever said or done aught that would suggest that I engage in sorcery?"

His eyes reluctantly met hers and something flickered in them that she couldn't quite decipher. "Nay," he said, shaking his head, "but neither have we been wed overly long."

"True, but I'm yer wife. Look around. This is the home where I grew up. Why would I be so eager to leave? Mayhap I should be trying to find a reason to stay?"

Mayhap he only needed reassurance from her. She inched close to him and touched his arm. "Bryce, I promise that I know of no treachery being plotted against ye. I simply had a dream that scared me. I want to go home and see for myself that Sim is okay. Have ye never had a dream that bothered ye?"

He looked down at her with his dark hair framing his handsome face. "Aye, after I witnessed my father's death, I dreamed of it for several years afterwards," he said gruffly, as if holding a raw emotion in check. "But, this is different." He lifted his hands in frustration. "Ye're claiming to have a dream about something before it happens."

Akira closed her eyes. *Dear God, how can I reach him?* It was then that she felt a gentle whisper in her heart. *Tell him about Me.* Suddenly, she knew what to do and how to approach him. "Bryce, has anyone ever told ye about the ancient scrolls that are now translated into Latin? How much do ye know of God's Word?"

"What does that have to do with Sim?" He sounded exasperated.

"Do ye know of Jesus?" she asked.

"Aye. I'm not a fool, Akira. He was the Christ, the Son of God."

"His father Joseph had several dreams before Jesus was born. Ye see, Jesus' mother, Mary, was pregnant and Joseph had not lain with her. So he could only assume 'twas by another man. He purposed in his heart to put Mary away, but an angel came to him in a dream and told him that the Holy Spirit of God had placed the seed in her womb."

"Aye, that is why she is called Mary, the virgin mother of Jesus." He paused in thoughtful silence and frowned. "But, I don't recall the part about Joseph having a dream."

"Aye," Akira nodded. "And after Jesus was born, King Herod decided to kill all the male bairns age two and under in the attempt to thwart the prophecy of Christ's birth. Joseph had another dream. An angel of the Lord came to him and warned him to leave the place where they were staying. That's how Jesus was saved."

Bryce gave her a look of hope. "If that's true, then mayhap yer dream is a divine warning from God. I don't know what to believe anymore." He shook his head as if to clear the confusion muddling his brain. "There doesn't seem to be any other alternative. For Sim's sake, I must believe ye."

Akira tried not to flinch, but his disbelief hurt nonetheless. "Bryce, we have to first prepare. No one knows of our departure this morn'. I'll talk to my da. He's familiar with my dreams, and he'll understand."

Akira turned from him and continued gathering her belongings while Bryce dressed. "Aye, I suppose yer right. I'll have Balloch and Kian prepare the men."

"Bryce, do ye believe Father Mike to be a man of God?" She hated how her voice trembled across the chamber.

"Aye, where are ye going with this, lass?"

She looked up at him, unable to hide the trembling that shook her body from the inside and out. "Ye sound as if ye still don't believe me. I'd appreciate yer taking the time this morn' to pay him a wee visit before we leave. He has one of the few Latin copies of the Bible. I'd like ye to see it for yerself."

A flutter of excitement swept through Akira when she first saw the MacPhearson Castle standing so strong and erect, welcoming her home. The gates loomed above them as they edged closer to the drawbridge over the moat. A flag of MacPhearson colors waved over the stone fortress. She wondered how she could feel such pride seeing it hoisted in the air like a crown in the sky. The mansion no longer seemed dreary, but exuded a secure feeling. A sense of belonging nearly overwhelmed her, and she breathed deeply of the fresh heather and pine surrounding the front entrance. It really felt like home.

"'Tis a welcome home," Kian said as if reading her thoughts. He pulled up beside her and allowed his destrier to travel at her mare's pace. "They always fly the MacPhearson banner when they first see our return. It lets us know all is well."

Akira glanced at him. "What do they fly when all is not well?"

"The MacPhearson flag carrying our crest." With a flick of his wrist he pulled his sword from his side and extended it to her, handle first. Akira accepted the heavy sword with both hands, using her thighs to keep her balance on her mare. She fingered the cat crouching on what appeared to be a tiny golden plate and then ran a finger along the blade.

"I'd like a sword this magnificent," she said in awe. "Mither thought it improper for a young lady to learn the art of wielding a sword, but Da thought 'twould be useful. So first he saw that I was trained, and then Mither took over teaching me the female arts, sewing and running a household."

"Where did ye get that sword?" Her husband's voice sliced through the air. Akira remembered that Bryce had not liked Elliot talking about her prowess with the sword and wondered if he still felt the same. He sat upon his mount like a glorious warrior with his back upright and his shoulders blocking most of the sun. "Where did ye get that sword, Akira?"

She stiffened at the sound of his clipped tone.

"I was showing her the MacPhearson crest," Kian spoke up. "She was intrigued by the MacPhearson flag." He pointed to the castle ahead. "She's been a MacPhearson bride much too long not to know the sight of the MacPhearson crest."

Bryce's jaw twitched. "She doesn't need to know the sight of it. We only fly it during battle, at which time she won't be present." He looked down at Akira from Ahern's great height. "Give that sword back to Kian and forget about having one of yer own."

Akira sighed with frustration as she handed it back to Kian. "Thank ye so kindly, Kian. My husband is a wee bit overprotective at times, but I choose to believe that he means well." She glanced in Bryce's direction for emphasis.

The sound of the drawbridge lowering caught their attention and they turned at the noise. When it slid into place, they rode across. Sim and Finella waited on the other side with a handful of servants to welcome them.

Akira slid from her mare and eagerly pulled Sim in a tight embrace. "I missed ye so much!" Ever since her vision, she'd been beside herself with worry for him.

"Akira, ye'll suffocate him." Bryce slapped him on the back with a wide grin in a brotherly greeting.

She ignored Bryce and leaned back to inspect Sim from head to toe. He looked healthy and appeared to be happy to see them. His eyes went to Bryce's momentarily, and he nodded in greeting before turning back to Akira. Sim motioned to them that they took long enough to return. Akira apologized, and they turned to enter the castle, communicating with their hands.

"I believe Sim requires yer wife's attention for the moment," Kian said to Bryce as they led their destriers away.

Bryce sighed. "What's a man to do?" He turned to Kian with a grin, leading Ahern's reins. "If he were a wee bit older, I might be jealous."

Kian chuckled. "I've never known ye to submit to that emotion."

Bryce didn't answer. He hated to admit to a weakness, and jealousy was the worst kind of weakness a man could own up to. "She's had some unsettling dreams of late, and Sim happened to be in one of them." They entered the stables.

Balloch followed behind them, leading his own horse. "Aye, m'lady told me about them," he said.

"She told ye about them?" Bryce couldn't help being surprised that Akira would mention them to anyone else.

"Aye, when it was my turn to keep watch over her, she told me about some of the dreams the Lord gave her."

Kian burst into laughter. "Bryce, I believe ye may be in for more than ye bargained for." He gave Bryce an affectionate slap on the back.

Bryce glared at him and turned to Balloch. "I'd appreciate it if ye wouldn't mention her dreams to anyone." He turned to Kian and said, "And that goes for ye. I think ye might've misunderstood her. We've all had a few unnerving dreams at one time or another." Akira's dream of Sim came to mind, and he pushed the mental picture away. For the most part, he managed not to think about it. The morning they left MacKenzie holdings, Bryce spent time in the chapel praying that Akira's dream wouldn't come true, and that God would send a legion of angels to protect his brother from any harm.

Bryce saw to the care of his horse and then went in search of his wife. He found her lying on the edge of their bed. She had fallen asleep fully clothed in her traveling attire. She must have been exhausted. Gently, he scooped her up and placed her closer to the center of the bed and covered her with a blanket.

The knocking and banging continued all morning until Akira thought her ears would grow as deaf as Sim's. She turned to look at him eagerly breaking his fast, completely unaware that her head hurt from all the noise around them. She felt pity for the lovely sounds he would never hear, and at the same time, grateful that he was being spared at the moment. The sounds echoed throughout the castle. Finally, she slammed her goblet on the table in exasperation and stood, pausing to give Sim a pleasant smile, and went in search of the chaos.

Outside on the west wing of the castle, men were scattered about working on various tasks. Stone lay in different piles, waiting to be carted off to its final destination. Men climbed up and down wooden towers built for hoisting the stones. Her husband stood in the middle of all the confusion, pointing to an unfinished patch and bellowing commands.

A feeling of pride swelled in Akira, and she smiled, watching him from a distance. Self-confidence radiated from his stance. They had returned home almost a sennight ago, and of late she noticed Bryce spending more time in the chapel with Vicar Forbes. Subtle changes slowly began to take place in her husband, and she liked it. He consulted the Lord more often before making decisions, and he seemed thankful that God answered his prayers for peace between their clans.

Three days ago, Bryce had started overseeing the project of repairing the west wing where it had deteriorated from old age. Pleased with his determination to see such an under-taking through, she also wished she could spend more time with her husband. The project seemed to consume him most days, and at night he collapsed early in a deep sleep from pure exhaustion.

An idea occurred to her. Mayhap if Bryce were to give her something to do, she could work alongside him. The two of them could make a wonderful team. After all, she wasn't help-less. Growing up with three brothers, Akira learned to play and do things that lads enjoyed or she would have spent most of her childhood alone.

Since it appeared that Bryce had no intention of taking a break anytime soon, she walked up behind him and tapped him on the shoulder. He turned in mid-sentence and folded his arms across his chest, waiting for her to speak. She leaned up toward his ear. "May I speak to ye for a moment?" Bryce looked mildly irritated, but she didn't let that deter her. "Please? 'Twill only take a moment of yer time."

He nodded. "Be quick about it then."

She pulled him around the corner for privacy. "Bryce, I would like to help with the repairs." She bit her bottom lip with uncertainty.

His thumb circled her knuckles as he stared down at her. Akira thought he might not have heard her. "Bryce, did ye hear me? I want to help."

"What did ye have in mind?"

Taking his question as a positive sign, she went into an explanation of her training with her brothers, projects she helped with, and emphasized how useful she could be with the repairs on the castle. His dark eyebrows drew together, looking as if they were almost one.

"Is this the only reason ye interrupted me?"

"Nay." She tried to ignore the tone of his voice. "The noise distracted me while I was trying to break my fast, and on my way out here to complain, it occurred to me that if I were somehow involved, I might not be so aggravated by it."

"Akira, don't ye have some household chores to see to? Ye're my wife. Ye have a whole castle with servants to manage. If ye want to be helpful, tend to household matters."

"Bryce, I'll manage the staff, but I don't want to be inside day after day missing out on the glorious creation that God intended for His people to enjoy. At least not now while it is warm and the days bright with sunshine."

He smiled down at her with a mischievous grin. "I suppose there's no harm in ye being outside a wee bit."

"Ye truly mean it?"

"Aye." He nodded his consent.

"Wonderful! As soon as I finish the morning chores and give the staff their duties for the day, I'll join ye out here."

Bryce shook his head. "Nay, lass. Ye misunderstand me. I'll find someone else to manage the castle." He stepped back from her and pointed a finger at her. "And I don't want ye anywhere near the west wing. The construction and unsteady structures aren't safe. I don't want ye to get hurt. Is that clear?"

"Very." She nodded, her smile fading.

"And do not get any ideas of training with my men. I know ye like swordplay and ye may even be good at it, but ye're to stay away from my warriors while they're training. Understood?"

"Absolutely." Her lips transformed into a tight line and anger replaced the uncertainty.

"Do ye have any other requests?" He folded his arms over his chest, his lips turned down in a slight frown.

"That depends. It seems I am to be punished with a new set of rules for each request I make. What would be the consequences if I were to make a demand?" She clenched her fists at her sides and tapped the toes of her right foot.

"Akira, I've not asked much of ye. I simply want ye to stay away from dangerous areas. Ye're my wife. I want ye to concentrate on wifely duties."

"I didn't say I wouldn't tend to my duties. I only meant that I didn't want to be confined inside all the time and allowed naught else. I only wanted to be useful, to work beside ye." Her throat ached with defeat. She backed away from him. "Never mind, being with ye is the last place I'd want to be right now."

"Lass, ye've got to understand that right now being out here with all this construction isn't a safe place for a woman." He reached for her, but Akira evaded his grasp and backed away.

She straightened to her full height and lifted her chin. "I'm certain I can find other activities that will keep me quite busy. I'm sorry to have bothered ye." Her voice held a cutting edge to it. She turned and left him.

11

Akira paced back and forth in front of the window of her chamber, waiting for Sim to finish his training lessons with Bryce. It seemed as if the hours would never end. Finally, her husband reached out a thick hand and tousled Sim's brown head, a sign that their training had come to an end for the day. Akira grabbed her basket and flew down the stairs on her way to intercept Sim before he could disappear. By the time she reached him, he headed toward the well and Bryce disappeared in the opposite direction.

She made a gesture with her hands to tell him she wanted to go riding. He hesitated, looking quite weary as he breathed heavily. He wiped beads of sweat from his brow.

Akira's hands tightened around her basket. Bryce worked him entirely too hard. Despite her opinions, Akira never interfered and did her best each day to keep it that way, yet she still wanted a chance to teach Sim. She pleaded with him again until he finally relented with a nod.

After he had drunk his fill and washed up, they selected their mounts and were soon on their way. They came to an empty field. Akira led him to the bottom of a steep hill, hoping it would be a good spot away from other distractions. They dismounted, and she spread a blanket on the ground. They sat facing each other. Akira pointed to her mouth and gestured that she wanted him to talk.

Sim gave her a disbelieving look and laughed. He could make a noise when he laughed, so she was convinced he could speak if he just learned how to control the muscles in his throat.

Akira shook his arm to gain his attention. She moved his fingers to her throat and began talking, letting him feel the muscles move in her throat. "Ye can feel me speak." A curious look entered his brown eyes, and she smiled, knowing she had managed to pique his interest. "I canna believe no one ever tried this with ye before. How can they expect ye to learn how to talk if they don't take the time to teach ye?" She reached over and touched her fingers to his throat. "Try to talk."

He moved his hand to his own throat and opened his mouth, but nothing came out. He looked at her as if to say, "What now?"

Akira nodded, determined to encourage him further. "Go ahead. Try it again."

He repeated the test. After a few more times, he shook his head and gave her a look that all but said this bordered on ridiculous.

"Nay." Akira shook her head. He grew impatient, and they engaged in a series of hand motions, arguing. Akira began to wonder about her sanity for what she attempted to do.

"Ye have a stubborn streak, ye do!" She grabbed his hand and held it against his throat. Sim always made strange noises when upset or excited. On impulse, she reached over and pinched him on the arm. He squealed in response. A look of amazement centered on his face as he realized the muscles in his throat had moved. Sim squealed again, just to make sure he hadn't imagined it. He gazed at her with wide eyes, and she laughed with delight, nodding that she understood.

Sim jumped up and bounced around the blanket, squealing and feeling the newly discovered sensation. His excitement bubbled over, and Akira stood, laughing with him. He stopped. Although he had grown over the last couple of months, he still stood an inch shorter than Akira. He pointed to her throat, and she realized he wanted to compare how the muscles in her throat felt to his. Akira leaned forward and sang a little ditty while he felt her throat.

Akira motioned for him to sit. She had to find a way to help him control the noise. The only sound he knew how to make, unfortunately, hurt one's ears after a while. Bryce would be furious if Sim continued running around the castle squealing like an injured bat. They worked on different levels of noise for the rest of the afternoon. They agreed to meet secretly each day to continue working on his speech, wanting it to be a surprise once Sim improved. They rode back to the castle before dark, regretting the end of an afternoon of discovery.

Akira entered the attached kitchen to return the rest of the leftover bread. She stopped in her tracks at the sight of the beautiful woman, ordering the cook about and sending the rest of the kitchen staff into a frenzy. The noise abruptly died, and everyone turned to look at Akira. Mirana noticed something had caught her staff's attention and turned a curious gaze toward the entrance.

A smile lit her ruby lips, apparently amused at the sight of Akira gaping at her. A moment later she made her way toward Akira. Her hips that narrowed into a slender waist swayed perfectly with each step. Her wavy blonde tresses brought Akira up to her full height. It should have been a sin to have hair that beautiful, Akira thought with envy, and then released a silent prayer, asking forgiveness from the Lord.

"So the mistress of the house wishes to relinquish all responsibility to me." She spoke with an air of confidence that matched her beauty and made Akira feel even smaller than Bryce managed earlier that day. "'Tis as well." Her voice dripped with mocking sympathy, and a bold challenge in her eyes. "I warned Bryce. I told him he couldn't be happy with the likes of ye. No one wants a MacKenzie here, least of all Bryce. Things are finally beginning to be as they were before ye came. I ran his household. Ye didn't know that, did ye?"

"If Bryce didn't wish me here, then he wouldn't have wed me," Akira said through clenched teeth, praying in her heart that the Lord would help her hold on to her temper.

The sly fox laughed. "Surely ye're not that naïve, are ye?" She threw her hands on her hips and shook her head, clicking her tongue. "He did it to save his people. Bryce wants no more bloodshed. Once he's sure that peace has been achieved, he'll only need ye for a legitimate heir. And now that I'm back, he'll remember how 'twas before ye came. I'm the woman he really wants. I always have been."

Color rose to Akira's cheeks. She hated the warmth flooding them, knowing Mirana would witness her shame. Her chest tightened as she searched her mind in her husband's defense, but her faith in him faltered. Ever since their return he'd been more distant and too busy for her. What could she say? Everyone knew he only wed her for peace and to keep the promise he made to his father. She and Bryce had no knowledge of each other before. His words echoed in her mind: *"Nay, lass. Ye misunderstand me. I'll find someone else to manage the castle."*

Akira thought she'd made it clear that she didn't mind managing the household duties. She struggled to hide the anguish searing her heart. Akira felt betrayed by her family when they left her here with the MacPhearsons, but this betrayal cut her to the core, and the knowledge of it sank deep inside her. Akira shook her head, unable to examine her feelings in the presence of Mirana and the kitchen staff.

She swept a disgusted look at Mirana and tried not to visibly flinch at how inadequate she felt beside her. To what extent did this woman's authority go? What had Bryce told her? Straightening her shoulders and lifting her chin, Akira thrust the basket at Mirana.

"See that ye don't waste the rest of that bread. I expect a superb meal tonight, and if I'm not pleased, we'll see if ye remain." Akira stomped out of the kitchen in search of her husband.

Ignoring her husband's rules, Akira strode to the west wing where she assumed Bryce would be. As his wife, he owed her more respect than hiring the likes of that woman. Akira fumed, huffing and puffing with each step. Bryce knew Mirana disliked her. He had witnessed the humiliation she bore from the woman's scorn on the first day they had met. How could he? Akira's anger grew the more she thought about the whole situation. She managed to work herself into a fine frenzy by the time she found him.

Bryce squatted on his haunches, talking with Kian, Balloch, and Tavis, as they huddled in a circle, pointing out stone markings in the dirt.

"Bryce, I need to speak with ye," she called to him from behind.

"Not now, Akira, I'm busy." His impatient tone did little for her mood. He didn't even spare her a simple glance.

Akira shook with fury. "Nay, Bryce, ye'll speak to me now, for I will not be ignored any longer." She shouted above the noise to make sure he heard her.

Not only he, but everyone else had too, as they stopped in the middle of their tasks and turned to stare. Bryce couldn't possibly ignore her challenge. His pride as the clan chief would demand he handle her properly in front of his men. This much she knew, being the daughter of the MacKenzie chieftain. Since she'd carried things this far, she might as well take it all the way.

"Akira, I told ye I'm busy," he quietly informed her a second time. His men gathered around with smirks on their faces.

"And I told ye I'll not be ignored." Her hands flew to her hips as she openly defied him. Akira's anger still controlled her, and she didn't have the good sense to know when to back down.

Both Kian and Balloch stepped back from Bryce.

"Ye've never had a wife before, so ye don't know how to behave," Akira dutifully informed him. Kian and Balloch stepped back again, both shooting concerned glances in Akira's direction.

"My behavior as a man is all I should be concerned about. Ye, on the other hand, I am without words to describe." He still hadn't moved.

Heat climbed Akira's face, and she knew her skin would soon be the same color as her hair. "Could we please speak privately or is it necessary to have our problems discussed in front of everyone?"

"Ye seem to be doing verra well right now," Bryce said dryly, crossing his arms over his chest. He gave her a level stare meant to make her retreat, but it didn't work.

Despite her fear, Akira insisted, "I would rather discuss this in private, if ye please." She inclined her head toward him for emphasis, but he either didn't get the hint, or he chose to ignore her. She figured it was the latter.

"Then ye should have chosen a more private time and place to approach me." He still hadn't moved. She now knew he wouldn't budge.

So be it. "I'll not share that wench with ye in my home. She is to be dismissed immediately," Akira informed him through clenched teeth. She prayed he wouldn't deny her now, in front of everyone. She stood rigid, hoping to hide the inner trembles seizing her stomach and chest in anticipation of his answer.

"Why is that, Akira? Ye said ye wanted to tend to other matters outside the castle."

Several of his men gasped in surprise.

Akira tightened her lips at the knowledge that she didn't even have to refer to the woman by name; he already knew to whom she referred.

"I didn't say that I wouldn't see to those duties. Ye've plenty of duties that ye find bothersome, but ye see to them anyway. I was only stating an opinion. I shall be careful how I phrase my words in the future."

"I canna dismiss her on those grounds. I only hired her this day."

Bryce baited her. Akira thought he knew why she wanted the woman dismissed and only wanted to hear her say it aloud. Akira resented him for what he pushed her to admit in front of his men.

"Then tell her ye were mistaken and ye no longer need her. Yer wife is perfectly capable of handling the household."

His startled laughter filled the air. "I canna have ye going around changing yer mind, Akira. Ye must decide what yer responsibilities around here will be and stick to them."

Akira moved closer to him so she could lower her voice. "She said I'm not welcome as a MacKenzie. Ye only married me to prevent bloodshed for yer people and that as soon as I produce an heir, I'll no longer be needed. She said she's the one ye've always wanted and now that she's back, ye'll soon see it."

The mirth disappeared from Bryce's face, and a sobering expression crossed his features as he folded his arms over his chest.

"Ye're a MacPhearson, not a MacKenzie. Ye're my wife and ye most certainly do belong here, and I should not have to remind ye of it. I'll speak to her about her ill-mannered behavior toward ye. She'll certainly be reprimanded."

Fire shot through Akira's soul, and she thought she felt the very roots of her hair burning. The world seemed to spin out of focus, and she closed her eyes to keep her balance, careful not to embarrass herself even further.

"I'm yer wife. I deserve more respect than that. I don't want her in our home." She opened her eyes in time to see a flicker of concern cross Bryce's dark features. It must have been her imagination, for as soon as she thought it, he stiffened.

"I'll consider it." He turned from her and motioned to his men, ending the discussion. "Balloch, let's go over those plans again."

Balloch glanced at her with sympathy before getting back to details with Bryce. Akira stood there a moment longer before she turned from them and headed to the stables. She needed a vigorous ride to allay her seething temper and hurt. The way she felt right now, she could murder someone, and she didn't know who would be her first victim—Bryce or Mirana.

After his daring wife departed, Bryce could hardly concentrate on what Balloch said. Akira had certainly taken him by surprise; he didn't know how to deal with her. He had told her not to go near the construction in the west wing, yet she openly challenged his authority in front of his men. A rebellious man he knew how to handle, but a rebellious wife left him baffled. He admired her bravery. She was as fearless as a MacPhearson should be, too much so for her own good. Some men in his position and authority would have her beaten for such public defiance, but Bryce couldn't bear the thought. He didn't believe in treating women that way.

As for Mirana, Bryce intended to dismiss her that night after supper. He would be a fool to mistake the pain Mirana's words caused Akira. He disliked the hurt he'd seen in her eyes. Bryce smiled to himself. It was nice to know that Akira seemed a bit jealous. Mayhap she cared for him whether she wanted to admit it or not.

"Bryce, did ye hear me?" Balloch asked.

"What? Uh, repeat what ye said." Bryce tried to give Balloch his full concentration.

"I said the bridge is here and the outer stone wall is fifty feet high and four feet wide, except here on the west side. 'Tis only two feet wide for about ten feet long. That will need to be restructured as well. The rest of it mildewed from the moat, and part of it crumbled."

"See to it then," Bryce commanded. "We'll discuss this further on the morn'."

He left his men to go in search of his wife. When he didn't find her anywhere, he went to the stables as a last resort.

"Tom, have ye seen Akira?" he asked the stable lad.

"Aye, m'lord." The lad looked up at him with wide, fearful eyes. "She rode Ahern out of here a little while ago."

"She took Ahern?" Fear gripped his insides. "Ahern has managed to throw a number of men who attempted to mount him. Of all the animals out here, why did ye allow her to take him?"

"She insisted, m'lord. I wanted to deny her, but she said I was being insubordinate." His chin trembled and his thin shoulders shook.

"Was she alone?" Bryce softened his tone. How could he expect a young lad to handle his wife when he struggled with the task?

He nodded vigorously. "Aye, she tore out o' here. I tried to convince her not to, truly, I did, but she was a wee bit angry." He looked down at his feet. "She wouldn't hear of it. I'm sorry, m'lord, truly I am." He wrung his hands in nervous anxiety.

"Ready the fastest horse ye've available." Bryce strode out of the stables in search of Balloch. He motioned for his trusted friend, who wasted no time in obeying his summons.

"Have Kian see to things for the moment. I want ye to watch for Akira if she returns before me. If that happens, snatch her."

"Aye, Bryce. Where did she go?"

"I don't know, but she took Ahern. He'll give her a time of it, and I only hope she's all right by the time I reach her."

He started to walk away, but Balloch grabbed his arm. "M'lord? What shall I do with her?"

"Lock her in her chamber. I don't care how ye get her in there. Carry her kicking and screaming if ye have to, but she is to be locked in her chamber until I return, though I expect ye to get her in her chamber without harming her, no matter how much trouble she gives ye."

Balloch nodded. "Aye, Bryce."

Three hours later Bryce still looked for Akira and his worry increased tenfold. He wondered if she'd returned home.

He turned the mare back toward the castle and nudged her into a gallop. Ahern's stall appeared to be empty still. No one was about. The stable lad must have gone home for dinner. He took care of his horse, hoping Akira would return before he left the stables. After he put the mare back in her stall, Bryce walked toward the courtyard like a man going to his doom, alternating between anger and fear.

At the dinner table, he couldn't keep his gaze from her empty chair. They were halfway through the meal when Balloch leaned over. "She'll turn up soon. She just went for a ride to release her anger on something else other than ye."

"I don't care that she went for a ride. I only wish she hadn't taken Ahern. He's a bit much for her."

"I can handle him just fine," Akira said from behind him.

Bryce jumped to his feet, but Balloch reached her first. "M'lord, remember yer temper, now." Balloch seemed worried that Bryce would turn his fury upon his wife. He pulled Akira's chair out for her. "We were worried for ye, m'lady."

She awarded him a sincere smile. "Why thank ye, Balloch. I'd come to the conclusion that no one much noticed whether I came or went in this household." Akira turned a particular jade eye in Bryce's direction. "Especially now that the household chores are being seen to."

Her words and the sarcasm in her tone were lost on him. At the moment, she looked so beautiful that Bryce didn't know if he would make it through his meal without pulling her tight into his arms. Instead, he lowered himself in his seat and picked up his goblet, gulping down the sweet cider. Akira's windblown, golden-red hair tumbled over her shoulders. She seemed to have a more peaceful air about her than when they last parted. Mayhap the ride did her some good.

Conversations resumed as Bryce and Akira ate in silence. Akira's appetite seemed to be ravenous. She ate everything on her plate and drank deeply of the cider in her goblet. While she waited for the next course to be served, Bryce met her gaze from across the long table. The deep significance of their visual exchange pulled at his already tight emotions. When he had realized the danger she could be in while riding Ahern, the fear of something happening to her nearly twisted his gut in two. Only in the last few hours did he finally admit to himself how much he'd begun to care for her.

Upon taking the council of Vicar Forbes and learning more of God's Word, Bryce prayed daily that Akira would come to love him. During that time he'd given little thought to him returning her love.

Guilt ripped through him. How selfish he'd been in thinking God would answer his prayer, while allowing Bryce to keep his own feelings at bay. Would God require him to first love her?

The servants set a cream spice cake before Akira. She stared at the dessert with a strange expression and then paled. Bryce frowned as she covered her mouth and scooted her chair back. She clutched her stomach with a groan and ran from the hall.

Bryce remained in his seat, wondering if she were truly ill or if she used a female ploy to avoid another tongue lashing for her most recent behavior.

His wondering ended a little while later when Finella burst into the hall. "Somethin's terribly wrong with our lady."

In his haste, Bryce knocked his heavy chair over. "What's wrong?" Even as he asked the question, a terrible feeling flipped in his gut, and he knew this wasn't a ploy.

"She's terribly ill, m'lord. She lost all of her meal and continues to lose her stomach. She hasn't stopped heaving since she made it up to her chamber where she finally collapsed."

Collapsed? His strong, stubborn wife who had challenged him in front of all his men only a few hours ago collapsed? His heart thumped in his ears.

"Balloch, send for Angus!" Bryce ordered as he sprinted from the hall.

Akira lay on the floor by the fire in her chamber. Bryce knelt, gently scooping her into his arms.

"Akira, speak to me." He laid her on the bed and shook her shoulders. He tried his best not to panic when her head limply rolled to the side. "Akira." He tapped her cheek.

"See? 'Twas the strangest thing. I've never seen anyone faint that way afore," Finella said with a worried frown, leaning around his shoulder.

Bryce turned to face her. "She had just entered the hall in fine health, recently returned from a vigorous ride." He couldn't understand it either.

Finella nodded and threaded her fingers in front of her. "She ran by me in the hallway. Out of concern, I followed her to the chamber. Not even when I carried my four wee bairns did I get that ill."

Bryce looked down at his wife again. Akira looked deathly pale. He bent to one knee and took her hand in his. Quickly, he dropped it as if it burned him.

"What is it?" Finella asked.

Bryce didn't answer. All he could think about was how cold Evan and his parents had been in death. She had that pale look to her now. He thought his legs would give out on him as he stumbled to the window for some fresh air.

"M'lord?" Finella followed him, but he didn't wish to speak his fears aloud. Too much death had plagued him lately. It was one thing to lose men in battle, but it was another to lose loved ones like this—through some mischief—an unseen evil.

"I'll go see if Balloch was able to find Angus," Finella mumbled over her shoulder.

Bryce stood at the window until he heard a muffled whisper. He moved to Akira's bedside, awkwardly bending over her.

"Akira?" He touched her cold forehead and hated the clammy feel of her skin. "Akira, did ye say something?" His hands moved to her arms and then her legs. Her limbs felt the same as the skin on her hands and forehead. He didn't know how to control his racing heart when he realized her whole body was this way. "Akira." His voice rose as he shook her again. "Akira, please speak to me, darling."

Bryce held her white, supple hand to his lips and barely twitched when Balloch burst through the door, looking harassed and angry.

"I know what's wrong with her, but I don't know what to do about it. All we can do is wait." Something in his fierce expression softened when his eyes rested on Akira.

"What's wrong with her?" Bryce sounded calmer than he felt.

"She's been poisoned." Balloch looked at him with awkward empathy and seemed to hesitate in the threshold as if he feared completely entering the chamber.

"How do ye know?" Bryce pressed Akira's cold fingers against his cheek waiting for Balloch to tell him what he didn't want to hear.

"Mirana confessed. When she heard yer reaction to Akira's illness, Mirana burst into tears. It took one of the servants a time of coaxing, but she finally wrestled the bitter truth out of her."

Another thought immediately occurred to Bryce. "Could anyone else be poisoned as well? What about Sim?"

Balloch shook his head. "Nay, Mirana said that Akira was the only one who ate the poisoned mushrooms."

"Mushrooms?" Bryce repeated, looking down at his wife. "But, she . . . could . . . " He couldn't say the word aloud, and he dropped his head on the bed by her side.

Balloch looked down at the floor, shuffling his feet from one to the other. Without saying another word, he backed out of the room and closed the door softly behind him.

Bryce didn't move for a while, ignoring his aching muscles. He kept replaying in his mind every conversation he'd ever had with Akira, as if seeing her laughing, smiling, and talking would make what happened unreal. He couldn't lose her now. He'd just begun to realize how much he needed her. With the exception of Sim, he'd lost everyone who ever mattered. Suddenly, she mattered more than anything in his life, and he wasn't ready to give her up.

A soft groan caused him to jerk. He blinked, wondering if his mind played tricks. Bryce grabbed her limp hand in his and squeezed as if he could force his own strength into her.

"I won't let ye leave me, Akira." New hope rose in his chest as he voiced the words aloud. "I've never known ye to give up on anything. I'll have the most noble of swords made for ye. 'Twill be grander than mine, and we'll engrave the MacPhearson crest on it," he promised, pressing her fingers to his lips. "Ye'll not have to stay inside. We'll find lots of things to do outside." He searched for more words that might gain her interest. "And if ye're real good, I might actually let ye swordfight me as well."

Akira stirred. Her eyes flickered but didn't open. Bryce brushed her beautiful golden-red hair from her forehead and pressed his lips to each eyelid.

"I love the color of yer hair. Everything about ye is perfect."

He wished she would wake up and talk to him, even if she yelled at him. The thought tugged at his conscience, and he choked on his emotion. If he hadn't been a fool and brought Mirana back, his wife would be healthy this very moment.

"Akira, please don't abandon me, now. I need ye, lass."

When he received no answer, he bowed his head and began to pray, pleading for his wife's life. His relationship with the Lord still felt new. In times past he always approached Father Forbes for divine guidance and repeated prayers he'd learned in childhood. Now he prayed directly to the Lord with an open and sincere heart.

Two hours later Balloch opened the door, leading Angus and Finella into the chamber. "I had to go a ways, but I found 'im," Balloch said, pleased with himself.

Angus nervously glanced in Bryce's direction and went directly to his patient. As Angus examined Akira, he asked them numerous questions. He nodded without looking up when he understood and asked another question if something didn't sound right. He glanced at the hearth.

"We need more wood for a larger fire. Her body is cold. We must try to warm her. 'Tis just as bad for the body to be too cold as it is for the body to be burning with fever. I need warm water and cloths."

Balloch left for the wood, and Finella went to see to the warm water and cloths.

"For the last hour her body has been unusually cold like this." Bryce touched Akira's arm and ran his hand down the length of it to make sure her body temperature was still the same. "Of all things, to be poisoned by mushrooms."

Angus walked to the foot of Akira's bed and jerked back the cover to feel her feet. He pointed to the corner of the chamber. "I need some wool blankets. We'll see her through this if it takes all night and all day on the morrow."

That was what Bryce wanted to hear. He opened the chest and pulled out a wool blanket. Together they wrapped her in it. Finella returned a moment later to tell them the warm water and cloths were on the way. "Keep some drinking water by her bedside. She should not go without liquids for long. If her stomach isn't sick anymore tonight, give her something warm first thing in the morn', preferably chicken broth. We'll know by then if she'll be able to handle it."

Angus obviously thought she would be here in the morning. Relief flooded through Bryce, and he dropped down in a nearby chair. He ran his fingers through his hair and rubbed the tender muscles in the back of his neck. Bryce had endured a long evening. He thought he might give way from worry and fatigue.

Angus walked over to stand in front of him. Bryce tried not to tense, and finally looked up at the sound of his voice.

"I won't lie and tell ye she'll make it," Angus said, "but I can give ye hope in that I've seen others live through such poisons before. Akira is a strong woman. 'Tis in her favor that she became sick so quickly after her meal. That means less of the poison was digested, giving her a better chance at surviving. The cider didn't sit well with her stomach and was even worse mixed with poison. 'Twas what prompted her to become so ill." He slapped Bryce on the arm. "Take good care of her. I'll stay close by here in the village if ye need me."

"Finella, give Angus a bedchamber," Bryce ordered.

Finella nodded and hurried to find something suitable for Angus.

Bryce concentrated on his next words to Angus. "I beg yer forgiveness for the way I acted when Evan passed away. I'm at yer service, and I'd like to offer ye a comfortable place to pass the night." Angus looked ready to refuse. "I'd also feel better if ye were in the castle, just in case."

Angus thought for a moment, and then he must have realized Bryce would soon resort to begging, so he nodded his consent. Two servants brought in hot water and cloths. When they left, Angus turned back to Bryce.

"Lad, ye're forgiven. Everyone is allowed their grief. Sometimes a person's only hope falls heavily upon my shoulders, and the cold truth is that I don't heal or perform miracles. I only do what I can. However, I would suggest ye call Father Forbes if ye've not already done so."

Bryce rightfully felt shameful and avoided replying when Finella conveniently reappeared.

"I've yer chamber ready, Angus. I'll show ye the way." Angus followed her out.

"Finella," Bryce called, before she could get far.

She reappeared, popping her head through the door. "Aye, m'lord?"

"Please fetch Father Forbes."

A sad frown crossed Finella's face and she nodded. "Aye, I'll do that right after I have Angus settled, I will."

Bryce moved to Akira's side and dipped the cloth left on a nearby dresser into the warm water. He gently patted Akira's face and hands as Balloch appeared carrying extra wood. He threw a couple of pieces on the fire and came to stand by the bed behind Bryce.

"Is there anything else ye might be needin'?"

"Aye," Bryce nodded, looking at him with a determined expression. "Ye may lock Mirana up until I've time to personally deal with her."

"I'll take care of her. Where would ye like for me to put her?"

Bryce shrugged. "If truth be known, I would rather the dungeon, but I feel even my wife wouldn't stand for a woman to be locked up down there, no matter how much she disliked Mirana. Take her to a chamber. Set a guard outside her door, and I'll deal with her on the morrow."

"I'll see to it," Balloch promised as he moved to leave.

"Balloch," Bryce called, before Balloch could close the door. "Thank ye, my friend."

Balloch nodded, closing the heavy wooden door behind him. No words were necessary.

12

*W*eakness claimed Akira from deep in her bones down to her soul. Her stomach seemed as though it were a large, empty hole in the middle of her body. Her lips were parched and her tongue heavy as stone. She looked to her left. Bryce lay slumped over in a chair by the bed. His dark head rested on his forearms, the heavy rhythm of his breathing a familiar sound.

"Bryce." Her voice was hardly above a whisper, foreign and distant to her own ears.

He didn't stir.

"Bryce."

Still, he didn't move.

Akira took a deep breath and called louder. "Bryce." She rubbed her fingers against his cheek. This time Bryce jerked and lifted his head. He rubbed his eyes to clear his vision, reminding her of the lad he had once been. At first, he stared at her as if he couldn't believe she'd awakened. Akira wanted to ask questions, but had no energy. "Thirsty," her voice croaked.

More alert now, he moved to a nearby table and poured a goblet of water. He tilted the small container to her lips and wiped her chin with a cloth.

"Careful, ye don't want to drink too much too quickly." He eased down on the edge of her bed, and she relaxed back against the pillows.

"Tired," she mumbled more clearly.

"Well, before ye doze back off, ye must eat a wee bit."

Wearily, she shook her head as her eyes slowly shut.

He knelt by the bed, taking her chin in his hand. "Akira." She struggled to stare at him. He bent toward her and kissed her cheek. "Angus said to make sure ye've something warm in yer belly first thing in the morn'. I have to do as he says and ye must let me."

She blinked once and slowly nodded.

He went to the door and called Finella. Akira was too tired to smile, although that's what she felt like doing as she listened to him call Finella a second time. A bit impatient, she thought, and made a mental note to tell him so when he returned to her bedside.

A moment later she heard Finella's voice, but Akira couldn't see her for Bryce's broad back blocking the doorway. His black hair hung to his shoulders in disheveled waves. It appeared he had been concerned for her.

When he closed the door and turned, she pointed to her dresser. "Brush."

He looked at her blankly and then a slow smile crossed his face.

"Sunshine," she whispered. She needed some light in this dreary chamber.

He grabbed her brush from the dresser and walked to the window, pulling back the drapes. The rising sun filtered through the darkness.

"Better," she whispered.

Bryce crouched by the bed, gently pushing her forward as he brought her brush up to her head.

"Nay." She shook her head, touched that he thought to brush her hair for her. She relaxed against the pillows and patted the bed beside her. He looked confused. She had to lick her lips. "I wish to brush yer hair."

He started to protest, but with effort she reached for the brush; their fingers lightly caressed, and with reluctance, he relinquished it.

"I insist." Akira patted the bed again. "Please, sit down and turn around. Ye look a mess."

Reluctantly, he dropped on the bed and crossed his arms over his chest. "Ye wouldn't be getting yer way so easily if ye hadn't nearly died last night. As it is, I know ye don't have the energy to argue and ye won't let the matter drop until I do what ye wish."

Akira brought the brush through his hair. "Then 'twould be best if ye let me have my way."

"Any other woman would be wanting her own hair brushed, but not ye." He glanced back at her, and she smiled up at him, pausing, "Just like ye'd rather be outside in the middle of a bunch of men working on construction."

Akira sighed. "'Twasn't the work that I longed to do as much as I wanted to be by yer side." He tensed, and Akira decided to change the subject. "Yer hair has such fine texture." She threaded her fingers through the thickness of it. "I wish I could have hair like yers. Although it isn't as red as Gavin's, I've always hated the color of my hair. Mayhap I could try and dye it."

"I would not like it. I love ye the way ye are."

Akira stilled, afraid to hope for what she thought she heard him say. "Ye love my hair or me?"

"Both."

"Water!" she croaked, pointing to the table.

He moved quickly, tilting it to her lips. Bryce set it back down when she motioned that she had drunk enough. He gathered her long curls in both hands on each side of her shoulders. "I forbid ye to dye yer hair, and I forbid ye to die, period."

Akira bit her lower lip, not knowing what to say. The moisture in his red eyes melted her heart at his sincerity, and she nearly fainted with relief. She couldn't move for fear that she would wake to find this was but a glorious dream—that fate had cheated her again.

Bryce tilted her chin to face him. "Akira, are ye all right, lass? Should I have not told ye? I know ye may not love me; after all, I am a MacPhearson. I had a talk with the Lord last night, and I came to the conclusion that I can accept that ye don't have the same feelings for me right now. Mayhap in time yer feelings will develop."

A warm glow flowed through her, and the emptiness she had been feeling earlier seemed to dissipate.

"Oh, Bryce, how I've prayed ye would come to love me." Happy tears surfaced. "It doesn't matter that yer a MacPhearson. Do ye not remember what I said that day in my father's hall after the brawl?" She sniffled, and wiped at her eyes, clearing her throat. "I meant what I said. I love the MacPhearsons as much as the MacKenzies. How could I despise ye for being a MacPhearson and then love Sim so much? 'Twouldn't be right."

Bryce chuckled as he gathered her in his arms and pulled her tight. "If that lad were a wee bit older, I might be jealous of all the attention ye dote on him."

Her body went limp in his arms, and when he released her, she relaxed back against the pillows.

Akira reached for his cheek. He bent forward, grabbing her hand in his, and gently rested it against his unshaven jaw.

"I need to know what happened," she said. "Why did I almost die last night?"

He turned his mouth into her palm and kissed her. How could she have once thought this gentle man a fierce barbarian? He pulled away, and his expression twisted into a frown at the reminder of last night's events.

His hands clenched at his sides, and he strode to the window as if looking for a distraction. Bryce leaned down on his elbows, and she wanted nothing more than to go to him, but she feared she wouldn't make it out of bed, much less across the chamber. She sensed his agitation, but couldn't understand from where it came.

"Bryce, ye didn't answer me."

He turned from the window and inhaled deeply. He moved, kneeling by her bed, allowing her to reach for him.

She searched his gray eyes. "What's bothering ye?"

"Mirana will be leaving immediately. I should have never hired her back, and I should have immediately dismissed her as ye asked me."

"Mayhap I overreacted."

Bryce vigorously shook his head. "Nay, lass. Ye were right. 'Twas Mirana that fed ye poisoned mushrooms. I don't know if she only intended to make ye sick, or if she truly tried to murder ye." A mixture of grief and anxiety filled his voice. His shoulders sagged beneath the heavy burden he bore. If Akira hadn't known better, she would have thought she saw his bottom lip tremble. "I'm so sorry."

"Are ye sure?"

Bryce nodded solemnly. "She confessed last night."

Speechless, Akira looked away at nothing in particular. She knew the woman didn't like her, but she hadn't realized her hatred ran so deep.

Bryce stroked her hair. His gaze longingly swept her face and then lowered to her mouth. He leaned forward and his warm lips joined hers. Warmth spread throughout her body until she thought she could feel her toes tingle.

The door opened, and it took them a moment to realize they were not alone. Reluctantly, they pulled apart. Finella set a tray on the table by the bed and turned to Bryce.

"What are ye trying to do? The lass needs her strength," she scolded, shaking her gray head in disapproval.

Bryce smiled as he rose. "Aye, and mayhap I was just testing her strength. Seems she'll recover her health in no time at all." He winked at Finella.

The top of Finella's head barely reached Bryce's chest, and she had to strain her neck to look up at him. Her eyes grew wide with disbelief with the realization that he had just winked at her.

"I apologize, m'lord, I was just concerned for the lass. I meant no disrepect."

"Finella, think naught of it. 'Twould seem I canna afford to have anyone in my home who wouldn't give Akira the same allegiance they would give to me."

Finella's stricken look suddenly changed to a radiant glow, and she squared her shoulders back.

"See that she eats and that she rests." He gave the old woman's shoulder a reassuring pat before heading toward the door. Bryce closed it softly behind him.

Outside in the hallway, Bryce paused to speak to Kian, who guarded Akira's chamber. "I'll send another guard to relieve ye."

"How is she?"

"She's a survivor. I didn't wed a weak woman. Has anyone tried to see her?"

Kian nodded. "Aye, Sim has been by at least thrice this morn'. I can hardly understand all of his hand talk. He seemed to be verra concerned."

"What of Mirana?"

"She's still locked in a servant's chamber. Balloch guarded her through the night."

"I'll see to her questioning." Bryce turned and headed down the long hall. Sim ran into him as he descended the stairs. His hands were moving so fast Bryce could hardly understand him, but Bryce knew he wanted news of Akira's condition. He communicated with Sim as best he could and granted him permission to go see her if she was still awake. Sim bounded up the stairs two at a time.

Bryce shook his head as he moved in the direction of the servant's quarters. He dreaded having to deal with Mirana, but it had to be done. He only hoped he managed to be somewhat civil to her.

Bryce met Balloch outside Mirana's door. "Have ye spoken to her?" He crossed his arms over his chest, stalling.

Balloch nodded. "Aye, but she refuses to speak. She's a stubborn wench."

Bryce sighed. "Well, I suppose I must speak to her." He opened the door, scowling at the loud creak it made. The door closed behind him with a heavy thud.

Mirana sat in a corner and jolted at his entrance. Bryce forced down the urge to throttle her. He sighed, halting in the middle of the small chamber that now served as her cell. Crossing his arms over his chest, he gave her a pointed look.

"Ye tried to murder my wife, Mirana! I thought I could depend on ye. I thought ye were loyal to me."

"I am loyal to ye. I've never wavered in my service to ye, Bryce MacPhearson." She lifted her chin, her eyes as defiant and prideful as ever. "Ye should never have wed her. She doesn't belong here."

"Is it true ye tried to poison Akira with bad mushrooms?" He waited with his arms crossed and grew impatient when she didn't answer. He leaned forward. "Is it true?"

"Aye." She dropped her gaze. "The only reason I confessed is because I feared the worst."

"What do ye mean?" Bryce demanded.

"I didn't intend to murder her." She cast a sideways glance at Bryce. "Did she survive the night?"

"Why did ye do it?" Bryce didn't bother answering her question. He was the one who wanted answers right now.

"I already told ye. She's a MacKenzie, and she doesn't belong here." Mirana's voice slashed through the silent chamber, bitterness dripping from her tone like a flask with a hole in it.

Bryce clenched his jaw in frustration. "Mirana, it sounds to me as though ye tried to kill her. I want answers. I've never known ye to be a coward." He shrugged. "But neither have I known ye to be a murderess."

"I'm no coward! I own up to what I do. I already confessed. What more do ye want?"

"I want to know why ye did it. Did ye act alone?"

"My confession is enough." She turned and gazed at the dark, empty wall.

"Is it necessary to have ye whipped? I must admit that such a punishment is quite a temptation after all I had to watch my wife suffer through last night."

She shook her head, her long hair swinging from side to side. "Nay." Mirana scratched at her neck. Bryce wondered if she imagined a thick rope around it. Thankful for the dark light in the room with the exception of the torch on the wall, Bryce watched Mirana's bent head.

"She taunted me," Mirana's voice burst through the silence. "She said I'd better see that she liked her food or she would decide whether or not I stay."

"That is hardly taunting ye. As the lady of the castle, it is her right to do as she pleases. That's no just cause to try and murder her."

"Ye only meant to use me," she accused.

"I simply offered ye a job that I knew ye were more than capable of handling. Ye've served this household well over the years. Ye always knew that one day Evan and I would wed and a mistress would take over the management of the castle. I never encouraged ye to think otherwise. Ye're responsible for yer own misguided thoughts."

"Ye love me, not her." Mirana swept toward him, reaching for his arm.

Bryce shoved her away. He wiped his hand over his face, praying for enough patience to deal with her.

"I think the best thing to do is let the people decide yer fate. I wash my hands of ye completely. And if they decide death is proper punishment for attempted murder, I'll do naught to stop them."

"Ye wouldn't!" she spat at him, her hands fisted at her sides.

"I've made up my mind." He kept his voice firm.

"They won't take a MacPhearson life for a hated MacKenzie." Her venom for his wife ran so deep and strong, he wondered how Akira managed to survive. He'd underestimated Mirana greatly.

"We shall see." He stormed out of the tiny chamber before she could pique his anger further.

He locked the door with the key and handed it to Balloch. Mirana banged on the door from the other side, ranting and raving against him. He ignored her as he walked down the hall, his thoughts already drifting to his next step. He headed toward the kitchen where he'd confront the staff. If Mirana's hatred ran so deep that she willingly betrayed him, could there be others who felt the same way? Bryce couldn't take the chance. He needed to know where he and Akira stood with his clan.

Akira seldom strolled through the village, knowing how some of the MacPhearson clan felt about her. But today Bryce had called the Council to a meeting, and she needed to speak with him.

As she walked down the side of the dirt road, Akira noticed people watching her. She hated the uncomfortable stares that made her feel as if she'd suddenly sprouted horns on top of her head. She kept her gaze down, doing her best to ignore people.

"Good day, Lady MacPhearson!"

Akira looked up to see Vika waving. Although Vika mostly kept to herself, she always went out of her way to greet Akira. On impulse, Akira motioned for Vika to join her. Vika nodded her blonde head, looked around before she crossed the dirt road, and scurried over like a runaway mouse.

"Vika, I canna help but feel heavy tension in the air. Did something happen while I was ill?"

"Naught that I'm aware of, m'lady." Vika shook her head.

Akira gave her a direct stare, knowing she wasn't telling her everything. "The Council is meeting today. Do ye know about it?"

Vika looked down at her worn brown boots, apparently feeling uneasy. Akira waited patiently. Vika then looked around her, still avoiding Akira's gaze.

"Are ye afraid of someone?" Akira wondered aloud.

"Nay," she shook her head.

"I know that many of the clan still think of me as a MacKenzie. Does it bother ye if someone should happen by while we're talking?" Akira decided to be direct.

Vika's fingers flew to her lips and she gasped, "Oh, nay, m'lady. 'Tis not that."

"Then what is it? I don't understand why everyone is staring at me so." Akira's agitation began to grow as she shifted her weight to her other foot and crossed her arms. "This is worse than how they treated me at Evan's funeral."

"They only wonder about ye, m'lady."

"I know that people wonder about me, but for some reason this day seems worse than normal, and I haven't the faintest idea why."

Akira lifted her shoulders in question. Several Mac-Phearsons had scorned her when she first visited the village, and some openly stared at her with hatred. She'd come to expect their behavior, but today something different lurked in the gazes that followed her.

"Vika, I pray ye'll tell me the truth. I've verra few friends here besides Bryce and Sim. What does everyone else know that I'm obviously unaware of?"

"Yer husband has declared that the clan should decide Mirana's fate, and some feel that if they choose in favor of ye then they're betraying the MacPhearsons. They question if ye're worthy of such an action. Bryce says he canna make the decision because his first loyalty is to his wife. Most of the men respect that and are now meeting to make a decision. I fear they're in a heated debate over the matter."

Akira blinked and tilted her head. "What are the women saying?" she asked, unsure if she wanted to know, but the question had already escaped her lips.

Vika waved a hand in dismissal. "It doesn't much matter what the women think, does it? I mean, the men are the ones making all the decisions."

"I still want to know." Akira watched her friend's uneasy expression, as her eyes shifted from one object to another. When Vika didn't answer, Akira reached out and tugged on Vika's elbow. "Please, ye must tell me. I canna allow yer people to be split amongst themselves because of me."

Gulping with wide eyes, Vika took a deep breath. "M'lady, 'tis mostly the women against their husbands on this issue, and women are not allowed in the meetings."

"Yet, 'tis a woman's fate they are now discussing," Akira said dryly. "Ye never answered me. What are the women saying?"

"The women feel ye were right in demanding Mirana leave. No wife should have to put up with another woman in her home. 'Tis bad enough that some of us have husbands who are not faithful, but to have to bear looking in another woman's eyes and seeing her presence in our own home is too much. The women have sided with ye, Lady MacPhearson."

Akira felt compelled to defend Bryce. "My husband has not been unfaithful to me. I knew Mirana's hatred against me ran deep. I simply felt that she and I would both be happier if she were under a different roof."

"Of course, m'lady." Vika lowered her eyes. Akira couldn't tell if Vika believed her or not.

A burst of energy lifted Akira's shoulders and her hands flew to her hips. "The fact that Mirana shouldn't have been in our home is irrelevant. The woman poisoned me and that is the true issue here."

"Precisely," Vika agreed as two passing women overheard their conversation and paused. "The men have completely changed the issue."

"When ye poison someone, what are ye hoping to accomplish?" Akira asked them.

"Murder," one woman answered.

"Or at least make someone deathly ill," the other woman chimed in.

Akira turned to the other woman. "Ye bring up a good point and one that Bryce and I have already discussed. We really don't know if Mirana intended to kill me, or if she only hoped to make me so ill I'd be sorry for asking Bryce to make her leave. How do ye determine a just punishment for someone without knowing the full cause of what motivated them, or what they really intended to happen?"

The women exchanged glances. Akira looked at them, realizing the root of all the strange stares she'd been receiving. Her poisoning brought unwanted division to their clan. While many of them didn't want to be perceived as betraying their clan in defending Akira, neither were they willing to excuse Mirana's promiscuous behavior. The men, on the other hand, had no problem overlooking Mirana's behavior, which brought arguments and division among husbands and wives.

Each woman took a turn to share her individual perspective while a few more joined them. Before long, several of the village women held their own council outside the very building where the men held theirs.

"I hope the men are discussing these same points," one of the women stated.

Akira thought about how at home a woman of standing could appear before the Council and give an account or speak on a particular subject. While women couldn't vote, they could at least be heard. She wondered if the MacPhearson Clan operated in the same way. "Does the Council hear individuals who may not be council members?"

Several of them nodded.

"Only men are allowed to attend the meetings. Some of them aren't members, but they're allowed to voice their concerns," another lady volunteered.

This piece of news disturbed Akira. She frowned in thoughtful silence. It would be best if she didn't bring up how the MacKenzies operated. She thought of another approach.

"Even though we're women, we are still part of the clan, and the person on trial here is a woman. I don't see why the Council canna at least hear our concerns."

Several of the women agreed, and separate conversations rose among them.

"Ladies . . . ladies!" A voice from the back rose above them. "Bryce MacPhearson said he wanted the clan to decide. Are we not also part of the clan?"

Heads bobbed up and down while a number of "ayes" echoed among them.

"What are we going to do?" Vika asked, looking at Akira.

Akira froze. At home she'd have no problem voicing her opinion, but here among these women, she hesitated. As the wife of their chief, she held a leadership role among them, but she needed to tread carefully. Only a few moments ago she still felt like an outsider among them. If she proposed something and it didn't go well, how many would turn on her?

"If ye intend to approach the Council, we need to have a plan."

"Aye, m'lady." Vika leaned toward her. "What's our plan?" The others gathered in close.

Akira took a deep breath. "Well, we canna approach the Council with all of us having different ideas. We need to be in agreement so the men won't think we haven't thought things through." Akira stepped out from among them and turned to their eager faces. "We canna prove what Mirana's motive was in poisoning me. Only one thing is certain: whatever the motive, we know she canna be trusted. She could be a possible danger to everyone around her." Akira lifted a finger. "I propose one solution: The Council should ban her from the clan."

More discussions took place as Akira listened to them. It seemed that few wives were fond of Mirana, and it made Akira wonder about Mirana's relationship with the other clansmen. She remembered back to the night Mirana had been dallying with Rae.

They finally agreed to approach the Council as one group and to request that Mirana be banned from the clan. Those who made the decision to approach the Council prepared themselves to face their husbands, brothers, and fathers. Akira took a deep breath, hoping and praying that this one action wouldn't put her and Bryce at odds. Their group had grown to about twenty women, and in the end only fifteen were willing to charge forward as planned.

"Wait!" Vika called. "Akira is our Lady. We should follow her into the Council." Akira wanted to give them full rein to do as they wished without her, but knew it would be cowardly, and besides, she would be standing up for what she believed. She walked to the front of the women and straightened her shoulders, purposefully striding toward the building that contained her husband and the men of the clan.

Akira's heart pounded as she passed through the entrance. Kian's words dissolved on his lips, and he gave them a look of disapproval. The men sat in circled rows and wore astonished frowns as the women filed in, crowding around the entrance. Akira slid her gaze across the room and found her husband sitting in a corner. Only mild curiosity marked his features. While the strange silence lengthened, all eyes eventually rested on Akira. She tore her gaze from her husband's and stepped forward. Kian's frown deepened, as he looked even more displeased at her approach.

"What's the meaning of this interruption?" an elder on the Council demanded. "We haven't called any of ye forward."

Akira stepped before him, lowered her eyes, and curtsied. "We beg yer pardon, gentlemen of the Council. We did not intend to interrupt. We will be content until it is our turn to speak."

The gray-headed man turned to Bryce. "Did ye invite them to speak?" Bryce shook his head, and Akira could tell he tried to hide a smile. The elder then turned to Tavis and Balloch, and they also shook their heads. The other men also claimed they hadn't invited the women to speak.

The elder member turned back to Akira. "It appears that ye haven't been called to speak."

Akira nervously linked her fingers together in front of her. "The women of this clan would like to be heard, regarding Mirana's punishment."

Her announcement stirred tempers and caused the men to murmur among themselves, while a few of them shouted for Bryce to cease this nonsense. Kian burst out laughing.

"Women have no place in such matters. It doesn't concern ye." A middle-aged man spoke up, and Akira recognized

Davis, the one who had claimed she wouldn't melt in the rain the day Bryce took her.

She unlinked her fingers and lifted her chin. "And why should it not concern us?"

"Lady MacPhearson, we are quite capable of handling what needs to be done with Mirana," Davis said, trying to placate Akira, but it only made her more determined.

"Were ye the one she poisoned?" Her voice held a stinging edge to it. "Nay, none of ye was," she answered for them, looking around the room and meeting their gazes with a challenge of her own. She realized how uncomfortable they felt when their eyes downshifted from hers. It was the encouragement she needed, for it told her that deep down they knew she was right.

Abruptly, she turned to where Bryce sat. He now leaned forward, his attention upon Davis.

"Bryce."

Her husband turned an interested gaze upon her.

"Aye?" he asked, hesitantly, as if he feared what she might require of him.

"Did ye not turn over the decision of Mirana's punishment to the people?"

"Aye," Bryce admitted.

"And are women not people as well?" A couple of men snickered at the question. "I pray, sir, that ye not jest in this matter, for we are speaking of a person's life," she warned, hoping the others would hush as well.

"Of course." He pretended contrite seriousness. "Aye, Akira, I must agree that women are people as well." She gazed around the room and noticed that some of the men were having an even harder time disciplining themselves. They elbowed each other and leaned over to tease.

"The person poisoned is a woman, and the guilty person in question is a woman, yet ye want to say that a woman has no place deciding her fate? Gentlemen," Akira said, turning to the rest of the room, "I'd like to know what ye've decided for Mirana's fate."

Deep voices rose, and a dozen conversations echoed throughout the room.

"I see ye've not made much progress. Ye seem to be in a great deal of disagreement." Akira raised her voice to be heard above the conversations.

Kian swore under his breath beside her. "Ye've interrupted our progress," he growled through clenched teeth.

He turned his back and strode out. Kian reminded her of Elliot in that moment.

The voices around her grew loud and confusing. Akira felt like she'd created more chaos when all she wanted to do was help the women earn the right to have their voices heard. Angry tones and facial expressions swam in her head, and then she felt a slight pressure on her arm. Vika held onto her, giving her the support she needed.

"We're still here, m'lady," Vika said in her ear, giving her the encouragement she needed.

With Kian forgotten, Akira looked over at the women still huddled near the entrance.

Their hopeful expressions touched a place in her heart, renewing her mission. They wanted to be a part of their husband's lives as much as she did. With Vika by her side, Akira stepped forward. "I would like a spokesperson to relay what has been discussed. 'Tis apparent that Kian has deserted us." To her profound relief, Tavis stepped forward.

"We voted a while ago that she should be stoned for attempting to murder ye. 'Twas won by only one vote, and we've been trying to decide by how much the majority should be."

Stoned? They wanted to stone her? "Is that the only choice ye've discussed?"

"Someone mentioned hanging her." At Akira's horrified look, he added, "'Tis a bitter betrayal to the clan chief to murder his wife. Death is the punishment for such betrayal. We consider it the same as treason, m'lady."

Akira nodded. "But the chieftain's wife has not been murdered. I am right here and am much alive, I assure ye."

"Her intent is clear. If she remains, she could succeed next time, mayhap, even with the chieftain's life. We are his people and we must protect him as he protects us."

"I agree," Akira said, "and at the same time we canna take a life without knowing her mind. Mirana has never made such an attempt in the past, has she?"

When Tavis didn't answer, Vika spoke up. "Nay, Akira, she has not."

"Then we must not take her life without knowing for sure what her intentions were. I . . . believe . . . Mirana thinks herself in love with Bryce." Akira's heart ached with the admission, but she had to state the obvious, since no one else would. "Mirana was angry with me for taking what she wanted. She might have intended to make me ill, never considering that I could die." A few gasps and angry retorts reached her ears. Determined, Akira continued, "I didn't die. Perhaps Mirana accomplished her goals to perfection. I became so ill that I wanted to die, but she knew how much to give me and 'twas perfect."

"But, my lady, she admitted to poisoning ye. No one in their right mind would admit to such a deed without their guilty conscience plaguing them as hers was." Tavis looked confused as he tried to reason out his earlier beliefs.

"Aye, but it could be a guilty conscience for wanting to see me suffer, not dead. I tell ye she loves Bryce, and she didn't confess until she found out how upset he was over it."

Tavis scratched his head in thought. The rest of the men listened. The women looked triumphant, and Bryce seemed pleased as he glanced down at Akira from his corner perch.

"Bryce is my husband, and I suffered horribly from what Mirana did, and if I can admit that she might not have intentionally tried to kill me, then surely the rest of ye can." Akira swept her arms, indicating everyone in the room.

"What would ye do with her, Akira?" Tavis finally asked.

Akira smiled. "We would banish her from the clan. She must leave with whatever belongings she can carry and never return. If she is caught back on MacPhearson land again, we'll assume her intentions were to kill, and she'll suffer a murderer's punishment."

Tavis stood still in thoughtful silence and then slowly nodded. "I'll agree to that." He looked back at the other Council members.

"I agree," Balloch said.

Most everyone in the room agreed. "Does anyone disagree with Akira's solution?" Tavis asked. No one spoke up. He turned to Akira. "Well, m'lady, it seems ye've spared Mirana her life."

Akira beamed. She had made a difference, and it felt wonderful. Husbands and wives joined each other as they slowly gathered outside. Akira stepped out into the afternoon sunlight. Finella rushed up to her, looking harrassed and deeply troubled. A trace of silver hair slipped from her headpiece as she doubled over, trying to catch her breath.

"Oh, m'lady. Somethin' terrible has happened." Her eyes watered, and her nose turned red. Her lined face wrinkled as the tears slipped from her lids.

"M'lady, Mirana has hung herself," Finella wailed. Akira stepped back, covering her mouth as she shook her head in denial. "Nay!"

"I saw it with me own eyes. I brung her the midday meal."

Akira hurried toward the castle.

Finella tried to keep pace with her. "The guard outside her door didn't even know." The older woman panted from exertion.

Akira faintly heard Bryce calling her name, but she kept moving. She had to see for herself. Concerned that Bryce would try to stop her, Akira broke into a run. Mirana would never hang herself. Finella was wrong. She headed for the servant's quarters and found the chamber where a guard stood by the door.

He stepped in front of Akira, blocking the door. "I'm sorry, m'lady, I canna let ye in."

"This is my home." Akira's voice rose. "Do not tell me where I can and canna go in it." The young warrior looked over her head for approval, and Akira realized her husband stood behind her. She felt his strength and feared it at the same time. For that reason, she did not turn around.

The guard stepped to the side, and a strong hand came down upon her shoulder while the other one reached around her to open the door. Instinctively, Akira stepped through the threshold. Mirana's lifeless figure hung from the rafters of the storage place in the ceiling. Her skin looked a chalky gray color, and her eyes were surrounded in purple circles. Akira felt sick at the waste of life and sank to her knees.

"Nay!" Silent tears slipped from her eyes as Bryce bent to wrap his arms around her. Taking refuge, she leaned against his strong chest. "I didn't dream this. Sometimes I dream of things before they happen, but I had no warning." Her voice dropped to a whisper, and she wondered why sometimes she was given a warning and other times not.

"Akira, ye couldn't have stopped it," Bryce tried to console her.

"I know and it hurts when I canna stop bad things from happening, but because I sometimes have this gift, it hurts even more when God doesn't warn me."

"Akira, that's when fate has to have its way, and God canna allow ye to interfere. What will be, will be."

"I didn't want her to die." Akira squeezed his strong muscular arm to her chest. "I don't think she intended to murder me."

"Shush." Bryce stroked her hair and cradled her in his arms. "I believe ye, lass. Ye defended her well, ye did. I was verra proud of ye this day." He kissed the top of her head and she closed her eyes. While his arms felt so very safe, she still knew she needed to visit the chapel. Right now she needed the comfort and understanding that only God could provide.

"I'd like to go to the chapel."

She rose, and Bryce let her go.

After Akira left for the chapel, Bryce sent for Balloch.

A few minutes later Balloch stood in the threshold. "Did ye send for me?"

"Aye." Bryce nodded. "I wanted ye to come see this for yerself."

Balloch walked over to the body and examined the sheets and rafters from where he stood.

"When I first arrived," Bryce explained, "I didn't get a chance to touch her or examine her, but there was still too much color in her skin for a lot of time to have passed." Bryce gestured toward the heavy dresser that had been dragged to the center of the small room.

As if guessing Bryce's thoughts, Balloch's eyes grew wide and he pointed to it. Bryce nodded. "Aye, are ye thinking what I'm thinking?"

"Possibly." Balloch moved on top of the dresser and examined the knots in the sheets more closely. Even he had difficulty reaching the rafters.

"Mirana did not have the strength to move that dresser." Bryce pointed at the scraping marks where someone had dragged it across the stone floor. "And even if she managed it, she wouldn't have been tall enough to reach the rafters."

Bryce nodded. "Then we agree. Mirana did not kill herself."

13

*B*ryce rose, rubbing his tense neck as he walked around his desk and over to Kian, giving him a level stare.

"Ye took one guard's place at Mirana's door for no more than ten minutes until the other guard came, and ye neither looked in on her, nor tried to communicate with her through the door?" Bryce asked for the third time.

"That's right." Kian met his gaze, keeping his unreadable expression the same.

Bryce raised his hands to the ceiling and looked up as if questioning his Creator. "Someone must have gotten into the chamber around that time. She wasn't dead for long before we arrived." Another sigh escaped him, and he wearily massaged his forehead in thoughtful silence. "One thing is for certain, if she did try to take her own life, she had help. Either way, I fear we have a murder on our hands."

Bryce pointed to Balloch sitting in a chair by the unlit hearth. "Question the other two guards one more time. If ye still get the same story, keep a close watch on them."

He turned to his other childhood friend. "Kian, I appreciate yer patience, and I hope ye understand that these questions are necessary."

"Aye." Kian nodded and scooted to the edge of his seat as if he were ready to bolt with the first sign of permission.

"Ye may go." Bryce dismissed Kian with a wave of his hand. Kian followed behind Balloch out the library door. Bryce dropped his head on his shoulders and rolled it from side to side, working out the kinks in his taut muscles. He walked over to a table in the corner and poured a goblet of water, drained it dry, and headed upstairs to his wife. This had been a long day.

Akira rolled over, rubbed her nose, and tried to go back to sleep. There it was again. Something kept tickling her. Deep laughter sounded in her ears. She yawned, stretched, and opened her eyes to bright sunlight filtering through the open window. The glare illuminated her husband's head in a silhouette, mere inches from her face.

He smiled and bent to kiss her. She embraced the warmth of his tender lips against hers. If she woke up to this blissful pleasure every morning, she would be a very content woman, indeed.

"My, yer cheerful this morn'." She brushed her hair from her face.

"Aye, I'm a man who has a lot to be thankful for. The Lord has blessed me abundantly."

Akira sat up, rubbing her eyes and blinking to clear her vision. "I suppose I should get up."

"Nay, not yet." Bryce rose from the bed. "I've something for ye." He bent and picked up a long object wrapped in thick material from the floor. The proud grin on his face made her suspicious.

"Bryce?" She looked at him skeptically, wondering what in the world he could be up to this early.

"It arrived yestereve. I promised it to ye while ye were sick." He laid the heavy gift in her lap. She searched her mind, trying to remember what he might have promised her, and couldn't for the life of her remember him making any promises. "Ye jest. I canna think of aught ye've promised."

"Aye, I did." Bryce nodded his dark head. "Ye might not have been conscious to hear it, but I did." The eagerness in his eyes reminded her of her youngest brother, Leith.

He sat in the perfect spot for the sun to cast a particular orange glow around him. "There are gold specks in yer gray eyes."

A grin slowly spread across his face. "Does that mean you think me handsome?" He leaned forward, waiting to hear her reply.

Akira giggled and shook her head. "Nay."

"Nay?" His dark eyebrows lifted and he tilted his head, perplexed. "Ye think me not handsome?" he asked as if it couldn't be possible.

Akira couldn't help giggling. The rogue knew he was handsome. Pity he didn't have the vanity to hide it. "Nay, I think ye're a handsome angel."

For a moment he looked startled and then leaned forward, his lips claiming hers. "Well then, I suppose that's even better." He pointed to the package. "M'lady, open yer gift. I'm eager to see what ye think."

Carefully, she unwrapped the material around it. Excitement gathered in her fast beating heart when she saw the gold handle encased in a heavy gold sheath.

"Oh, Bryce! It's beautiful." Akira pulled it free and examined the handle more closely.

"The MacPhearson crest." Bryce pointed to the carved engraving. "I thought about it and decided Kian was right. Ye should know the MacPhearson crest by sight. As my wife I want ye to carry my name with pride. I expect ye to wear my plaid, and now I want ye to bear the MacPhearson crest. Our marriage began as two enemies striking a bargain in an attempt at peace, but now God has truly made our union a holy matrimony the way 'twas meant to be."

"Bryce MacPhearson, ye're making me cry too much of late." Akira placed the magnificent sword back in its sheath. "But, whatever ye do, I forbid ye to stop." She reached over and hugged him, burying her face in the corded muscles of his chest. Gently, he tilted her chin and lowered his head until their lips met in a tender kiss.

Later that morning they were in the dining room breaking their fast when Balloch came rushing in. "Bryce! The stone wall we've been repairing crumbled on top of Tavis."

Bryce threw down his napkin. "How bad is it? Is he alive?" He rose, following Balloch to the west wing.

"For the moment. We've sent for Angus. I'm not sure if he can last."

Akira swallowed her eggs and drank her water to wash it down. Hastily, she followed behind them. Balloch glanced back at Akira.

"M'lady, Angus may need yer assistance. We have a mess to clean, and Bryce will be needed to restore and keep order. There are other injuries, but none as serious as Tavis."

Akira nodded. "Of course. I'll do what I can."

In the end they couldn't save Tavis. The internal wounds continued bleeding while Akira prayed and tried to comfort him as best she could. Someone went in search of Vika, his wife. When Tavis's head finally rolled to the side, and she could no longer see his chest rise and fall with his labored breathing, Akira knew there was no more they could do.

Her gaze lifted to Angus, his expression full of sorrow and worry. Akira placed her hand over his. "Angus, there was naught ye could do for him. The stones were too heavy."

"Bryce hasn't forgiven me for not saving Evan." He wearily rubbed his eyes, looking away from her in shame.

"'Tis not true." She squeezed his hand for encouragement, waiting for him to look at her. When he did, she continued, "Ye canna save everyone, and Bryce is well aware of that. As ye once said, ye're not a healer or a miracle worker. God is in control, and we must accept His will, as hard as it sometimes seems."

"Tavis and I were like brothers," Angus mumbled while looking at the face of what used to be his best friend. His bearded chin trembled.

"I'm sorry, Angus." Akira thought he needed to be alone and patted his hand one more time before moving to the end of the bed.

"I'll inform Bryce." She quietly left the room, closing the door behind her to give him privacy.

Akira reached her husband's side a moment later. Bryce helped clear the rubble from the crumbled wall that had killed Tavis. She stared at the massive pieces of stone lying about.

Bryce must have sensed her presence, for he turned in that moment and came to her. She continued staring at the half-crumbled wall. He shook her shoulders when her eyes didn't move. "Akira?" He searched her face while her eyes remained fixed and she didn't reply. "Akira." He shook her again.

"I thought ye should know." Her voice barely rose above a whisper as she continued to stare, hating to be the bearer of more bad news.

"Know what?"

"He didn't make it."

A cold shiver raced over her skin as recognition dawned in his troubled eyes. Her heart went out to him, and she touched her hand to his arm.

"Tavis didn't make it?" he repeated as if he didn't want to believe it.

"We did all we could." Akira watched her husband's head drop. He half-turned to move away when Akira tightened her grip on him. "I must have yer word that ye'll be easy with Angus." Bryce gave her his full attention, looking slightly flustered. "Angus is taking this hard. Tavis and he were close."

Bryce looked wounded by her words. "Don't worry, lass. I'm well aware of their friendship."

The ache in her heart pierced deeper. "Angus still believes ye blame him for not saving Evan and that the death of Tavis will unleash yer fury again."

"When ye were sick from the poison, I apologized to Angus and asked him to forgive me. I was sincere in my request." Bryce stared down at the stone debris and sighed.

Akira cleared her dry throat. "I'm sorry, I didn't know. He just mentioned to me of his worry on the matter."

Bryce nodded sadly. "I can see where he might be concerned that I would turn on him again." He looked back at Akira. "Ye've my word that I'll be a true friend to Angus." Bryce bent close to her ear. "Tavis was a true friend to me as well." He choked on his emotion.

Her heart lurched at his pain, but there was naught she could do, so she simply bit her tongue. Determined to console him somehow, Akira brought her hand to his jaw and rubbed the back of her fingers against the rough texture of his unshaven face. "I know ye will. Ye're a loyal friend and a true husband."

Their gazes were so intense that Balloch had to cough to gain their attention. Akira jerked in surprise, and Bryce swiftly turned to him.

"Aye?" he asked.

Akira could feel him tense as if bracing himself for more bad news.

A keening sob shrilled in the distance.

"I thought ye should be aware that the rest of the clan already knows of Tavis's death." Balloch swallowed uncomfortably.

Akira stepped toward the huge warrior, her hands balled into fists at her side. "Who told them?" Fury swelled in her as she stared him down. "Vika is his wife, and we've not yet found her. They should not have been told before his own wife."

Bryce's strong hands gripped her shoulders, but Akira jerked away. "Akira is right. I sent for Vika as soon as we found him. Who told the people before we could inform his wife as is proper?"

"I did." Kian walked up behind them.

Akira whirled from Balloch and moved toward him. "Ye had no right."

Kian glanced in Bryce's direction. "The servants were spreading rumors, and people were panicking, especially after what happened to Mirana. They needed to be told it was a simple mistake, that there is no murderer running around."

"Kian, it wasn't yer responsibility to make a formal announcement. I'm not completely convinced that Mirana's death was by her own hand, and I'm certainly not ready to say that Tavis's death was not a murder. His family should have been informed first, and I should have been the one to make the announcement."

"Vika wasn't around. And the rumors were spreading with or without her." Kian's defensive tone was unusual, but Bryce seemed to be holding on to his temper.

"Even so," Bryce said, "ye've worked by my side for years. Since when are ye incapable of making the correct decision? Ye knew I should have been the one to make the formal announcement to the clan."

Bryce's eyes clouded over and his voice grew calm—too calm. Akira watched his jaw clench as he stared at Kian. She sensed the two of them were close to erupting. She tugged on Bryce's tunic, but it neither moved him nor drew his attention as she had hoped.

The fierceness suddenly disappeared from Kian's face, and a look of bewilderment came over him.

"I'm sorry, Bryce. I wasn't thinking. I'll go and apologize to Vika immediately."

"Nay." Bryce shook his black head. "Ye and Balloch oversee the cleanup of the wall. My wife and I will see to the clan as is our duty."

Kian nodded and turned to follow Balloch.

Akira sighed with relief when they were gone. "I don't like it when ye're angry with each other."

"He was wrong."

Akira hurried beside him, trying to keep up with his quick pace. "Ye don't think it was an accident?"

"Now is not the time to discuss it, Akira. We have to deal with Tavis's family."

Taken back by his abruptness, Akira tried to console herself that his harsh tone wasn't directed at her. "Ye believe that Mirana and Tavis were both murdered?" She couldn't let it go. She had to know what he thought.

"I said now isn't the time to discuss it."

"But, Bryce—"

"Not now, Akira!"

His raised voice and increasing pace made her feel rejected, but she wasn't appeased. "I have a right to know if I'm in danger."

Abruptly, he stopped, grabbed her by the shoulders and turned her to face him. "Woman, ye really know how to pester a man."

"I'm yer wife. 'Tis my responsibility to nag at ye," she reminded him. A grin suddenly broke his tense features, and his hands came to hold both sides of her face.

"Aye woman, ye are my wife an' ye're sometimes a bother, but I thank God for ye." He kissed her forehead. "An' no one will harm ye," he promised. "No one." The vehemence in his voice betrayed his thoughts on the matter.

"Ye believe they were both murdered." The new revelation seeped further into her mind. She trusted his instincts as much as her own. Something still plagued her from the moment they found Mirana's body. Akira glanced at Bryce, but he quickly turned from her.

"Ye're not telling me everything."

Bryce shrugged, pulling her hand in his and leading them back to the sounds of the wailing and keening. "There is naught to tell."

"Naught else to tell, but something else ye suspect?" she prompted, leaning toward him and stepping into stride beside him. He faced the other direction, purposely keeping his gaze from hers. Akira jerked on his hand to let him know what she thought about his avoiding her.

"Ye're becoming a bother again," he teased, and she could tell that he would like to distract her from asking more questions, but Akira wasn't about to let it go.

"Ye don't trust yer own wife?" She couldn't hide the pain in her voice. Why else would he withhold information from her?

"I trust ye. I feel there is no need to frighten ye without reason."

"There is verra little ye could say that would frighten me more than I am right now."

Bryce turned to look at her, and in that moment, she could not mistake the fear in his eyes. His hand tightened around hers, and she realized his fears were for her and that was why he hadn't wanted to discuss it with her. An eerie chill coursed through her body, making her blood run cold.

"M'lady?" Finella interrupted. Akira sat on her knees planting more spring flowers in the courtyard. Covered in dirt, she couldn't help smearing it across her face as she brought up her sleeve to mop her brow.

"Aye?"

"A messenger has a letter for ye an' he said he was to give it to ye personally. Shall I bring him to ye?"

Akira's mind raced. Who would need to send a messenger to her? It must be terribly important to be personally delivered. She gathered her tools in her hand and straightened.

"Of course, bring him to me. I'll be at the well washing my hands." Akira splayed them out in front of her for them both to inspect.

Finella nodded. "'Twould be the least ye could do. Wouldn't want to scare the lad off afore he states his business, now would we?"

"Nay, Finella, I suppose not."

Finella gave her a sympathetic grin. "They might not come clean a'tall. Ye work too hard, lass." She turned on her heel and disappeared, leaving Akira to her task.

A moment later, Finella ushered a young lad over. He patiently waited for her to dry her hands and face. He appeared to be close to Sim's age, with rugged red hair. His thin frame barely held his clothes on his body, and Akira wondered when he'd last eaten a decent meal. She glanced at Finella protectively hovering behind him.

"Finella, see that his stomach is satisfied for his trouble."

"Aye, m'lady."

"I must wait for yer answer." The lad stood proud, his bony shoulders squared back like a warrior on duty. Akira rewarded him with a smile.

"I wouldn't want ye to neglect yer responsibilities." She held her hand out for the letter. "Verra well then, I shall read it now, if ye please."

The lad thrust the letter in her hand and Akira's fingers eagerly curled around the parchment. She tried to keep them from trembling as she allowed her mind to imagine all sorts of bad news. She tore open the MacKenzie seal. Unfolding the letter, Akira skimmed the words across the page as excitement filled her.

> *Dearest Sister,*
>
> *I feel I have wronged ye and would greatly appreciate it if ye would meet me on Thursday of next. By the time this letter reaches ye, I will already be on my way. I have news concerning a betrayer among yer husband's warriors. It is most important that ye do not tell him of our meeting. Together we will decide how to handle the situation until I can prove it is true. I trust I may confide*

in ye, dear sister, and remember: Bryce must not know we are meeting. I fear he wouldn't trust me and might forbid ye to meet with me. I have yer best interests at heart.

Elliot

Akira stared at the letter a little while longer before turning back to the lad still waiting.

"Tell him to meet me . . . " Her mind searched for a convenient place, and a picture of the meadow where she and Sim had often met to practice his speech came to remembrance. No one had ever come across them or even suspected them there. Her lips curled into a triumphant smile. "Tell him to meet me at the meadow of daisies."

Akira knew Elliot would wonder where that was but he would have to pass by it on his way to MacPhearson Castle, and he could not miss it, for at the moment daisies completely covered the entire field.

"I shall expect him shortly after sunrise," she added, thinking that would be the best time to meet since Bryce was an early riser. He'd either be training his men or working on repairs to the west wing of the castle.

Akira turned to Finella, who waited nearby. "Finella, please see that the lad has a chamber to sleep in if he wishes to stay the night."

"Aye, m'lady." Finella motioned for him to follow her.

Akira's thoughts returned to Elliot's letter. She shivered and wrapped her arms around her middle. It wasn't cold. The end of spring and the budding of summer promised more heat-filled days. A shimmer of fear coursed through her at the knowledge that her brother could possibly know about a dangerous murderer running rampant at MacPhearson Castle.

"Akira, ye look like a force to be reckoned with," Kian commented from behind. She hadn't heard him approach and turned to smile up at him.

"I feel like it." She looked down at her old, dirty dress and laughed. "I have no intention of meeting with the queen today at any rate."

Kian laughed. "M'lady, I'm sure ye could charm the king and queen in any state, if ye've a mind to."

Akira blushed crimson. "Ye have a way with flattery, Kian."

"'Tis no flattery, but the truth." He walked over to the bucket, dipped his hands in the water, and splashed his face. "Ah, that feels good."

"Ye and Bryce are getting along well?" Akira inquired, knowing they had been testy around each other of late.

"We've always gotten along. Ye can have an argument with yer brother one minute and die for him in the next. We've always been like that. Even when Evan was the chieftain, it was because of Bryce I gave my allegiance to the MacPhearson clan."

"I see."

"Ye're a woman, and a woman doesn't give her allegiance to anyone." Kian turned to look at her, leaning his elbow on the well.

"A woman must give her loyalty to her husband," Akira countered, trying not to be defensive. She was expected to obey the chieftain, the same as he, only she wasn't required to swear an oath as a warrior must.

"True, but a woman doesn't die for him in battle."

"Many women have died bearing children because their husbands wanted sons. Women may not die in battle, but for the widows left behind, sometimes 'tis harder to continue on."

"Ye've a way with words yerself. No wonder Bryce is completely taken with ye." Kian's curious expression turned into something else that Akira could not decipher. "I've never met another female quite like ye, Akira. Ye would have been perfect had ye been born a MacPhearson." A grin slid across his face, and she realized he teased her.

"Well, I did the next best thing. I married one so my children could be born as MacPhearsons."

"Yer wit is beyond comprehension. I imagine Bryce has a hard time keeping his own wits about him when ye begin to weave flowery words at him. He is the brightest of men I know, but I believe he's finally met his match."

"Kian! Quit dallying with my wife and come along. Ye hold the rest of us up," Bryce called from the other end of the courtyard.

Akira waved to Bryce and he waved back, while he waited for Kian to reach him. The two men immersed themselves in conversation as they headed toward the west wing of the castle. Akira went to her chamber to change clothes and then headed toward the kitchen to oversee the menu for the coming night.

"I'm convinced the wall collapsed because the mortar didn't have enough time to settle within the wood frames," Bryce said, thinking aloud.

"Aye, but the wood ties would be strong enough to keep the wall from collapsing. That's the whole purpose of using the wood frames until the mortar sets," Balloch argued.

"I agree; therefore, I want ye to see to the task of checking all wood ties and frames holding the rest of the mortar intact. Only a portion of the wall collapsed, and I want the rest of it checked. Use the crane wheels if ye must. I want to know if anything appears to have been tampered with. In the meantime, I'll see that the repairs continue," said Bryce.

"I'll see to the wood, Bryce," Kian volunteered.

"Nay." Bryce shook his head. "I need ye for something else. Let Balloch see to that."

"But—"

"Balloch will see to it." Bryce cut him off.

"Aye," Kian said, backing down.

"I fear I will need to repair the rest of the castle in the future if I don't take certain measures now," said Bryce. "The castle was built on a solid foundation, and there couldn't have been a better location, but the walls were made of layers of rock covered with a crust of clay when the family ran out of funds for limestone. That is why the west wing decayed so quickly. I have a shipment of limestone coming along with the ashlar stone I ordered yestereve.

"Kian, I want ye to form a party of men to help ye encase the east wing in the ashlar stone. 'Tis much smoother and will be a good outside finish. When ye complete a wall ye need to coat it with plaster and whitewash it. If we are going to rebuild, we're going to do it right." Bryce looked around at his men, meeting each gaze to assess their understanding.

Bryce proceeded to assign men to certain tasks and then left it up to Balloch and Kian to carry out his wishes. Bryce pulled his own group of men, and they began working where they had left off the day before.

By mid-afternoon, Bryce held up one end of a heavy timber being tied to another. They needed to create a new frame for the mortar they planned to prepare. Balloch's huge body appeared, casting a deep shadow upon him from the setting sun. Bryce could taste the salt of sweat upon his upper lip as he grunted with the heavy pressure on his shoulder.

"Don't stand there, mon. We could use yer muscle," Bryce shouted to him.

"Aye, m'lord. I came to talk to ye," Balloch said as he bent and lifted some of the pressure from Bryce's shoulders.

"I was hoping ye would say that. Where is Akira?" Bryce hadn't seen his wife all day and wondered what she had been up to.

"She is with Vika. She took her some food. If she has her way, I believe ye might soon have a guest in the castle."

They lowered the timber and waited for the men at the other end to finish setting their side down. "Leave it until the morrow at sunrise," Bryce told them. He gave Balloch his full attention while they walked to the courtyard. "I thought as much. Vika and her son are welcome in my home anytime. Tavis was a great friend and a loyal warrior. I would consider it an honor. 'Tis the least I can do. Where is Sim?"

"I believe he joined Kian and his group after he and Akira returned."

"Akira still found time for him even after all her good duties, did she?"

Balloch returned his grin. "Aye, she's a sweet one. Always worried about everyone else." Balloch's expression grew serious, and he rubbed his chin with his fingers. "There's something I need to tell ye. We found the most peculiar thing, and it canna be mistaken for naught but tampering."

"What is it?" Bryce reached for the double doors to the entrance of the castle. Swinging them wide, he said, "Let's go to the library. We can talk more privately there."

Balloch waited until they were behind the closed doors, each with a goblet of cider in hand. Balloch pulled out a rope he had been keeping in the fold of his plaid. " 'Twas purposely severed, and there were at least three others."

Bryce took the rope and examined it. The cut was clean and precise, something that had to be made by a blade. The rope certainly hadn't torn from wear or bad threads. Bryce threw the rope in a nearby chair.

"It certainly proves that it was tampered with, but how would they know who would be near the wall or when for that matter?" Bryce took another swallow from his goblet. "The real question is why?"

Balloch shrugged. "I'm as baffled by it as ye."

"Exactly when did the stone wall crumble?"

"At daybreak."

"Who was working on the daybreak shift for those repairs?" Bryce swallowed more cider from his goblet.

"Tavis, Rae, Davis, and Iain. Lady Akira usually brings the men water within that hour."

"Then someone would have cut the ropes sometime during the night, before sunrise, and their target could possibly be someone in that group. We need to be more careful. Akira isn't to be left alone. She isn't going to like having a guard, so ye and a few others will have to pretend to be interested in her affairs so that ye can accompany her wherever she goes without her suspecting she's being guarded. I want ye to arrange the same thing for Sim. I know he is in training, but he still has so much to learn. I dislike the idea of him not being able to hear someone sneaking up on him."

"I'll take care of it," Balloch said. "Sim won't be as hard to keep up with as yer lady."

"If Vika moves in, Akira will be more inclined to spend time with her and that will ease my mind a bit. She's better off even with female company than being alone. Have ye discovered anything else concerning Mirana's death?"

Balloch shook his head.

"There must be something we're missing." Bryce rubbed his forehead. "Inspect that room from top to bottom. Make sure there are no secret passages leading to that chamber that I don't know about. That is the only way for someone to enter without a guard noticing. Without a window in that room, there's no other explanation. We've got to find it."

"I'll check it out again on the morrow," Balloch promised. He held out his goblet for Bryce to refill.

"Aye, nothing better than the sweetness of good cider on occasion." After refilling Balloch's goblet, the laird leaned back with his hands behind his head in thoughtful concentration.

"I suppose we'll need to replace Tavis," Bryce said at last. He grew silent for a moment, considering who might be up to the task. "See that Rae completes Tavis's duties for a while. If he proves trustworthy and competent, we'll select him."

Balloch nodded and took another swallow.

"How do ye think Sim is doing with his training?" Bryce asked, changing the subject.

"Splendid, considering his drawbacks. He's faster on the attacks than he is on the defensive. As we feared, he has trouble detecting a backward assault and fares better with the frontal and side assaults. He's developing muscle and becoming solid enough. I believe yer wife is teaching him a few sword tricks. He's becoming quite handy with a sword, but is still developing the strength of a man. One thing Sim has learned from Akira is speed. There may be a need for a swordswoman after all. She has learned that her speed makes up for her lack of strength. If Sim develops both speed and strength, along with using his wit when fighting, he'll more than make up for his lack of hearing."

"Keep up the good work, and if he and Akira are sword-fighting, don't stop them. However, if she tries to fight anyone else, interfere immediately. It appears we have a murderer on our hands, and right now I trust no one."

They finished their drinks and retired from the library. Bryce went upstairs to clean and change before the evening meal. Akira wasn't in her chamber, and he questioned everyone he passed as to her whereabouts, but no one seemed to know. By the time he settled in his chair at the head of the table, Akira still had not appeared. Finella hustled into the great hall carrying a basket of bread.

"Finella, where is Akira?"

"She said to tell ye she'll be dining with Vika tonight. She was worried about her being alone. Akira is trying to convince her to come to the castle and live, but Vika has refused thus far. She doesn't want to be a burden."

"I'm going after them. If I wish to see my wife, I suppose I must beg Vika to move in," Bryce muttered as he left the hall. His men exchanged knowing smiles as the great door to the foyer slammed behind him.

14

*B*ryce went to the stables, saddled Ahern, and rode out the gate into the village. He would not have Akira wandering about at night with a murderer on the loose. How could she be so careless knowing the recent events that had taken place? He rode Ahern hard in the dark, eager to ensure his wife's safety. After spending the day with his men, he had grown weary of their company and missed Akira. He needed her.

He mulled over the day's events in his mind. It occurred to him that the murderer might be someone close to him, and he feared Akira could be their target. Based on the strength required to move that dresser, and the height needed to reach the rafters, Bryce suspected a man to be the most likely culprit.

Something spooked Ahern and he reared. Wrestled from his thoughts, Bryce grappled with the reins. "Whoa!" He eased Ahern, gaining command as best he could. Bryce squinted in the dark, but could see naught in the scarce light of the quarter moon. He thought he heard a slight rustle, but had no time to decide what it was before Ahern reared again, throwing him to the ground. Bryce had just enough time to roll to the side and miss Ahern's hooves before his horse took off in the opposite direction.

Bryce shook his head, trying to clear his mind and stay awake. Nausea overcame him, and he fought to keep his stomach. Wetness dripped down his face from the intense pounding in his right temple, where he must have struck a rock. He wiped the blood away and tried to stand, but dizziness hit him, and he fell to his knees. Taking a deep breath, Bryce growled with determination and managed to sway to his feet. He wasn't far from Vika's home. He would continue. He concentrated on putting one foot in front of the other. His progress was slow, but he finally staggered to Vika's house.

Vika answered his knock and yelled for Akira. He must have looked a sight. The throbbing in his head heightened, and he was tempted to yell along with her to shut out the pain. Akira hurried to the door, and bless her, she did not scream. Instead, she pulled him in and led him to a nearby couch.

"Nay, I don't want to lie down," he protested, but when Akira pushed him down, he willingly lay there. He hadn't the strength to argue.

Vika brought a cloth and warm water. She watched Akira clean his head wound.

"What happened? Would ye care to explain?" Akira sounded ready to scold him.

"Not particularly," he said, with a lazy grin, pleased to be near her again. He thought the short walk to Vika's would take him forever after Ahern left him, but here he was with Akira's warm, gentle hands attending him.

"Well, I would particularly like to know how ye came about this large lump on the side of yer head. Ye've managed a huge gash, and I fear it might swell as large as an onion."

She leaned over and kissed his forehead.

Bryce chuckled. "Well, I canna exactly complain about the attention it's getting me."

"I can think of at least half a dozen other things that would earn ye lots of attention without yer getting knocked senseless." She brushed her lips against his, relief apparent in her face. "Don't ever scare me like that again," she scolded. "Is yer head the only thing that's hurt?" Akira checked the rest of his limbs, apparently concerned he might not remember with the huge lump on his head.

"The rest of me is fine."

"I'm still waiting to hear what happened."

Bryce sighed, hating the pain of trying to remember. "Something or someone spooked Ahern. I lost my balance, fell, and my head must have struck a rock."

Akira patted his arm. "I believe we shall be Vika's guests for the night. There is no way ye're getting up. That head of yers would start bleeding again, and I refuse to walk back without Ahern." A curious look crossed Akira's face. "What were ye doing out anyway? Ye should have been having yer evening meal."

Bryce looked disgruntled.

"I was, until Finella informed me that ye were dining with Vika tonight. I decided to come after ye—the both of ye," he clarified, closing his eyes from the pain of talking.

Akira patted his cheeks, and his eyes fluttered open in wonder.

"I'm sorry, darling, but I canna allow ye to fall asleep. Angus says it isn't good to allow someone to fall asleep with a head wound."

Bryce rolled his eyes. "Trust me, Akira, I wasn't sleeping. My head is pounding worse than the surf on the shore." She looked uncertain and moved to better settle a pillow behind his head. "Nay," he moaned. "Don't touch it."

Akira bit her bottom lip in a worried frown, unsure of what to do for him.

"Could ye make me something to eat?" he asked softly. She nodded and stood when Vika interrupted her.

"Sit down. I'll make him some soup. My poor Tavis always loved a broth to soothe his stomach when he wasn't feeling well."

The mention of Tavis reminded Bryce of his other reason for coming for his wife. "Vika, I've been meaning to talk to ye."

Vika didn't answer him as she bustled around pouring ingredients into a pot and hanging it over the fire. Her home was small like most houses in the village. Made of mud, clay, and stone, the walls were simple, the dirt floor compact and hard, and no spare rooms existed for privacy. Life would now be hard on her without Tavis, unless she were to remarry.

"I would like ye and yer son to come and live with us. Without Tavis, ye'll need protection, and I can provide it better at the castle. There is plenty of room for ye both, and I know Tavis would prefer it. Ye'd want for naught. Yer lad could train in my army when he grows older."

Vika looked nervous as she continued to remain busy. "I appreciate the offer, but we canna take it. Tavis wouldn't like a handout, and he'd prefer me to make me own way."

"Not if I were here to offer a way out, and I am. He would rather ye have protection and comfort over the struggles and hardships ye would have to endure here alone."

Vika clasped her hands together in front of her and bowed, looking down at the floor. She kept quiet a long time before looking up. Silent tears ran down her face.

"'Tis kind of ye, m'lord. If I agree, 'twould be because of my son, and on the condition that I could work in yer household to pay my way."

"We agree," Akira said before Bryce could answer. She jumped up and hugged Vika, jubilant that she would soon have a friend in the castle.

Bryce half closed his eyes. He wasn't asleep, only dreaming of blissful peace. As the hours passed, if he closed his eyes Akira would shake his arm or poke at his chest. After Vika retired, Akira sat and told him funny little stories and joked with him. At one time she sang to him, until she realized her voice lulled him to sleep. Finally, she fell asleep on top of his chest, and he thanked the heavens above for the pestering angel in his arms. He said a quick prayer for their safety and the ability to catch the murderer before he hurt someone else. Bryce blinked several times, but his heavy lids wouldn't stay open. In spite of his efforts to stay awake, he too entered the blissful surrender of sleep.

Akira splashed around in the water, wishing she hadn't agreed to Sim's crazy scheme. He thought it a wonderful idea for him to teach her to swim since she had taught him how to speak a few words. Now as she held her lungs until she thought they would burst and continued kicking only to get nowhere, she feared this was the worst idea of the century and prayed she would get through the afternoon alive. If and when she ever made it back to dry land, she wouldn't allow him to tempt her into going swimming again.

Akira's head surfaced and she sputtered, gulping water while trying to catch her breath.

"Sim!" she screamed, when her lungs had enough air. "How dare ye to trick me into this."

Knowing her words were falling on deaf ears, she roughly thumped him on the back of the head to gain his attention and repeated herself so that he could read her lips. Sim only laughed as he struggled to keep a serious expression and failed miserably. A chuckle escaped him. Akira found herself smiling in spite of her fright.

Sometimes it still amazed her to hear sound coming from him. Just the thought of what he'd accomplished was a miracle, and she would never forget the agonizing hours he spent trying to pronounce words he'd never heard, and achieving what so many others took for granted—the spoken word.

"Akira." He said her name so easily now that it almost sounded like music to her ears.

"Aye?" She gave him her full attention.

"Ye . . . twead . . . wa-ter," he pointed out, almost as excited to see her swim as to feel his throat muscles move the first time he felt them.

Akira gasped in disbelief. She glanced at her arms moving of their own accord and noticed that her legs had been moving on their own as well. She stayed afloat all by herself.

"Maybe my fate isn't to die by drowning after all." She breathed heavily, beginning to feel the fatigue in her muscles and lungs. Somehow being aware of her success made her all the more tired.

"Ye . . . for-got . . . drown-ing." Sim swam toward the bank.

Unaware of his intent, Akira struggled to follow him, realizing he was right. If she kept her mind on other things besides drowning, she didn't panic as easily. Before she knew it, her feet were touching the sodden ground beneath. Akira sighed with relief, increasing her speed to the dry ground a few feet beyond.

"How ever did ye convince me to do it?" Her lungs expanded and contracted with each breath and word. She tried to slow her breathing and ended up coughing. Even her throat hurt. Mayhap she had swallowed too much water.

"Did . . . good." Sim grinned at her.

Akira folded to her knees, pressing her hands into solid ground. She slid to her stomach, allowing herself to relax with the side of her face buried in the thick grass. After spending the past couple of hours worried she would sink and die of suffocation, she welcomed the wonderful feeling of security beneath her—and fresh air.

She pulled a handful of green grass from its roots and gripped it in her fingers.

"'Tis amazing how simple some things may seem and how heavenly they can be when we miss them."

"What?" Sim leaned toward her from where he leisurely lay on his side.

Akira realized she had spoken without looking at him. She sat up and held out her hand for him to inspect, repeating her words once more. She let the dirt and grass slip through her fingers, watching it fall to the earth where it belonged.

"I suppose I should thank ye for today." Akira looked directly at him so he could not mistake her words.

To her surprise Sim blushed. "Ye g-gave . . . my . . . v-voice."

She shook her head. "Nay, God gave ye yer voice. I only helped ye find and use it." Akira stood and wrung out the excess water from her skirt and then her hair.

The day already proved to be warm as the sun started to rise and touch her skin. They had slipped into summer a couple of months ago, and with the quick passage of time, only had a few more warm weeks left that they could enjoy.

The scent of pine and sycamore trees thickened around them as the morning came alive, the birds and insects stirring. The loch was nestled between two rolling moors of heather and daisies. Mountains painted the distant sky in hues of purple, dark blue, and gray in uneven peaks and round hills.

Today she would meet with Elliot. Akira knew she would dry before she reached the castle and actually regretted having to leave their peaceful surroundings. It was the first time she'd ever felt comfortable in water and could appreciate the beauty by reveling in it, rather than watching it from afar.

"I'm glad we didn't ride today. I would rather walk." She bent to put her shoes back on her feet.

"Whaaat?" Sim's tone held a hint of frustration.

She had forgotten to look at him before speaking again. "Ye've become more natural to converse with, and I forget to face ye. Think of it as a compliment."

Sim gave her an uncertain glance and then a smile crawled over his face. "Aye," he announced proudly, straightening his shoulders and puffing out his broadening chest.

"Ye're not allowed to let yer ego become conceited, no matter how much ye wish to join the ranks of other men. I insist ye remain different." Akira winked at him with an affectionate grin.

"Al-wayz . . . dif-ent." Sim pointed to his mouth, frowning and shaking his head. He pulled his sword from its sheath and threw Akira's to her with his other hand. "Fight!"

Off balance, she had to jump high enough to reach it. She nearly fell with the weight of it. Even though Bryce had them design it smaller for her, it was still quite heavy. Glancing at Sim, she noticed the protruding muscle in his arm as he swung his sword in a wide arc, waiting for her attack.

"Not today, Sim." Akira shook her head. "I've other plans."

He looked insulted as he tilted his head, and his lips puckered in a frown. "Al-ways fight . . . af-ta . . . ye near-ly . . . drown."

"But today is different. I didn't nearly drown. Ye saw me yerself. I was an excellent swimmer."

"Ye twead-ed . . . w-wat-er." Sim twisted his mouth in response to her dry humor. He leaped toward her with one fist on his hip and the other swinging his sword.

Deciding that she didn't want to lose her head, Akira brought her sword up, and the sound of steel rang in the air.

"I don't have time to fight," she shouted at him, but he ignored her as he waved his sword and forced her to duck and lunge sideways to miss his swing-back attack. Sim's sword clashed with Akira's once again. "I have things to do."

"Fight." Sim went in for a side attack. Akira longed to just stand there, but she knew better. He wouldn't expect it of her, and he might not have enough time to pull back from his attack. She would have no choice but to fight him and be quick about it, or she would be late meeting Elliot.

Akira had kept her word and told no one about their meeting. If she didn't hurry, Sim would still be here fighting her when her brother arrived, and Elliot would think she deliberately set him up. She fought with all her might, but fatique from treading water and Sim's excellent stamina wore her out. He fought well. Too well, she thought as she barely held onto her sword in a deadlock. Sim broke away, and their swords clashed again.

Deep into the fight now, Akira was taken by surprise when her brother emerged from the woods. He must have thought she and Sim were really fighting for he ran at them with his sword raised and a beastly yell that heightened her senses and fell on Sim's deaf ears, unnoticed. He raced up to Sim from behind.

"Elliot, stop!" Akira screamed.

Elliot's eyes were fixed on his target. He kept his sword raised, ready to strike and kill. Akira knew that look in Elliot's eyes and nothing would stop him. He intended to finish his foe. Flashes of Sim's bleeding head against a rock crossed her mind. With no time to spare, she did the only thing she could to protect the lad. She lunged at Elliot.

Sim paused, a confused frown marring his features as his gaze switched from hers to something behind her. An expression of horror claimed his features as his eyes widened, and he yelled a warning, charging around her.

Her breath caught in her throat as Elliot threw his sword a scarce inch by her head. She had meant to knock his sword out of his hand, but she had not correctly anticipated Elliot's intent. At the last minute, he had moved the wrong way, tripped over her foot and fell into her sword.

The world stood still. Her heart beat like thunder in her ears, as his eyes flew to hers, a look of betrayal stinging so deep that the sword might as well have passed through her own body. She looked at Elliot's blood on the tip of her sword and threw it to the ground, screaming and running toward him. Elliot made no sound as he slowly slid to his knees, gripping his side and falling forward against Akira's skirts.

"Elliot? Oh, Elliot, I didn't mean it." Akira wrapped her arms around him, carrying his weight upon her as she helped him to the ground. She *must* make him understand that she didn't mean it. She could feel her own blood storming through her temples; she could hardly think coherently.

His head sank onto her lap. She rubbed his dark hair from his forehead, her hands trembling so violently she could hardly accomplish the task. "I only intended to knock yer sword from yer hand, but ye threw it instead. What in the world possessed ye, Elliot?" She wiped at the tears streaming down her face; her hands were stained with his blood. "Elliot, please don't die. I canna bear it if ye die."

Stop the bleeding, a voice chanted in her mind. In obedience, she ripped a part of her skirt and tore his clothes to assess the wound. Elliot winced as blood poured from his side. She mopped at it and pressed her garment against the opening. Elliot groaned, wincing in pain.

Once she had done all she could, Akira gathered him close. How could fate be so cruel? "Elliot, I love ye. Please, don't die." She would plead, beg, give anything to save him. He rolled to his unhurt side, and she leaned over his body to make sure the garment was still pressed tight against him.

Elliot groaned, jerking from her. "Don't put yer hand there, lass. Don't ye know that a man hurts where he's bleedin?"

His Scottish burr was an imitation of their grandfather, and when she was younger, it would make Akira laugh and forget whatever ailed her. The tender thought that he would make an effort to try and comfort her now when he lay dying, made her burst into tears. She bent to hug him.

"I'm so sorry," she whispered again. "I never meant it."

"Shush. I know, lass. Ye didn't see the demon behind ye." He reached up and rubbed the back of her head. "Go take care of the lad. He needs ye more than I." Elliot nodded in the direction behind her.

"Demon? Who was behind me?" She raised her head and looked her brother in the eyes. She saw the raw pain in them and almost flinched, but he squeezed her arm to gain her attention.

"He wore a mask. He must be the traitor I warned ye about. Listen to me, lass." He clenched his jaw tightly, and she knew it was an effort for him to talk, but he seemed determined to have his way. "Only my side is wounded. I don't believe any of my organs are punctured. I'm just a little weak from a loss of blood." She began to protest, but he placed a finger against her lips.

"Akira, the lad has a severe head wound. Ye must take him home to yer husband and send someone back for me. Ye canna carry the both of us."

The words "head wound" caught her attention and without further prompting she jumped to her feet and turned to see Sim lying in the grass beside a huge rock where they had often sat and talked. Akira could clearly see the blood splashed across the front of the large rock where he had struck his head. Sim's face looked ashen beneath the blood covering most of his body. Her dream re-played before her.

Cold chills slid up her spine. Akira ran to him. "Sim? Sim!" She knelt at his side, but he lay as limp as a blade of grass. "Oh, dear God in heaven. Why let me see it if there is naught I can do to stop it?" Angered, scared, and frustrated, Akira turned to Elliot, who watched from where he still lay. She wondered what to do, as she chewed her bottom lip.

As if reading her thoughts, Elliot nodded. "Save him, Akira. I will still be here when ye come back for me."

Elliot's voice sounded weaker, and she knew he would fight her on the matter. He closed his eyes and his face wrinkled in pain. Akira's guilty heart went out to him once more as she stepped toward him.

"Akira, I meant every word in my letter. I want ye to know how sorry I am for the way I acted, and that I'll always love ye no matter what."

Akira started toward Elliot again, but he stopped her. "Save him! Ye're taking the last of my strength to argue with ye."

She choked down her sobs as she backed away from him.

"I've a horse tied to a tree on the other side of the field. Go get him and put the lad on his back."

Akira ran to do his bidding. She rode the horse back and slid down his side to the ground. Akira struggled to lift Sim over her shoulders as she hoisted him with all her might onto the animal's back. She worked to situate Sim's body just right, hoping she wouldn't jar his head wound worse. He had grown heavy with muscle because of his training over the past few months.

Once she felt comfortable with Sim's position, she turned back to her brother. "I love ye, Elliot. I'll be back before ye know it." She mounted up in front of Sim. Akira listened to the stillness, sparing only a few precious moments to see if he responded, but there was no reply. She prayed he'd only fallen asleep or was too stubborn to answer.

Her muscles ached and she felt weary to the bone, but she kept going. She couldn't stop just because of fatigue. Elliot lay alone in the wilderness with God only knew what animals to prey upon him without the strength to protect himself. And she would forever be partly responsible. The thought of her own folly caused a lump to rise in her throat, but she forced it down and concentrated on what she had to do.

By the time she reached the castle she looked a mess and the guards didn't recognize her. They shouted for her to give her name. Akira tried to answer them as best she could, but her throat felt dry. She ended up sounding more like a croaking frog.

"Lady MacPhearson?" One of them recognized her after all.

Her energy drained from the summer heat and the morning's events, Akira nodded as fresh tears stung her eyes. She took a deep breath, thankful she was almost there. She glanced behind her, but couldn't tell if Sim still breathed. *Please let him live, Lord. And keep Elliot safe and alive.* The gate slowly opened.

They sounded the MacPhearson alarm. She urged Elliot's horse forward. Bryce's men rushed to meet her. The ranking warrior ordered someone to find Bryce, Angus, and Father

Forbes. Someone lifted Sim from the horse. She fought with a warrior who tried to lift her up.

"Nay! Nay!" she shouted, but her cries were muffled and hardly heard. "Bryce!" She kept calling his name over and over.

"What happened?"

Akira barely recognized Balloch as she lifted her tired eyes in the direction of his voice. She held her arms out to him, and tears of relief flowed so incoherently, he couldn't understand a word she said. Balloch lifted her into his strong arms and carried her off.

"My brother," she whispered.

"What?" Balloch bent his head closer to her, trying to understand. When she didn't repeat herself he continued rushing toward the castle. "There will be war over this, and if Bryce doesn't kill the one who did this, then I surely will."

The mention of killing sent her into hysterics as she struggled against him. Balloch almost dropped her. "I've got to go back to my brother." Akira jerked from him and searched wildly around her. "Sim?"

"Akira, they carried him upstairs. Angus is looking after him. He must also see ye as well."

"Nay. There's no time." She backed out of reach, shoving her tangled mass of curls out of her face. "I must go to Elliot. I won't rest until I do."

"Akira!" Bryce called to her. She looked to the stairs leading into the castle, waiting for him to show himself. He ran out the double doors and stopped in his tracks when he saw her. "Akira?" Bryce looked uncertain.

"Aye, Bryce." She nodded. "'Tis me."

He rushed to her then. "What happened?" She looked down at herself, realizing what he must think with all the blood and dirt covering her. Akira held her hands out in front of her, and it was like seeing them for the first time.

"'Tis not my blood." She saw the confusion in her husband's eyes and realized his fear. "I haven't been harmed. My dream of Sim came to pass, but I didn't see the danger for Elliot. We must go to him. He will die if we do not."

"What does Elliot have to do with all this?" His suspicious tone made her fear for Elliot if his men were to go after him without her.

"I'll explain on the way, but right now we have no time to waste. I must go to him. If he dies, 'twill be my fault. Bryce, ye've got to help me," Akira pleaded, clutching his shirt in her fingers and twisting it against his chest.

"I canna leave Sim. He's struggling with his verra life." Bryce choked the words out as if in agony.

"Balloch will come with me." She glanced behind Bryce to make sure Balloch still stood there. He wore a confused and concerned expression with his fists on his hips.

"Ye'll go nowhere. I forbid ye to leave my side again. I've nearly lost ye more times than I care to think on."

"At this moment, I would gladly give up my life for that of Elliot's."

"Akira, don't be a fool. Ye're distraught and ye don't know what ye're saying." Bryce tried to coax her toward the stairs, but she shoved him away.

"Ye don't understand. I am a fool!" she cried. "'Tis because of me that Elliot lies in a pool of his own blood, stabbed by my sword. He tried to save us from an attacker and tripped and fell into my sword. He insisted I bring Sim home and come back for him. Bryce, I've got to go back for Elliot. I canna allow him to die any more than ye can allow Sim to die."

The struggle in his expression showed him wrestling with indecision. He closed his eyes and growled. "Ready my horse. I'll check on Sim one more time and then we'll leave." Bryce and Balloch exchanged a look above her head.

"Ye stay with Sim, but I want at least a dozen men I can trust to come with us in case of an ambush."

Bryce swung Akira into his arms and headed for the nearest wash basin. After she had swallowed a glass of water and most of her face, hands, and arms were clean, Bryce returned from visiting Sim's chamber. The lad still had not awakened. Angus and Finella tended to him.

Akira and Bryce rode Ahern through the open gates and over the drawbridge. Twelve warriors accompanied them. They traveled fast and hard, reaching the field of daisies in record speed. She scanned the area, searching for a glimpse of her brother lying in the tall grass where she had left him.

He was gone.

Her heart beat faster as she jumped from her husband's hold, down the side of Ahern, and ran past the rock where Sim had fallen to the place where she knew Elliot should have been. Akira fell to her knees searching the area. Her hand slipped into the soft puddle of blood lying hidden beneath the tall grass that had cradled her brother's body only a short while ago.

Bryce moved to her side and pulled his plaid from his shoulders to wipe her hand clean, his grip gentled as he avoided her eyes. He turned to his men. "Search the area. He couldn't have gone far if he's wounded. Check for signs of other riders in case someone came for him."

They scattered in different directions, their destriers charging past her. Akira's head felt so heavy, and her shoulders seemed to be carrying a mountain full of stones. Her chest tightened until it felt like no air would be able to move in and out of her lungs. She touched her hand to her breast, gasping.

"Akira?" Bryce wrapped his arm around her shoulders.

"'Tis Elliot's blood, the life of his body, and I took it from him."

15

"Tis not true." Bryce reached for her chin, but she turned her head from him, unwilling to be comforted.

"Aye, it is," she said.

"Akira, someone could have taken him. I don't see a trail of blood, so more than likely, his wound was bound and someone carried him home."

She sat up on her knees. "Elliot said I didn't see the demon behind me. By the time I turned around, whoever he saw was gone, but not before he struck Sim where he fell and hit his head on the rock." Akira looked at Bryce with a new fire of determination in her eyes. "Elliot said he wore a mask. Whoever it was could have taken Elliot." New worry creased the frown already etched across her face. "Bryce, we must find him."

"My men are already looking, Akira. We canna do more than that." He squeezed her shoulders in a warm, reassuring hug. "I promise ye, we'll find the man, and when we do, he'll pay for all the pain he's caused the both of us. Ye know I do all I can to keep my promises."

"Aye, I know," she said. "Someone could be deliberately trying to cause a war between the two clans."

Bryce stroked his chin in thought. Silence fell between them and lengthened as they both considered the possibilities. "I'm convinced of a conspiracy. I didn't believe the deaths of Tavis or Mirana were accidental, and now I'm certain of it."

Akira glanced up at him. "Someone is either trying to weaken ye by hurting Sim and me, or trying to provoke ye to fight. We canna stand for it."

"They know me well enough to know I love ye. The MacKenzies think I'm a barbarian, but the MacPhearsons know what kind of man I really am."

"Love is as hard to hide as hate."

"How do ye know what kind of evil lurks beneath the skin of a man? There is evil all around me, threatening to destroy all that I love, and I canna even see it. No one could get so close to me if I didn't trust them. Yer life could be in mortal danger, Akira. I want ye to keep yer sword with ye at all times. I trust yer skill with it. I would lock ye up if I thought it would protect ye, but being locked away didn't protect Mirana."

Guilt consumed her again. "Bryce, I don't have my sword. I threw it down after I pulled it out of Elliot, and I didn't pick it back up when I carried Sim home. Now I canna find it. It's disappeared with Elliot."

Bryce pulled a large hunting knife from the scabbard at his side. The blade sparkled in the sunlight. Momentary fear curdled his gut. What if the man overpowered her and wrestled it from her? He dismissed the concern. She was better off with something than nothing.

"Keep this with ye and don't hesitate to use it if ye must to protect yer life. Trust no one, lass. I don't care how well ye think ye know them." He thrust it back in his scabbard, untied it from the belt around his waist, and handed it to her. "Hide it. Ye'll be safer if no one knows ye carry it."

"Bryce—"

"Shush." He placed his finger over her lips. "I won't let anyone take ye from me if I can help it."

"But, I have something to tell ye."

"We must go." He pulled her up by her hand and led her to Ahern.

"'Tis important!" Akira hastened to keep up with his pace.

"M'lord!" One of his men called as he guided his horse toward them. "We found something."

His warriors found recent tracks of another horse nearby. For several miles they followed the tracks until the late afternoon when it began to rain, cooling off the summer heat. It ended their search. The tracks seemed to be heading toward the direction of the MacKenzie holdings, but it neither proved nor disproved their suspicions.

By the time they reached MacPhearson Castle, their clothes were soaked through and Akira so weary she would have fallen from Ahern's back if Bryce hadn't held on to her. He dismounted, keeping a firm hand on her.

"Take me to Sim," she mumbled, as he gathered her in his arms and pulled her down.

"Ye need rest, lass," he said softly in her ear.

"Nay, I need peace from my dreams, and sleep will not bring it." She buried her face in the crook of his shoulder as Bryce paused over the threshold nodding for Balloch to follow them. "Please, take me to Sim."

Bryce could have ignored her request and taken her to their chamber as he thought best, but he took her to Sim's chamber instead. She was grateful, rewarding him with a weak smile. His heart lifted at the small gesture. He set her on her feet. She leaned over Sim, stroking a lock of hair across his forehead.

"He sleeps so soundly. I wonder if he dreams?" For the briefest moment, her lips touched Sim's forehead. She lifted his hand and locked her fingers with the lad's. His wife would make an excellent mither.

Balloch appeared in the threshold. "The lad hasn't woken at all."

"What does Angus say?" Bryce asked, glancing over at the sleeping physician, sitting uncomfortably in a chair beside Sim's bed.

"He's afraid ye'll kill him if Sim dies," Balloch answered honestly.

Bryce rolled his eyes and crossed his arms over his chest. "What has he said about Sim's condition?"

"He says that head wounds are hard to tell. He could wake up and not remember what happened, or he might not remember his own name. The worst possibility is that he may never wake up. The important thing is that the wound in his head has stopped bleeding, so it will now begin to heal."

Akira nearly dozed. Her arm fell off the bed and her head jerked, slightly startled. She had slid to her knees, leaning over the bed.

"Woman, ye won't listen to reason." Bryce bundled her in his arms. "What good will ye be to the lad if ye collapse yerself?"

Bryce turned to Balloch. "Sim is to have someone here at all times. No one but ye, Kian, or Rae is to stand guard inside this chamber. And I want someone stationed outside the door. I'm taking Akira to bed where she belongs."

Akira folded her letter to her father and sealed it with the MacPhearson seal. She wrote his name on the outside and marked it urgent.

Rain poured as she made her way through the courtyard. She cuddled her letter between her bosom and her arms to keep it from being ruined. Blinking several times to see, she nearly missed the mail carrier as he mounted his horse and rode away.

"Wait! I've a letter!" she called. Either he didn't hear, or he simply ignored her. "Please!"

Fearing she would miss him, Akira ran. She couldn't afford to fail. She must inform her father before he discovered the news from someone else. Her feet splashed through the thick mud puddles, ruining the hem of her dress by the time she caught up with him.

At least he had slowed. She reached up and pulled on his arm, while still clutching her letter protectively under her other arm.

"I've a letter that must go with ye."

The thin man looked down at her. Irritation burned in his dark gaze. "Hurry, lass! 'Tis bad enough I'll have to ride all night in this mess."

She thrust the letter at him. As she feared, the rain seeped into the fragile parchment before he could slip it into his leather bag. "Thank ye." Akira forced a smile, blinking uncontrollably as the water poured into her eyes.

He rode off. She covered her face with her arms as the horse kicked up mud in her direction. Akira turned to rush back inside, but her feet slid. She swung her arms wide in an attempt to keep her balance. Akira groaned as she felt herself going down. Two strong hands gripped her around the waist and hauled her against a hard body.

She gasped as she turned, gazing into a pair of dark gray eyes. She cleared her throat, unsure of her husband's intent as he stared at her with raindrops running down his face, his eyes rapidly blinking.

"What is so important that ye must chase the mail carrier out into the rain?"

"I wrote to Da." She crossed her arms and looked up at him, ready to defend herself if he thought it a silly notion.

"What is so important about that particular letter?" He pointed in the mail carrier's direction with his black brows raised in question. She licked her lips in thought, tasting the sweet water fresh from the sky. Why did he have to make her feel like a child caught at doing something she shouldn't be doing? "I thought to warn him of what I did to Elliot. Da should hear it from me first. I wanted a chance to tell my version of the story."

"Ye've already judged yerself guilty of his death?" Bryce raised a black brow. He sighed wearily. "Lass, if the stab wound was in the side as ye claim, then most likely, he isn't dead, merely wishing he were at the moment."

"Well, we canna know for sure, can we, since he's nowhere to be found."

"Ye neglected to tell me why Elliot was here in the first place. How did ye know he would be there?"

She hesitated. After Elliot disappeared, Akira planned to tell Bryce about the letter. But since then, it seemed less important. Now she wondered if he would be angry with her.

At her hesitation, he sighed wearily and his shoulders hunched forward in disappointment. His expression grew grim and bleak with sorrow as he watched her, waiting. When the sound of the downpour grew heavier between them, he started to reach for something tucked in his folded plaid.

"He wrote to me." Akira's voice stilled his hand in mid-motion and he seemed strained as he patiently listened to the rest of her explanation. "I would have told ye sooner, but he specifically asked me not to." She reached for his hands and squeezed them. "Bryce, ye've got to understand that he didn't want me to tell ye because he feared ye wouldn't let him meet with me."

Silence lengthened between them.

"Elliot wanted to meet alone with me, but his letter didn't say why. It only hinted of danger and that he trusted no one. He didn't think ye would believe him after his reaction to our marriage." She pulled his hands to her lips. "I'm sorry if I hurt ye."

Relief poured into his expression faster than the rain beating down upon their wet heads. "How did Sim happen to be there?"

"We were swimming, and he wanted to sword fight afterward. I kept telling him I had to be somewhere. He wouldn't leave, and before I knew it, Elliot arrived."

"Ye were to meet in that field then?"

"Aye." Her voice grew heavy with the weight of guilt she bore. "I'm sorry I made the wrong decision. I thought I should at least hear what he had to say. I was scared that he wouldn't talk to me if ye came, and I too feared ye wouldn't let me meet him alone if ye knew. Now I realize that if ye'd been there, he and Sim might not have been hurt." She paused, and another more frightful thought occurred to her. "Or it might have been ye who was wounded instead!" she gasped, covering her mouth with her hand.

"Ye made the right decision in telling me now." Bryce paused. "I have a confession to make of my own. When ye were gone from yer chamber, I noticed ye left yer drawer open, and I saw the letter. I picked it up, and I read it. I, too, am sorry."

Stunned, Akira hesitated for a moment, but quickly recovered with a genuine smile of forgiveness. "Then I have another confession." She laughed aloud at his worried frown. "I probably would have done the same thing, so consider yerself warned."

His face relaxed into a wide grin, his tense body easing.

"I love ye, Bryce MacPhearson." Leaning up on her tiptoes, she wrapped her arms around his neck.

Bryce pulled back from her and gazed into her eyes. "I sought ye because I have a favor to ask. Will ye take a turn watching Sim while I collect a few men to send a messenger to yer Da?"

"But—"

"Ye should trust in me more." Bryce touched the tip of her wet nose. "I planned to send a messenger to him concerning Elliot. A messenger will reach him much faster than a letter carrier would, and I didn't just want to send anyone. Whoever hurt Sim could still be lurking about, and I wanted someone capable of handling the unexpected."

Akira's arms circled around him in gratitude. He picked her up and carted her off. "We are both soaked through and ye need a bath and a change of clothes."

"Not before ye handle yer mission," she insisted.

"Soon after," Bryce agreed, hurrying with her to the castle. "I believe ye've gained a bit of weight," he teased.

She playfully slapped his arm. "Yer a rogue if there ever was one, Bryce MacPhearson."

"Aye, I believe ye have." He pretended to huff and puff his way through the side door.

"Off with ye, m'lord. I've no need of yer insults at the moment. I'm a bit heavy due to this soggy skirt o' mine." She pulled him down by his tunic, giving him one more kiss before sending him on his way.

Akira rushed to Sim's room, greeting Kian outside the door where he stood guard. "If ye were not wearing a skirt and lacking a bit of height, I'd swear I just saw ye pass me not a moment ago." He shook his brown head with a lopsided grin as if he knew a secret about her.

"Ye and the laird match quite nicely, all soggy and wet with yer shoes squishing down the hallway."

"I suppose I must look a sight." Akira blushed, looking down at herself and lifting her muddied hem from the floor.

"A raving beauty." Kian peered intently at her as if he couldn't believe his eyes.

Akira shivered and wrapped her arms around her middle, suddenly feeling the chill of the rain. She looked around her, barely able to see anything in the dark. The castle always seemed so gloomy on cloudy days. "'Tis my turn to sit with Sim."

"Rae will welcome the break."

She stepped into the room, leaving the wooden door ajar, hoping her eyes would adjust to the even gloomier darkness. Burning candles were all that lit the room. The hearth contained no fire as the elevated temperatures didn't require such warmth. "Bryce would like for ye to meet him in the bailey."

"Thank ye, m'lady." Rae bowed and left the chamber, closing the door behind him. Akira turned to look at the still unconscious form on the bed. With it pouring rain outside, she couldn't open the only window in the chamber. It wouldn't provide enough light anyway. Too many dark clouds floated through the sky on this day. She walked over to the logs by the unlit fireplace and pulled one from the pile. She would light as many torches as it would take to brighten this dreadful room.

Satisfied with more light, Akira watched Sim's chest rise and fall with his even breathing.

He looked like he slept, resting through an afternoon nap. Except for the huge bruise on the side of his face, he looked to be only dreaming rather than hovering on the verge of death. A peaceful glow about him mystified her.

Akira tried to imagine what he could be dreaming, but her thoughts kept retreating to one question. Why Sim? He happened to be the one person in the world who seemed incapable of earning an enemy. Had the attacker really been after her and Sim merely in the wrong place at the wrong time?

As the memory of what she had done came crashing back to her, Akira sank to her knees beside the bed, gripping the edge for support. The memory would haunt her for the rest of her days. Elliot had to be alive. Her mind and heart clung to hope. She couldn't bear the thought of his death, much less the responsibility of it. Akira began to pray.

⌁♥

The next morning Akira overheard a disturbing coversation coming from the library as she walked through the great hall. Bryce's voice rose in anger as she hastened to discover the cause. Two other voices echoed with her husband's through the corridor.

"What do ye mean the MacKenzies are on their way?" Bryce demanded.

"M'lord, I jest not. They are armed for battle, at least eighty or more men. I came straight back to warn ye." She recognized Rae's voice.

"Ye didn't give my da the message about Elliot?" Akira asked from the doorway. All eyes turned to her, but she kept her gaze on Rae, waiting for his answer.

"Nay, m'lady. Yer father rides at this very moment armed for battle, and I fear we are his destination."

"Ye think he plans to wage war against his only daughter?" She looked at him as if he were mad. When Rae nodded without hesitation, she felt a need to defend her father's honor.

"That's absurd." She turned to look at Bryce for confirmation, but he wasn't looking at her. He kept his back to them, staring out the window as if the fresh air would help him reason through their words.

"M'lady, he already knows about yer brother and he's fighting mad about it. 'Twould have been a wasted effort to give 'im the message."

"But how could ye be so sure?" she demanded. "Just because they're armed and heading this way doesn't mean they aim to attack us." She looked to Bryce again, but he offered no assistance. Why wouldn't he defend her father? He knew they had made an agreement before both clans, and no highlander of his word would break it—least of all Birk MacKenzie. "How do ye know he doesn't come asking Bryce to join forces with him against another enemy?"

Rae rolled his eyes heavenward as if asking for divine patience. "M'lady, their faces were painted for warfare and their destriers dressed for battle. They fly the MacKenzie crest, and they are chanting war songs against the MacPhearsons."

"Ye were close enough to hear them?" Bryce turned from the window.

"Aye, I was. An' I tell ye, we must prepare." He raised his fist.

To Akira's surprise Bryce didn't contradict him.

"Is it true?" Kian quietly asked from the entrance.

"Of course not." Akira whirled on him. "Tell them, Bryce," she demanded, but he didn't speak up. He averted his gaze. "Tell them." Appalled that he wouldn't stand with her, Akira marched over to his desk and slammed her fist against the surface. "Tell them, Bryce," she said through clenched teeth.

Calmly he lifted his gaze, and her heart broke.

"Nay," he said.

Akira straightened, blinking as if she'd been slapped in the face. Shock reverberated through her system as she searched her mind for an appropriate response that wouldn't sound disobedient.

"I canna promise what I do not know." Bryce turned to the men behind her. "I'll wait to see if he comes as an enemy or as family."

Rae jumped forward. "M'lord, ye know what that means if we don't prepare for the worst."

"Rae's right." Kian snorted with disgust.

Balloch remained silent, staring at the floor.

Akira, slightly recovered from her shock, felt relieved that he planned to at least give her father the benefit of the doubt.

"Thank ye," she murmured, still angry that he didn't think Rae's accusations against her father were false. "They are family," she couldn't help adding as she turned to glare at Rae.

"What will ye do if he attacks?" Balloch finally asked.

Akira watched Balloch, wounded that he would even have to voice the question aloud, but her friend avoided her gaze, staring at Bryce.

"I suppose we shall prepare for battle," Bryce reluctantly said, sighing. He rubbed his eyebrows.

Akira glared at her husband, but she knew he avoided her gaze on purpose. Her ears rang with warning. She couldn't believe the lot of them. Her husband most of all.

"Then? Not now?" Rae questioned, not bothering to hide his distrust in Bryce's decision. "Why not invite them to burn the castle down? We haven't even finished the repairs." He looked up at the ceiling as if questioning the justice of it all.

Akira realized he honestly believed her father planned to attack them. Icy fear twisted up her spine. She shivered.

"Bryce, there must be some mistake." She approached him around the desk. "Da wouldn't attack us for naught. I'm his only daughter. He knows I could be killed."

"Akira," Kian said, shaking his head. "A daughter is important to a man when she is to wed and that is all. I don't want to hurt ye, lass, but ye're a MacPhearson now, or have ye forgotten?" The subtle implication was hard to ignore, but she managed.

"Balloch, reason with him. He won't listen to me." She ignored Kian, pointing at Bryce.

"Akira, ye must be reasonable. Bryce is chief of our clan. If yer father attacks, he will be forced to defend his people. He has sworn to protect them. 'Tis the way it is." Balloch's sympathetic expression didn't appease her.

"All of ye are mad." She glanced around the room at them. "How dare ye not give him the respect he deserves?"

Bryce whirled from the window in one swift motion and slammed his hands on his desk, leaning foward. "I have. I wait until he comes, to see with my own eyes whether he will attack or come as family. And understand me well, Akira MacPhearson. That is more courtesy than I have ever extended to any man. If he plans to attack and I've made no preparations, 'twill take a miracle to survive. Do ye understand, lass? I'm giving yer father more than I'm giving my own people, so don't tell me I owe him aught."

They stared at each other for a long moment. No one in the room dared to make a sound. Their fierce breathing was all that could be heard, although Akira felt certain Bryce could hear her pounding heart. It sounded so loud to her own ears that she thought her blood would pump straight out of her head.

She turned and stomped from the room, leaving the ill-bred heathens to weave a web of their own making. She would be no part of it.

Bryce closed his eyes, rubbing his face as his wife fled in anger. The look on her face had pierced him through, but he couldn't give her more than he'd offered her at the expense of his clan.

Rae turned to him. "I didn't want to say this in front of Akira, but Elliot is dead."

Bryce grew concerned and walked around his desk toward Rae. "Are ye sure? How do ye know?"

"I trailed them. They were traveling fast, but I managed to hear of his death. They talked of the MacPhearson sword that took his life. I saw Birk MacPhearson studying it often. The man is deeply grieved. His other son, Gavin, is riding with him and is much the same. There is no telling what they'll do when they arrive."

Bryce considered this bit of news. "I appreciate yer saying naught about it in front of Akira. But I need to know everything. What else did ye hear? How did they find him?"

"Gavin said someone had dragged his body to the gates."

Bryce listened and let his mind wonder over the possibilities.

"There's something else." Rae hesitated.

"What is it?" Bryce motioned him to continue with a feeling of dread centering in the pit of his stomach.

"The mail carrier ran into them and camped with them the night they stopped. He gave Akira's letter to her father.

I watched from the woods as he read the letter, crumpled it up, and threw it into the campfire. Then he stood shouting in grief." Rae stopped, as if to gauge Bryce's reaction. Bryce nodded for him to continue. "That's when they began chanting against the MacPhearsons. I rode through the night, but they aren't far behind. They're pushing their destriers hard."

Bryce remained silent while the room grew increasingly tense. The sudden chill in the air wasn't imagined when Bryce swiftly lifted an empty goblet and threw it across the room. He gave Rae an intense look that would make any man's skin crawl. "If ye lie, I'll come to know the truth and ye'll wish ye hadn't. Are ye telling the truth of Birk MacKenzie's reaction to Akira's letter?"

Rae nodded. He swallowed uneasily. "Aye, 'tis the truth."

16

The alarm sounded at the entrance gate to the castle. Akira halted in the corridor, uncertain what to do, and rashly decided to run the other way. She would greet her father. There was no reason why she should assume he was there for naught else but a visit. The sound of the alarm bell tolled again, but it made no difference as she stepped into the courtyard and dodged through her husband's warriors arming themselves and hastening to their posts.

Akira couldn't hear her father's approaching army for all the noise within the castle gates.

"The MacKenzies look as though they plan to ride right through the walls!" a warrior shouted.

Fear seized her as she slipped through the doorway leading to the tower stairs, hoping no one would notice. Akira ran up the steps as fast as she could. She had to get to the top so her father could see her. Maybe he would cease in his anger if he saw a glimpse of her.

When she reached the top of the tower she paused, gasping to catch her breath. Then she shoved her way toward the edge. Only one more step, and she could lean over the stone wall and see him. A guard stepped in front of her, blocking her view.

"M'lady, I canna allow ye any closer. M'lord has ordered yer safety. I must follow orders. Ye must go back to the keep."

"Nonsense, I merely wish to greet my da like any loving daughter would." She straightened her shoulders and met his stubborn gaze.

"Ye may greet him when he makes it plain that greetings are all he plans to bestow upon us. The chieftain is on his way, and he'll decide."

"Move out of my way," Akira yelled above the surrounding noise.

The warrior simply crossed his arms and shook his head. "I canna."

Before she could yell an insult, the doorway to the tower stairs burst open and her husband strode purposely toward her. He gripped her arm in a fierce hold and pulled her along.

"Ow! Ye're hurting me, Bryce." She stumbled to keep up with him as he pulled her off to the side. He stopped and jerked her around to face him. His jaw clenched, and she knew by the fierce dark clouds swirling in his eyes that he was angry beyond belief. Akira swallowed convulsively, but she determined to be brave and face him. What had she done other than try to keep peace between him and her father, the two men she loved beyond anything in life?

"Ye've betrayed me, haven't ye?" he growled, careful to keep his voice low, ignoring the looks they received from his men.

Akira shook her head in denial, unsure of what he meant. Bryce jerked her arm so tight behind her back that any squirming would cause intense pain.

"Whatever ye told yer father in that letter caused this. Ye've endangered hundreds of lives."

"What are ye talking about?" She couldn't think of anything in her letter that would cause her father to come barreling upon them in an act of war.

"Bryce, I promised ye my allegiance. I love ye. I would never betray ye. Something else happened, but 'tis naught to do with me."

"Don't speak to me of love," he snarled. "How can I believe ye now?" His cold eyes raked over her face in disgust.

She shriveled from his hateful words and loathsome expression. None of what he said made sense. Akira tried to reason it all out, but she had no time to question him further. Her father's angry voice bellowed from below.

"Bryce MacPhearson!" Birk MacKenzie called.

Bryce gave her one more scathing look that cut her to the core before pointing a finger in her face. "Don't move from this spot until I know his intent." He released her arm, and she rubbed her aching muscles with her other hand, glaring after him. "If ye disobey me, ye'll be sorry," he warned over his shoulder.

"I'm already sorry," Akira whispered to his back as she stood staring after him. Birk MacKenzie called for Bryce once more. Bryce reached the edge of the tower wall and leaned over the side to greet his father-in-law.

"Good day, Birk MacKenzie. Have ye finally come for a visit with yer family?"

"Bryce MacPhearson! Ye owe me an explanation, and I plan to have it this day or I'll tear down what's left of yer castle walls."

Her grief over her husband's treatment temporarily forgotten, Akira concentrated on her father's words. They left no doubt her father harbored deep anger and that he directed it toward Bryce, but why? And why would Bryce think she had betrayed him? What had happened? Akira listened to a flurry of motion and heard what sounded like a sword being unsheathed. She nearly forgot Bryce's orders and took a step forward, but her father's voice halted Akira in her steps.

"Do ye deny this is a MacPhearson sword with the MacPhearson crest on the handle?"

"Nay, even from this distance it looks like ours. Where did ye get it?"

℘

Birk's eyes grew bitter and his face turned red from rage. "I pulled it from my son's verra own heart." He lifted the sword and threw it up in the air where it flipped several times, and the tip of the blade landed in the ground. "It still carries the stain of Elliot's blood."

Alarmed, Bryce breathed deeply and tried to still his fast beating heart. He'd never gone into battle with the Lord on his mind and in his heart, but today might be the first day, though he prayed not. He gripped the stone rail and closed his eyes.

"Lord, give me wise words and help me prevent war with Akira's family this day," he whispered. Bryce opened his eyes and leaned forward, pointing to the ground. "I'm coming down to meet ye!" he called.

Bryce turned to see that Akira had gone completely pale. He felt the urge to comfort her, but there was no time as he strode by her. Could she have been mistaken about Elliot's wound? Mayhap she thought it had been his side, but it had actually been a mortal blow. It was possible she was so grief stricken with guilt that she couldn't admit to her deed, no matter how innocent her intentions might have been.

Even as these thoughts crossed his confused mind, something in him didn't feel right, and he turned to look at her one more time, pausing before the entrance to the tower stairs. She leaned against the tower wall as if all strength bled from her soul, and her spirit lay bare and broken. Her eyes crept to his, and as long as he lived, he would never forget the heart-wrenching sorrow lurking beneath the pool of tears shimmering in her jade eyes. His gut clenched. A weak wail built up through her as she pushed into the wall behind her, as if trying to dissolve right through it. Her vulnerable state tore at his conscience, and he knew in his heart he had wrongly accused her of betrayal. Clearly, she hadn't known Elliot was dead until the moment her father confirmed it. Someone had betrayed him, but it wasn't Akira.

Bryce ripped his gaze from Akira and hurried down the stairs to meet her father. He ached to apologize, but at the moment he knew her grief would be too strong to comprehend any words of sorrow and comfort. Besides, right now he had to try and prevent another war.

At his command, the drawbridge lowered, and he only allowed Birk MacKenzie to cross it. Bryce walked out to meet him. They conversed in the middle of the bridge, speaking in tones too low for the others to hear.

"May I see the sword?" Bryce asked, cautiously holding out his hand. Birk handed it to him, and the pained expression in the older man's eyes reminded him too easily of Akira's. The moment he gripped it, he quickly recognized his gift to his wife. He looked it over carefully, hoping to find a clue as to who else might have used it.

"Do ye know who it belongs to?" Birk's voice interrupted Bryce's concentration.

"Aye." Bryce nodded, regretting to tell him.

"Speak up, man. I'll not have ye protecting a murderer." Birk bellowed in anxious satisfaction. His hands balled into fists at his side. "I'm eager to get my hands on 'im," he growled.

"Before I tell ye, I want to know how many times Elliot was stabbed and where ye found him?"

Birk stood taller and eyed him carefully. "I don't know why ye need to know."

"I want to know everything. This sword belongs to someone in my clan, and I want to know if there is the possibility of others being involved. The guilty will be punished."

"The guilty will die," Birk challenged. He rubbed his chin with his thumb and crossed his arms. He looked Bryce up and down as if to measure his worth and finally growled. "Humph! He was stabbed in the side and through the heart. We found him outside the castle wall at daybreak two days ago. Someone dragged him to the spot right outside the gate." Birk leaned toward Bryce. "Now whose sword is this?"

"Yer daughter's." Bryce waited for the color to come back to the other man's face, and when it did, Birk's eyes grew wide in disbelief. He raised a heavy fist, and it landed on Bryce's jaw. "Ye dare to jest over my son's life?" he yelled with a murderous glare. He swung at Bryce again, but missed the second time when Bryce ducked.

"'Tis no jest." Bryce wiped blood from his lip. "I gave her this sword as a gift. Here." He pulled his own sword from his scabbard and sighed when Birk jumped back out of reach.

Bryce held the two beside each other. "I had it made smaller for her."

"Are ye saying Akira killed Elliot?" He looked at Bryce as if he had gone mad.

"Akira was supposed to have sent ye a letter explaining what she knew. Did ye get it?"

"Aye, I received it from a messenger the day before. Akira wounded Elliot in the side, not in the heart." Birk took a moment to collect his thoughts and compose himself. "Elliot was strong and healthy. He would have survived Akira's wound. 'Twasn't a mortal wound."

Bryce was relieved that she hadn't betrayed him as Rae thought and felt guilty for wrongly accusing her. He swallowed with difficulty and turned to Birk.

"After Akira accidentally stabbed Elliot, she dropped her sword. When we returned for Elliot, both he and the sword were missing without a trace. Akira didn't see the person attacking them from behind, but Elliot told her 'twas a man with a mask. My younger brother, Sim, might have seen him, but Sim is deaf and mute. And right now he is still unconscious from a head wound he received from the villain."

"I want to see Akira," Birk demanded.

"She isn't well right now." Bryce hoped Birk would agree to leave her alone.

"What do ye mean? What's wrong with her?"

"She didn't know Elliot was dead until ye yelled it awhile ago. She didn't take the news verra well."

"No woman does." Birk waved his hand in the air as a dismissal. "Nara cries often."

A frown creased Bryce's forehead, and he looked at the bloodstained sword still in his hand. "For now, yer men must remain outside the castle walls."

Birk nodded. "Aye."

Bryce waited while Birk returned to his men and dispensed orders. A moment later he rejoined Bryce. They walked over the bridge and through the castle gates. Bryce told one of his men to find Akira for him. He waited until his warrior returned.

"Lady MacPhearson is no longer in the tower."

"She must have returned to the castle. See that she is told to meet us in the library."

Bryce turned to Birk, and they continued to the castle discussing who could have put Elliot's body outside the MacKenzie gates and why. Once they settled in the library, they grew weary of conversing, and each man lapsed into a tense silence. After a considerable amount of time, Bryce excused himself and left to call on his servants.

Finella immediately appeared. "Aye, Bryce?"

"Where's my wife?"

Finella's expression grew concerned. "With all the commotion going on this day, I've not seen her."

He turned around at the sound of booted footsteps and saw Balloch striding toward him. Bryce glanced at Finella still standing behind him.

"Look for her," he ordered, turning his attention to Balloch. "What is it?" he demanded irritably, dreading more bad news.

"The men informed me that ye're looking for Akira."

"And?" Bryce raised black eyebrows, growing increasingly impatient. Why couldn't anyone finish a sentence or a complete thought without him constantly having to prompt them to continue?

"I have twenty men searching the castle and the grounds for her. She's disappeared without a trace."

"That isn't possible," Bryce growled, rubbing his forehead in concentration, and began to pace while Balloch continued. "The guards insist she didn't pass through the gates. I even took the liberty of speaking to Gavin, and he promises she hasn't escaped to see him. In light of the situation with the MacKenzie clan, I didn't know if ye would want me to put more men on the search."

"Twenty more," Bryce said without hesitation. "Akira must be found immediately. There is a murderer in this castle, and I want my wife found."

"Do I take it ye've lost my daughter?" Birk appeared behind Bryce.

Bryce rolled his eyes heavenward and turned, not knowing what to tell the man.

Balloch quietly backed away, leaving him alone to deal with his father-in-law. Bryce paced.

"Nay, I haven't lost her," he finally answered. "She likes to disappear when she's upset."

"Then ye've lost her until ye've found her," Birk corrected, well aware of his daughter's habits. "What do ye mean a murderer is in this castle? Have ye had more deaths?"

"Two deaths here in the last two weeks, and Elliot makes the third. It must be someone I know and trust." Suddenly, Bryce began to laugh at his own folly so hard he doubled over as the stress of it all got the better of him, and he couldn't stop. His eyes began to water until Birk pounded him on the back.

"Lad, now isn't the time to go mad," Birk said harshly.

Bryce pounded his fist into his other hand.

"Ye might want to save yer knuckles for someone else," Birk suggested. "Keep yer wits about ye. I want my daughter found."

Bryce laughed even harder. "'Tis someone I trust, and I was fool enough to even think 'twas Akira. I thought she betrayed me and that's why ye came the way ye did. I doubt she'll be able to forgive me for the things I said."

"Ye better hope she does. Akira's the only reason I've not wasted this place."

"Go ahead. I'll not fight her father. I thought I could, but that's the one thing she'll not forgive me for."

"Where does she like to go to be alone? When she was home, there were particular places we could go to find her if she had disappeared. Think, lad! Think!" Birk demanded.

Bryce paced in circles, trying to think of places within the keep that Akira would go besides the chapel and her chamber, both of which had already been searched.

"Stop pacing. Ye're making me dizzy." Birk rubbed his temples.

Bryce suddenly stopped and looked at Birk. "What if one of the men searching for her is the murderer? I need yer help, Birk." Bryce rushed to Birk's side, fully intent on carrying out a new plan. "I want to pair them up. Each of my men will be paired with one of yers. I don't know how many of mine are involved and yers will surely not hide it if anything goes amiss. 'Tis humiliating, but I don't trust my men right now."

"Ye'll have my help, lad." Birk slapped Bryce on the back. "Excellent plan. We'll pair them up, we will."

Birk went back to his men to discuss the plan with Gavin. Balloch rounded up the MacPhearson men, and they were each paired with a MacKenzie. It appeared that they understood the situation well and were more than willing to watch each other.

Bryce called their attention. "If just one of ye comes back bruised or bleeding, I'll lock ye up in the dungeon, and ye'll not see the light of day until I decide to let ye out. If ye're fighting, ye canna be looking for Akira. Is that clear?" They nodded and were dismissed to their designated search areas.

Several hours later they all returned with no sign of her. By midnight, Bryce grew increasingly worried as the search continued. He sent Balloch and Kian to search the west wing again, while he and Birk searched the east. Gavin headed off to the stables, the courtyard, and the chapel, while Rae checked the second level and Fergus the third.

Sometime early the next morning, Bryce fell asleep, sitting in Akira's chair by her harp in the solar. He dreamed of her on the tower and slept little. What sleep he did manage felt extremely uncomfortable in Akira's small chair. After a couple of hours he woke with a start and rubbed his tired eyes.

Bryce looked at Gavin, who sat across the room, watching him. "I'm going to my bedchamber. She might have gone there when she grew weary." He made his way to the stairs.

To Bryce's disappointment, Akira wasn't in their chamber. He walked over to their bed, running his fingers lightly over the still-made bed.

"Where are ye?" he asked aloud to the empty chamber.

Sighing, he walked over to the wash basin and splashed cold water on his face. He rolled back his sleeves to bathe his arms when he realized he was using Akira's basin. His was on the other side of the room on his dresser. He restrained himself not to shatter something within reach. This desolate emptiness he felt without her grated on his nerves.

His instincts often kept him alive in battle, and this time he knew Akira's disappearance wasn't because she wished it. Danger permeated the air, and he feared for her. Bryce wiped the dripping water from his face as a scream rippled through the quiet morning. He ran down the hall to Sim's room where Finella called his name.

"M'lord! M'lord! He's awakened." She ran toward him.

"Sim's awake?" He felt one burden on his shoulders lift and continued past her.

"He's asking for Akira."

Bryce stopped. "Did ye tell him?"

The color drained from her face as she paused, shaking her head. "Nay, ye don't understand."

Bryce waved a hand. "Never mind. I need to see him."

Finella tugged on his arm. "M'lord, he's speaking. Sim *asked* for her."

"Sim's speaking? Impossible." He looked at her in question. When she nodded, his curiosity outweighed his disbelief, and he hurried to Sim's chamber. He stopped in the doorway, afraid to believe, afraid to hope. Sim struggled to sit up, situating his pillow just right. He didn't notice Bryce at first until he turned. Sim's expression broke into a huge grin. The bruise on the side of his jaw looked fainter.

"I . . . scared . . . ye, heh?"

"'Tis true then, ye're speaking?" Bryce slowly came forward as tears filled his eyes. His voice sounded young, but squeaky like a lad going through the change into manhood. It was both strange and wonderful to hear his brother speak for the first time.

"Aye." Sim nodded his brown head. "Akira . . . taught . . . me."

Bryce narrowed his gaze. "What do ye mean?"

"To . . . speak." Sim touched his throat, patting it. "See?"

Bryce reached out for the bedpost to steady himself. "This is unbelievable." His amazement was contained by the grief and stress of the current situation. "I'm glad yer awake." Bryce pulled a chair closer to his bed and sat down. "The two of ye managed a miracle."

Sim nodded. "Aye." He looked at the entrance and back to Bryce.

"Akira?"

Bryce's smile faded. "I don't know, Sim. She disappeared a day ago."

Sim frowned. His brown eyes clouded with confusion. "Why?"

"I need to know what happened." Bryce leaned toward his brother, still hardly believing he could now carry on a conversation with him. He listened intently while Sim spoke.

Sim's expression wrinkled in concentration as he leaned back against his pillow. With the advent of speech still so new, Sim spoke slowly, sometimes confusing certain words with others or mispronouncing them. He stopped a moment and motioned to the goblet on his dresser.

Bryce got up and handed the goblet to Sim. He drank deeply and gave it back to Bryce. He continued relaying the same story as Akira had told him. Bryce scooted to the edge of his seat as Sim came to the part where he was attacked from behind.

"He . . . m-mask." Sim made a motion as if to pull a mask from his face. He shook his head in disbelief. "Sor-ry."

"Sim, I know someone I trust has betrayed me. I must know who. I believe he's taken Akira."

Sim touched the side of his face, remembering.

"Who was it?" Bryce prompted.

Sim looked at Bryce. "K . . . Kian."

Bryce stood and crossed to the window. He opened it and leaned out, breathing deeply. The betrayal hurt. The day they went back for Elliot, Bryce began to suspect someone close to him, but Balloch or Kian never crossed his mind. He closed his eyes, asking himself why. And most of all, what did Kian hope to gain by taking his wife?

He walked back to the bed and knelt by his younger brother, considering the situation. "Then Kian knows ye know 'twas him, and he's been sharing the responsibility of guarding yer chamber. He's had ample opportunity to put an end to ye if he wanted."

"Mute." Sim covered his mouth with two fingers.

Bryce snapped his fingers. "'Tis true. I still don't know his motive or what he wants." Bryce stood and stretched, raising his arms and yawning. His two hours of sleep would have to do. "We can sit here and try to reason this out all day, but we still won't know his reasons. We know that he's not to be trusted, but what we don't know is who else might be involved." Bryce pointed at Sim. "Ye canna let anyone else know ye can speak. I'll go see who Finella might have already told."

Sim nodded and Bryce ruffled his head.

"Food." Sim called out before Bryce could pass through the threshold.

Bryce turned. "I'll send Finella up with something right after I've talked to her." Bryce placed a finger over his lips and reminded him not to speak. For a lad who had been silent nearly all his life, Bryce knew he was asking for a bit much. "For Akira," Bryce reminded him, and Sim nodded his agreement.

Akira groaned and tried to move, but her hands and feet were bound. The gag between her teeth made her mouth ache, and although she knew her eyes were open, everything looked pitch black. She wiggled on her stomach against the stone floor and ignored the searing pain in her ribs. Someone gripped her hair and yanked her head back.

"Stop that squirmin, lass! Ye'll scare the rats away, and I plan to feed ye to them."

The burning in her scalp ceased when he let her go. *Rats!* her mind screamed. She silently prayed that the man lied and no rats would find her.

In the next instant, he hauled her up and over his shoulder. Her ribs pained her even more as he roughly jostled her along to who knew where. She wiggled forward, trying to move her ribs off his shoulder, but he tightened his grip and held her still.

"Keep that up and I'll throw ye down the rest of the stairs," a familiar voice roared. For a moment, she considered pounding her bound fists into his back, but decided to save her strength for a better opportunity to escape.

She squeezed her eyes shut, trying to remember how she had ended up in this predicament. The last thing she remembered, Bryce had left her in the tower to go down and meet her father. She had no memory beyond that. She did remember that Elliot had been stabbed in the heart. At least she hadn't killed her brother. She could take consolation in that knowledge. Akira vowed she would find out the truth of who murdered him.

Lord, help me. I don't want to die, she prayed in her heart.

An orange light glowed in the direction they headed. Akira lifted her head, trying to peer around her captor's shoulder.

"Be still," he ordered.

The voice sounded so familiar, but she couldn't place it. The orange glow grew brighter, and her captor increased his pace.

"Did ye have any trouble?" a woman asked.

"Nay, of course not." He threw Akira off his shoulder. She landed in a heap on the floor, gripping her aching hip from the impact.

"Oh!" the other woman exclaimed. "But Kian, ye didn't cover her eyes."

A fearful jolt shot through Akira's chest. She glanced up to see if she heard them correctly. Kian stood proudly before her with his heavy arms crossed over his chest, grinning down at her as if he had just won a prize. Her cousin Odara stood by his side with wide, frightened eyes, holding her hand over her mouth, struggling to keep quiet.

"It doesn't matter," Kian said. "She'll not live long enough to talk."

Akira already accepted the fact that they planned to kill her, but what she couldn't have known was that Kian and Odara planned her fearsome fate together. It pained her deeply to know of their betrayal. She would almost rather not have known. And Bryce thought it had been her?

"Did ye kill Elliot?" She dared to ask, but the gag prevented her from coherently forming her words so they could understand her.

Kian's laughter boomed around them. He leaned back as if savoring the moment. "I've waited a long time for this." He turned to Odara. "Remove her gag. I believe I'd like to hear what she has to say and to hear her beg for mercy."

Odara took the knife Kian offered and bent to cut away the gag. Akira kept herself extremely still, giving her cousin no reason to slice her skin.

"What was it ye wanted to know, lass?" Kian put his hand up to his ear, teasing her.

"Did ye kill Elliot?"

"Aye." He seemed to enjoy his sickening humor. "Does that make ye hate me?" He rubbed his hands together.

"Who dragged his body to the MacKenzie gates?"

"Full of questions, are ye?" He shrugged. "Are ye sure ye want to know it all? Mayhap 'twill be too painful."

His blue eyes glazed over, and suddenly, he seemed to be in another world, but he snapped right back out of his momentary trance and grinned at Akira. "I met Odara halfway. I rode all through the day and night. Bryce occupied himself with so many other worries, he hardly missed me. With Balloch always running around to do his bidding, I slipped away unnoticed. Odara conveniently dragged his body to yer father's castle gate."

"Ye wanted it to look like I did it."

"Elliot had two different wounds. I knew they would eventually figure it out, but using yer sword gave them more to consider. It brought a bit more confusion." He seemed proud of all they had accomplished.

"How did ye manage to get Odara to go along?" Akira shot a scathing look at her cousin, who stood faithfully beside him.

"Odara and I have something in common. She despises ye an' so do I."

Akira always knew her cousin disliked her, but she never realized to what degree. Somehow that didn't seem to bother her half as much as Kian's disloyalty to Bryce. "I thought ye liked me, Kian."

"He never did," Odara declared.

"Hush." Kian glanced in Odara's direction, shaking her off his arm and moving to bend toward Akira. "Oh, I like ye just fine for a woman, but not as a MacPhearson or the chieftain's wife." Kian gave her a level stare. "What else do ye want to know?"

"What about Bryce? Where's yer loyalty to him?"

A grin broadened his face. "Well, Bryce has always been there for me and that's why I'm here for him now, when he can no longer make the best decisions for our clan."

"Why do ye believe that?" She moved to sit on her bottom, unable to lean her sore elbow into the stone floor any longer. She grunted as she swung her bound feet around and pushed herself up.

"'Tis simple. 'Tis all because of ye." He looked at her pointedly. "'Twould have been okay to wed ye, so long as he didn't fall in love with ye, but he had to come to care for ye, and that ruined all his plans. 'Twas only supposed to be for convenience." Kian laughed again. "But then, our dear Bryce always believes peace is the best way, and he isn't always right—at least not where the MacKenzies are concerned."

"What about her?" Akira indicated her cousin, who still pouted behind him. "She's a MacKenzie, and yet she's helping ye." Akira could not understand his illogical thinking.

"Aye, and she's only here because she serves my purpose and is a convenience." He paused. "Mirana was convenient as well, until she began to feel guilty, and then she became a threat to my plans."

"I see," Akira murmured, realizing how much imminent danger both she and her cousin were in at the moment. She looked up at Odara and noticed her face had gone quite pale. She clutched her throat and then her stomach. "What's wrong, Odara?"

Kian laughed. "Odara has lost her usefulness to me as well. She's beginning to feel the effects of the poison I slipped into her food earlier." Odara slid to the floor with a hard thump.

Akira tried to hide the panic running wildly through her heart. She stared at Kian, wondering how he could be so cruel. His hair wasn't as dark as Bryce's, but it fell in the same intricate waves to his shoulders. They both had the same square face, but there the resemblance ended. Kian's dark blue eyes bore through her hatred.

"Bryce believes I betrayed him." Akira tried to distract him. If she could prolong their conversation, mayhap Bryce would have time to find her.

Kian lifted her chin. "And ye hate me for making him believe it?"

"Nay," she answered honestly. "I'm angry and hurt that he would believe it so easily." Her heart felt so badly bruised by what Bryce had said that she wasn't sure what she felt anymore. Numbness claimed her feelings; only the physical pain bothered her now. Maybe she could survive this whole ordeal if her body would stop feeling and just go as numb as her heart.

"Why do ye hate my clan so much?" She cocked her head to the side, studying him as he considered her question.

"Do ye know where we are, Akira?" He waved his arms and moved them in a circle, ignoring her question.

She scanned the dingy surroundings and noticed the decaying bars, old clothes lying here and there, scattered rocks, broken cracks, and crevices dancing in the torchlight. The darkness and coldness seemed to enter her senses more than anything—that and the foul smell filling her nostrils. "The dungeon?"

"Aye." Kian grew anxious. "The west wing dungeons are nearly thirty feet below ground. Not even Bryce has been down here since we were children. He's probably forgotten about them."

"Why do ye plan to kill me? I thought Bryce was yer friend?"

"Bryce and I have been close friends since we were small lads, but he's forgotten that MacKenzies canna be trusted. Evan isn't here to remind him of that. Sim canna speak and lend him support. So in a sense Balloch and I are his only family. I've taken matters into my own hands. I intend to exact revenge against yer family." He leaned forward.

Disliking his closeness, Akira forced herself to continue facing him. "Killing me is yer revenge?" She swallowed a lump in her throat and hoped he would have some compassion for her.

"Not even yer life is enough to exact revenge for what the MacKenzies have caused." His voice lowered to a dangerous pitch. How could a person be so crafty at hiding their true inner self as Kian had done? And how should she deal with him?

"Kian, I don't want to die. Why not accept peace between the MacPhearsons and the MacKenzies?" She searched his blue eyes for a sign of the Kian she thought she had known.

"Birk MacKenzie killed my da in battle. I saw it. 'Twas my first time in battle, and I've never forgotten it. I'm taking ye because I want Birk to pay, and that's why I killed Elliot. Gavin will be next."

"I'm sorry about yer father," Akira said sincerely. "But, there is naught ye can do that will bring him back or change what happened."

"Birk will come for ye," he persisted. Akira dared to breathe and licked her dry lips.

"Nay." She shook her head. "If that were true, then he would have come for me when Bryce took me. He's only here now because of Elliot. 'Tis no secret that a son is worth much more to a father than his daughter. Yer the one that reminded me of that just the other day." Her heart wasn't as numb as she had hoped; the truth in her words pierced her soul. "Ye know that as well as I." She hated the trembling in her voice, but the encompassing pain and fear overwhelmed her ability to remain calm. Her chest constricted, and she bent her knees, determined not to concentrate on that pain right now. She had more immediate problems to deal with—like how to survive this madman. Akira blinked back the tears, summoning the inner strength she prayed still existed inside her.

Kian released her with a sigh and rose, pacing the small area. "Hush, lass. I don't have much patience for weeping women."

He turned away, but not before she glimpsed the tenderness he desperately wanted to hide from her. She half-crawled and half-wiggled over to him.

"Kian, look at these hands." She thrust her palms out to him. "These hands have never harmed a soul. I canna say the MacKenzies are angels, and I won't say that I'm one, but I can say I've never harmed a MacPhearson. I'm sorry for what my father did, but these hands are not responsible. Making these hands bleed or cease to exist will not bring yer da back, and 'twill not make ye feel any better."

He took her trembling hands in his and rubbed his thumb over her knuckles. For several moments he didn't say anything as he stared at them. Akira watched him closely, still unable to read his expression. If she must die, she wished for a quick death. *But Lord, I'd rather live. Please help me*, she pleaded silently.

Without warning, Kian pulled a knife from the belt at his side and brought it down to her hands. Akira winced, thinking the blade would slice right through her skin. She held her breath as the blade slid through the bonds around her wrists. Akira glanced down at her feet still bound by the rope.

"Yer feet will stay bound."

One victory at a time, she reminded herself. Gain his confidence and trust, and then use it against him.

"Ye know too much, and I still don't trust ye," Kian said.

"We've been gone too long for Bryce not to have noticed. He'll come looking for us. What do ye plan to do then? Will ye fight Bryce as well?"

"I'm loyal to Bryce. 'Tis for him that I do this. I only need ye to lure Birk MacKenzie down here."

"Do ye honestly think that Bryce will not be involved? He'll try and stop ye."

"Aye, I'm aware of that. I have a plan for Bryce if all goes well."

Kian moved to pick up Odara's lifeless body, as if she were nothing more than a rag doll. He carried the corpse to the wall on the other side and dropped her on the hard stone floor. He pushed on several stones, loosening them one by one, until they revealed another room.

Akira's curiosity grew, and she hopped over to him. "What's back there?"

He pulled another stone loose. She leaned forward. Did he plan to put her back there with Odara's body?

"What will ye do?" Her whispered voice sounded childlike to her ears as she swallowed, trying to keep from fainting.

"This is where we'll bury Odara." He turned to her with an evil grin. "This castle has many secrets."

Her pale face probably glowed in the torchlight. She couldn't possibly hide her growing fear. *God, please help me,* she thought, trying not to panic. Akira took several deep breaths to steady her racing heart.

Kian grunted as he pulled another stone loose. "These stones are heavy, but sturdy and very useful." He chuckled.

A chill surrounded Akira as she looked into the dark hole. Kian was insane. It could be hours before anyone found them. She wouldn't allow herself to think beyond hours. She glanced down at Odara's corpse and decided she didn't want to end up like her cousin.

Bryce went to their chamber to think. He didn't know if any of his other men were privy to Kian's scheme, but with Birk's men teamed up with his, no one would be out of anyone's sight for long.

He thought long and hard, racking his brain for clues as to where Kian might have taken Akira. He went back to the tower where she was last seen and searched for missing clues that didn't seem to exist. He searched Kian's chamber, to no avail.

Bryce knelt by their box bed in a position of prayer. He prayed for guidance, but now he held one of Akira's nightgowns as if cherishing her memory. Sensing he wasn't alone, he looked up through sleepless eyes that felt tired and swollen.

Sim stood in the threshold, watching him. "F-find . . . her," Sim said, walking into the chamber. Bryce said nothing, only wadded Akira's gown in his hands and brought it against his cheek. The scent of lavender assailed him, burning a hole in his heart that he feared would never be mended.

"I was mean to her." Bryce closed his eyes, remembering her pained expression on the tower. "I accused her of betraying me."

Bryce squeezed her nightgown into a ball. "I was wrong, and I knew I was wrong, but I didn't take the time to tell her." He dropped his head and buried his face in her garment. His shoulders shook with the force of his pent-up frustration and grief. Bryce made no sound, holding it all in.

Sim hurried to his side and touched his shoulder. "Akira . . . knows."

Bryce stood with her gown still in his hands and turned from Sim to hide his face. He walked to the window. Where else could he look? He had searched every room that he knew existed in the castle. Suddenly, his mind snapped to the past. Yes, he'd searched all the rooms, but there was one place he'd forgotten about.

"The tunnels in the dungeon!" Bryce whirled from the window with renewed hope. He repeated what he'd said for Sim's sake. "There are dungeons in the west wing where Kian and I played as lads. Da condemned them and wouldn't allow us back down there. At the time he didn't have the funds to repair the west wing, so he simply forbade us from going down. He boarded up several areas. That must be where Kian's taken Akira." Bryce moved to the door and motioned for Sim to follow.

He shouted to anyone within hearing distance as he descended the stairs. One by one his men returned with Birk's men. Bryce ordered Balloch and Sim to light torches while he explained how they would conduct the search in the west wing dungeons.

Akira wanted to scream, but it was no use. No one would hear her down here. Kian had chained her in one of the cells, and now he held a whip. He slapped it against the floor. She jerked, hating the thought and fear of it slicing through her flesh.

"How do ye think this will feel against yer skin?" he taunted her.

She winced from the pain in her ribs. Her arms ached in the chains. Her stomach growled with hunger. How sad that her life would end here and now like this.

Kian slapped the whip against the floor, and she jumped. The sound echoed through the dungeon.

"Hear that, Akira?" He had no reason to intimidate her further, but he seemed to enjoy a sickening pleasure from it. "I imagine that's going to hurt that pretty soft flesh of yers." He moved closer.

In her mind she screamed, *Jesus! Jesus! Help me! Please don't let him torture me like this.*

"Well, let's see then." He moved his arm back, poised, ready to strike.

Akira closed her eyes, gritted her teeth, and braced for the pain, but it never came.

"Let's do," another voice said, echoing around them. She thought she must be dreaming.

Kian had already swung his arm, but Bryce intercepted, moving just in time to prevent the whip from slashing into Akira's body as it wrapped around his arm. Realizing what had happened, Kian pulled on the whip and caused it to rip into Bryce's flesh even deeper.

Bryce growled and pulled his sword out with his other hand and threw it into Kian's belly.

Kian staggered forward as he let go of the whip and fell to his knees, clutching the sword in his middle.

"I was getting rid of her for ye, because ye're too weak to do it yerself." Kian fell forward.

"I don't want to be rid of her." Bryce pulled the whip off his arm as blood poured from his open wound. The whip had wrapped around his forearm thrice, and it looked as if his flesh had been flayed. He could only imagine what it would have done to Akira's soft skin. He closed his eyes. "Thank ye, God, for leading me here in time."

Balloch went to Kian. "Why, Kian? Why?" He pulled out Bryce's sword, and Kian fell forward, never to speak again.

Birk rushed to Akira and released her wrists from the chains. He pulled out a knife and cut loose the rope that bound her ankles.

Tears of relief flooded her face as she rubbed her aching shoulders. "Oh, thank God, ye found me." Her physical strength was depleted, but her heart beat strong with hope. "Da, did ye really come for me this time? I didn't think ye would come."

Her father gently pushed her hair back, and moisture gathered in his dark eyes. His chin trembled, and his voice sounded gruff with emotion. "Akira, don't ye know I love ye, lass? I'd give my last breath for ye. Ye're my child."

A sob broke from Akira. "But ye never came for me when Bryce took me."

He pulled her into his embrace. "Oh, lass, I never really thought ye were in any real danger from Bryce or Evan. If they are anything like their father Cedric, they are God-fearing men who would do right by ye. I can think of several MacKenzie men I'd rather not see ye wed over Bryce or Evan."

Akira sobbed into her father's shirt, allowing the tears and pain to dissolve into forgiveness and peace.

Blood dripped on the floor as Bryce moved to Akira's side.

Akira pulled away from her father. "No matter what ye think of me, Bryce, please know I didn't betray ye." A mixture of exhaustion and relief engulfed her, and her legs gave way beneath her.

Bryce caught her with his good arm. "I know, lass. Please forgive me."

Akira's body felt sore all over, but determined to leave the bedchamber, she could hardly wait to walk outdoors. She smiled as Finella pulled open the window to allow the breeze to float in and the glorious sunlight to filter into the shadows.

"Ah, that's much better, Finella," Akira sighed.

Nara pulled a pale yellow gown from her wardrobe and held it up. "How's this?" Her eyebrows rose inquiringly.

Akira glanced at the gown and walked toward her mother. "'Twill do. Hurry and help me dress. I've been in this chamber for far too long."

Finella scoffed and turned from the window. She picked up her skirts in wrinkled hands and strode to them, taking the gown from Nara, fully in charge. "Turn around, lass. Ye act like ye've been in bed for more than a week, an' 'tis only three days."

Akira did as she was bid, exchanging a smile with her mother. "Well, it feels like longer."

The idea that she had only been recovering three days reminded her of how much distance her mother had to travel in such a short time.

"Mither?" Akira held her long hair up while Finella buttoned her dress in the back. "How did ye ever arrive here so quickly?"

Amusement touched Akira as she watched her mother flush.

"Once I found out yer father led his warriors to MacPhearson Castle, Leith and I quickly packed and came after him." Her shoulders straightened proudly, and she met Akira's gaze. "I refused to allow him to lead an attack against our only daughter. Only he didn't plan to attack the MacPhearsons; he only wanted to get down to the bottom of Elliot's murder.

"And ye can imagine his surprise when I arrived and ye were missing. I told him he'd better find ye, or I would never go back home, and he'd have to run the house and tend to his own needs."

Akira giggled, imagining the shocked surprise on Birk MacKenzie's face. She leaned forward and hugged her mother. "'Twas something ye should have done a long time ago. Men like it when women aren't so weak. They want to know that we'll stand by their side and be there when times get rough."

Her mother nodded in agreement, and Finella patted Akira's back to let her know she had finished.

"Ye'd better remember yer own wee bit of advice, lass. Bryce MacPhearson can be as stubborn as they come," Finella warned.

"Ye've known Bryce all his life. I intend to rely more on yer advice, Finella—" She patted her abdomen. "—especially now that there could soon be a wee one among us."

Finella bent and kissed her cheek with an affectionate smile. "'Tis good to have ye home, m'lady."

"'Tis good to be home."

Nara led Akira from her bedchamber, down the stairs, and out to the corridor. The sight that awaited her all but melted Akira's heart. The good news that she and Bryce were expecting had spread quickly. Smiling faces greeted her with shouts of congratulations for the wee bairn, while others clapped and cheered for her safe return. The casual comfort between the MacKenzies and the MacPhearsons touched her the most. One could hardly tell the clans apart. It was an answer to prayer—a miracle.

Sim and Leith played games. Gavin and Rae had been in a deep discussion about something. And Fergus and Balloch carried hunting weapons, planning an afternoon excursion.

Bryce appeared at her side. She struggled to blink back tears of happiness. Things had turned out far better than she had ever dared hope. His arm slipped around her, and he bent to speak in her ear.

"I think our idea of pairing a MacKenzie with a MacPhearson for yer search might have helped speed progress along."

She turned a watery gaze in his direction. "Ye did what?"

He held up a hand. "I didn't trust my men, and I knew no one could do anything with a MacKenzie trailing them everywhere. I feared someone was in league with Kian." He gestured around them. "It appears that our clans are truly at peace, and we are happy and in love."

"My darling," she whispered in his ear, "God has blessed us beyond measure. He answered all our prayers and kept all His promised blessings. We are indeed fortunate."

"We are indeed, m'love." Bryce lowered his head, his warm lips melting upon hers.

Author's Note

If you are wondering why Bryce and his warriors weren't wearing kilts, it is because the modern kilt as we know it only dates back to around 1725. It is similar to a skirt with pleats from the waist down to slightly below the knees.

The Great Kilt or Belted Plaid dates back to 1594. The Great Kilt was an untailored garment made of cloth gathered up into pleats by hand and secured by a wide belt. The upper half could be worn as a cloak draped over the left shoulder and secured by a clip of some sort or draped down over the belt and gathered up at the front. In cold or wet weather, they might have brought it up over the shoulders or head for protection against weather.

Before the Great Kilt or Belted Plaid, they wore a long shirt that is known as a *leine* in Gaelic and thought of as a "tunic" in English. A plaid of wool cloth would have been draped over the shoulders and around the arm and fastened by a clip. The tunic came down to the knees on a man and was much longer on a woman. Because of the length on a woman it was similar to what we think of as an English chemise.

The association of clan family-specific tartan colors and plaid designs was a late development in the seventeenth and eighteenth centuries. However, much earlier family clans that lived within a region would wear similar plaids and colors because they used the same seamstresses in the area. And, of course, families that intermarried typically lived in the same region in medieval Scotland, especially in the Highlands. Most of the clan colors and design patterns associated with specific family clans probably derived from this regional practice. This is why Bryce and Akira had different plaids with different colors, since the MacKenzies and MacPhearsons didn't live on neighboring lands.

You can learn more from my blog at: http://carolinascots-irish.blogspot.com.

Want to learn more about author
Jennifer Hudson Taylor and check out other great fiction
from Abingdon Press?

Sign up for our fiction newsletter at
www.AbingdonPress.com
to read interviews with your favorite authors, find tips
for starting a reading group, and stay posted on what
new titles are on the horizon. It's a place to connect
with other fiction readers or post a
comment about this book.

Be sure to visit Jennifer online!

www.jenniferhudsontaylor.com
http://jenniferswriting.blogspot.com
http://carolinascots-irish.blogspot.com

What they're saying about...

Gone to Green, by Judy Christie
"...Refreshingly realistic religious fiction, this novel is unafraid to address the injustices of sexism, racism, and corruption as well as the spiritual devastation that often accompanies the loss of loved ones. Yet these darker narrative tones beautifully highlight the novel's message of friendship, community, and God's reassuring and transformative love." —*Publishers Weekly* starred review

The Call of Zulina, by Kay Marshall Strom
"This compelling drama will challenge readers to remember slavery's brutal history, and its heroic characters will inspire them. Highly recommended."
—*Library Journal* starred review

Surrender the Wind, by Rita Gerlach
"I am purely a romance reader, and yet you hooked me in with a war scene, of all things! I would have never believed it. You set the mood beautifully and have a clean, strong, lyrical way with words. You have done your research well enough to transport me back to the war-torn period of colonial times."
—Julie Lessman, author of *The Daughters of Boston* series

One Imperfect Christmas, by Myra Johnson
"Debut novelist Myra Johnson ushers us into the Christmas season with a fresh and exciting story that will give you a chuckle and a special warmth."
—DiAnn Mills, author of *Awaken My Heart* and *Breach of Trust*

The Prayers of Agnes Sparrow, by Joyce Magnin
"Beware of *The Prayers of Agnes Sparrow*. Just when you have become fully enchanted by its marvelous quirky zaniness, you will suddenly be taken to your knees by its poignant truth-telling about what it means to be divinely human. I'm convinced that 'on our knees' is exactly where Joyce Magnin planned for us to land all along." —Nancy Rue, co-author of *Healing Waters* (*Sullivan Crisp* Series)
                2009 Novel of the Year

The Fence My Father Built, by Linda S. Clare
"...Linda Clare reminds us with her writing that is wise, funny, and heartbreaking, that what matters most in life are the people we love and the One who gave them to us."—Gina Ochsner, Dark Horse Literary, winner of the Oregon Book Award and the Flannery O'Connor Award for Short Fiction

eye of the god, by Ariel Allison
"Filled with action on three continents, *eye of the god* is a riveting fast-paced thriller, but it is Abby—who, in spite of another letdown by a man, remains filled with hope—who makes Ariel Allison's tale a super read."—Harriet Klausner

www.AbingdonPress.com/fiction